S0-BHV-282

MOTHER OF GOLD

By EMERSON HOUGH

NORTH OF 36

THE COVERED WAGON

THE SAGEBRUSHER

THE WAY OUT

THE BROKEN GATE

THE MAN NEXT DOOR

LET US GO AFIELD

OUT OF DOORS

THE STORY OF THE COWBOY

THE GIRL AT THE HALFWAY HOUSE

D. APPLETON AND COMPANY
Publishers New York

HALLOCK ROSE, REMOVING HIS HAT

[Page 109]

MOTHER OF GOLD

BY

EMERSON HOUGH

AUTHOR OF "THE COVERED WAGON," "NORTH OF 36," ETC.

D. APPLETON AND COMPANY
NEW YORK :: 1924 :: LONDON

PRINTED IN THE UNITED STATES OF AMERICA

CONTENTS

MOTHER OF GOLD

CHAPTER I

THE DESERT RENDEZVOUS

"WE are only soldiers three," said Hallock, bending toward the camp fire in order more easily to read the letter he held in his hand. "Ought to be soldiers four, all present or accounted for. Wonder what's the matter with Allison, anyhow?"

Neither of his two companions made immediate reply. John Palmer, the oldest of the three—perhaps fifty years he showed of sun and saddle, or pick and pan—continued his intent gaze at the long-handled spider which he manipulated over the sagebrush blaze. Dan Silsby still moodily gazed into the fire, with no more than a grunt to show he had heard.

The first speaker—"Pug" Hallock, they called him in Harvard football days—was of age about the same as that of Silsby. Either might have claimed twenty-five, twenty-eight years. Both were strong, tawny-haired, blue-eyed young men, hard-bitten and brown now, by reason of life in the open. Both wore the half-military garb now so common in the west—flannel shirt, breeches, puttees, wide hat.

The older man, John Palmer, dated to earlier days by many ineradicable tokens. His dress was the loose wool of the old frontier, and he and his garb had the strange, inseparable quality of the real western man and his apparel. You could not think of John Palmer as dressed in any other way but precisely this any more than you could ever think of him as in any way aware of his own clothing. He was designed for utility himself—or had come to that through years of knockabout. The mountains and the desert had taught him their silence. Their suns had given him his khaki skin, their nights the veiled blue of his hidden eye. He made no unnecessary movement. It was plain the bacon and cottontail would be done just as the black coffeepot came to the boil. He was old-timer of ancient right: if a prospector, one who never had lost decision in desert dreams. His gray sandy hair was abundant under his slouched hat, his jaw and chin were hard and strong.

Travelers these three obviously were, as four saddle animals, as many pack mules, with their gear neatly aligned back of the bed rolls and the kitchen pannier, attested. Rifles leaned against the luggage, each man had a belt weapon. But that they were not hunting for sport might be guessed from the four picks, the two gold pans that had made part of the little pack train's burden.

It was the semidesert of north Chihuahua, in old

Mexico, that lay around them here in the brilliant moonlight which always marks that arid region. That they were no more than transients was obvious. For some cause, for some purpose, over some trail, from some point not indicated, they had come hither from the American side of the Mexican line. Their clean and workmanlike encampment, their way of picketing their live stock, their ease in attitude toward conditions as they found them, their small but efficient means of transport, all bespoke them travelers by no means on their first trail. They were at home, even in this wild and uncertain land of touch-and-go.

"No," grumbled Hallock once more, "Allison ought not to be holding us all up in this way. He knew the rendezvous as well as any of us. He only had to come from Chicago, on good trains. I came from Colorado, and John here is up from the other end of Mexico. And this is the time and the place."

"The time, the place—and the girl!" grinned Silsby, slowly, still looking at the browning rabbit legs. "I should think you might be charitable." He nodded toward the letter Hallock was reading. But that young man was unabashed.

"At least, Edie isn't holding up the party," said he. "She's slipped me! I'm here. *Adsum! Me voici!* No more girl for me. But Barry Allison isn't either present or accounted for, and this is the third day. As though time wasn't anything on a job like ours!"

"Give him time," murmured Silsby, hypnotized by the advancing rabbit ripeness in the skillet, just now indicated as John Palmer shifted the pieces by a flip of the pan. "I saw a picture of his girl once. He has taste."

John Palmer turned from the little fire, drew off his coffeepot with a hooked stick, and set the spider on the ground before them.

"Girls!" said he, at length. "Every night I hear that, over everything else. If there's going to be anything to balk us, knock us out, it's going to be girls!"

The two younger men looked at him soberly, with a contrition apparently admitting a contract broken. Each man found the bone of a rabbit leg. Palmer poured himself a tin cup of coffee.

"I made it plain to you all," he went on presently, "that if we went into this it was to win, and not to fail. We all agreed this should be first, and every other earthly thing should come after that. We all swore to that. If we begin this soon to forget, what's the chance later, when we're really into the hard part of the game?"

"Oh, well, John," began Hallock, "we've not any of us let anything handicap us yet. Weren't you young? Didn't my father tell me about you in Harvard '82?"

"Never mind. I'm old and I'm alone—now. I've put all that behind me. I learned long ago that in these times you can't make a States girl happy if you're broke. Come back in a year broke and your girl's married some other man who isn't. Come back with the big secret solved that we're on now and there's no queen on any throne of the world who wouldn't look with longing on any one of you—or us."

"But, John," argued Dan Silsby, holding his rabbit leg aside for a moment, "a man, or anyhow a young man, is organized for love as well as for bread and butter."

"Humph! you'd jolly well better get the bread and butter settled first. What I want to say is, I've studied this problem all my life, this one we're on now. If we win, we can wipe out even the years that are gone. That was what we all agreed when we made our bargain at the Cornell school of mines, where we took the post-grad—I was a little old for that.

"I knew your fathers, boys. I knew it would take youth and strength and cash resources to put this thing to the test. We all agreed that if any of us ever fell on to a good thing, we'd send for the other three, and we'd all come, and we'd let nothing hinder. Well, we couldn't have guessed that I'd blunder into the biggest of all the big secrets the Rockies, the Cordilleras ever had—the one great secret of time! But since I have, and since we've come, we must remember our oath together. I can't succeed alone, I know that. But if I'm not to do so, let's know it while there's time.

"If I thought Barry Allison was holding us up on account of some woman, I'd shake this outfit right now, because I'd know that we'd fail. This is no brass-band proposition we're taking on. We're soldiers. So was

Cortes a soldier. So were the men who for untold ages have kept this secret soldiers. Soldiers and celibates, by the lord! Men of one great purpose. Consecrated, if you please. I don't know, but my great feeling in all this is not one of what it's going to mean to me—that's too little. It's what it will mean to my country; what it'll mean to all the world."

The two young men who heard John Palmer's words listened in silence, wholly sobered. Lean and hard as greyhounds, hardened by work in the open, blue of eye and keen of mind, they seemed a type of the fighting man. Evidently the proposition at hand was not new to them, nor did either show any sign of surrendering it.

"How long can we give Allison, John?" demanded Silsby after a time.

The other turned to him impatiently. "It isn't a question of days or months; it isn't a question of time at all. The great fact is that we four men share this knowledge, and share it under an oath as binding as any that held the ancient guardians. One leak, one back sliding, one weakness—it's all gone."

"Barry's a hustler," said Silsby. "We'd have to concede that. Besides, you must remember, it was he who ran across that old volume put out by the Bureau of Mines. That story, pieced to what old Pedro told you in Lower California, really was what started you south, eh?"

"Yes. My contribution has been eight years of work

and risk and study and exploration—of happiness and despair—in lower Mexico. I didn't issue the call till I was sure, or reasonably sure, that the time had come for the final work on it all. Maybe I'm a little nervous."

"Well," said Hallock, "I've gambled, to the bone; I've put into it every dollar I had and some I didn't have, and quit my job besides—and lost a girl I wasn't so sorry to lose. So's Silsby—he's put up his professional chance against it. I think Allison's putting up a woman's happiness in it—maybe each of us is, what? And, of course, there's no actual proof."

"Proof!" The older man's scorn was supreme. "Do you think the luck will bring you proof in a chance like this? That's the chance we take. That's what we pay. So large a something—are we to have it for nothing?

"Yes, Allison's stumbling over that old book was what gave me the proof that the great valley was not in our own country. I've been all over the big Blue Bucket land slip in east Oregon—where the emigrants in 1848 found solid chunks of gold. I've found the bed in Death Valley, where again she was taken out of sight. There's only one true mother vein in all the United States, of course, and that's the old Comstock—twenty miles, fifty, but deep, deep. When we've found her, she's sunk, always—nature has taken her back. Why? Because otherwise it would have been found and used in America too soon—too soon.

"This country here"—he waved a hand—"has been

left slothful and backward and impoverished for some inscrutable purpose. We couldn't have held the great secret! Mexico could, did, has done so, for centuries. Luck alone let us in to the door of it. It will take luck and destiny both to unlock the door—and it is indeed the door I've found. Surrender something, give up something, pay a little self-obligation? I should say we might!"

"Or pay more!" said Silsby, quietly.

"Yes! Or pay more! Or pay all! We thrashed that all out before we made our agreement. It's life or death for me, literally, for I'll never come back from that country if I fail now. I've known happiness—and despair."

"Pay?" Palmer mused. "Why, yes, pay. That is how the secret has been kept since before Solomon. The Madre d'Oro has taken toll, always! She never will let in any man who is not ready to pay what may be asked. It is sacrifice, renunciation that one may pay, yes. But pay we must—all that is asked; not one of us can tell how much."

"Listen at the old desert rat!" smiled Hallock. "You'd think he's the worst mystic in the world instead of the safest mining engineer."

John Palmer did not smile. "Yes," said he, "I've found some mines, and some I've never disclosed to my company. Nowadays I'd be watched every time I punched a burro into the mountains. Look here"—he spread a sheet of brown paper on the ground in the firelight—"I could sell this hand-made map in New York—with one hour's talk, besides—for five million, ten million. Would that be success? Not as I figure it. That would not be my great dream."

"Dream?" smiled Pug Hallock. "Thought you called it a cinch, now!"

"As near to it as so vast a thing may be. But I estimate our success by the intangibles—by the radio, the submarine, the airplane. If these things may be, the time may now be ripe for our own divulgence. Who shall say the immortal gods have no hand in all these things? They only take their time, that's all. It is luck which agency they choose. He may be in silk, in armor, or in jeans; we can't tell. But if a great finger is laid on a man's shoulder—if he's led to the very door of the Madre d'Oro—it's not for him to vaunt himself, that's sure. Neither is it for him to hold back in any way. Neither may he hesitate about the price he may have to pay."

Unconsciously, all three of them looked about them. Under the blaze of the southern moon the high plain lay wide, mysterious, ominous. There came no sound save the wild thin quavering wail of a coyote slinking near.

"I suppose a million men have died hunting for the same thing we're after," continued the older man. "Thirteen men on the dead man's chest? Say thirteen hundred thousand! Sometimes I think Spain has had the secret up her sleeve for four hundred years. We don't know how many may have held back the story. Some old Diego Vasquez, 'high admiral of Spain,' may have burned the records behind him, and concluded that breadfruit on a sunny beach was better than the gold of the valley—I don't know. What I do know is that the world, that mankind, always has had touch with the greatest secret of the world.

"Now, call it accident, if you please, that Allison chanced to go into the congressional library and rummage around and get his tip about it. Call it accident that I, down in the San Andreas, ran across the young woman in the village that Villa had destroyed and who said I was headed right—call it accident that we met as we did and made our compact. That was before the World War! I never knew there had been a World War. I was buried, down in here, for eight years. Happiness! Despair! That's what it costs to buy your way in to the Madre d'Oro. Accident? I don't know. Sometimes I think there's no such thing."

"Your words have a dulcet sound, Uncle John!" said Pug Hallock. "They say much sheep herding maketh a man mad. How about much prospecting?"

The older man only smiled. "Maybe—maybe—I don't know. But take good care of your crazy Uncle John, boys, because if I die, my secret dies with me. I've never written down a line of directions and never shall. What I call the San Andreas are not the San Andreas. To leave one specific written, carved, or printed word about the entrance to the great valley, the ancient Madre d'Oro, mother of all the gold of all the world—that would be fatal! The Aztecs, who did know the valley, knew that much—they never left a record, not in all those centuries!

"That's tradition, eh? I'll say so. The greatest piece of knowledge, the most epochal of all discoveries ever made or unmade, is unwritten and unrecorded in its perpetuity! Its secret was known—and it is known to-day—by three men only in all the world. It was written in the brains and hearts of loyal men, men who had been ready to pay for the trust given them. Eh? I'm crazy? I'm a mystic? Why, Allison's old book told you that much."

"Go on, John Palmer," half whispered Silsby. "Tell us all over again!"

"I can tell you little more than I have, my son. I can't specify much more—just yet. But when you stand, as I have stood, at the door of the Madre d'Oro, and have felt her, just beyond—why, then, it will be an easy oath that never, for any price, shall you set down word or leave any trace that will lead any other man to that same spot.

"If you did," he smiled, "then the old Aztec curse would come! The mountains would fold themselves once more around her—as maybe they did in Oregon, as maybe they did in Death Valley—and take her back again for their own—to wait how long? Perhaps till time comes to pay for another World War!

"Eh? Crazy—a mystic? I don't know. Maybe so."

"Why did you take us on, John?" demanded Silsby suddenly.

"Why? Because of our old agreement at Cornell. Because I knew your fathers, clean Americans. And because," he added, "it will take men who have something left to pay! Youth only can open the door of the Madre d'Oro! Me?—I had nothing left to pay! I was lived out, had nothing more to lose, nothing more to sacrifice, when I knew I was at the door. Happiness! Despair!"

"You make me feel creepy, you desert rat!" said Silsby, smiling. "Got a Minotaur, or something, huh? Want a nice virgin-mining expert fresh from Cripple Creek to feed on, eh?"

Old John Palmer, smoking his pipe, his hands falling limp before his knees, grinned as amiably. "You still want to put me in the visionary class, eh? You can't think of the Madre d'Oro as an actual mother lode of actual gold, actual free gold? Is that more wonderful than it is for you to go to Mexico City, or Chihuahua, and ask your mother by radiophone what she is going to have for breakfast? It is not so utterly impossible as that last. Yet that last abstract, impossible thing is true, it is done. It seems simple. So will it be simple when you see the valley. Franklin, Edison, Marconi —all simple men. What chose them? I don't know. Who chooses us? I don't know that.

"But, of course, my boy," he added, placing an affectionate hand on Silsby's knee, "if it comes to Galahadding around after grails and things, I do like to think that a clean knight—'the most worthy knight' of them all, as they called old Colonel Bedivere—some nice, clean-cut young American chap who had good ideals and who'd always done his duty as I know you three did, would have the best chance, if really there was anything in all that mysticism which has grown up about the undying legend of the Mother of All the Gold. Eh? At least we're here, eh? We'll try?"

The two stalwart young men who heard him looked at him gravely and steadily. Already they had taken certain degrees in the great lodge of life.

"I wish Allison'd come along, you know," remarked Silsby at last.

"So do I," said John Palmer. "But most I wish that when he comes he may come with no entanglements. No man who ever stood at the door of the Madre d'Oro did so with a woman on his arm."

"Fie! Fie! John Palmer. You were not always a hater of women and a lover of gold!" Silsby grinned at him. "Don't they go together?"

"In sequence—in the right sequence!" The older man smiled as he answered. He flung open his bed roll on the sand. His face was sad in repose. "We'll give him a week to show up or send word," he added. "Though how he'd send word, five days from the border and four from the rails, is more than I could say."

MOTHER OF GOLD

The friends of Barry Allison, tarrying for him in the desert encampment, had spoken of the annihilation of distance so far as one of the five senses of man is concerned. The other four still await the magician. What man shall bring present to the eye across all the leagues the sight of the woman a young man loves? How shall he touch her hand, know the nectar of her lips, scent the fragrance of her hair? The sound of her voice does not replace all these, efface them; it only intensifies the need of them.

At least so felt that lover after telephoning Mary Westlake by long distance from Chicago to her home in upper Ohio. Her voice was there, in his ear. It was not enough. He was going away on a long and far journey, a man journey, from which he might never return. As to the nature of that, he was sworn to secrecy. But surely, so he reasoned, it would be a sin against the truth if he left and did not let Mary know at least a little of the reasons she might not see him for a year, two years—he did not know how many years. And already she had waited for him to seek his fortune these five years since he had left Cornell and gone west as a mining engineer. The two years of the War had not brought the fortune nearer. He could not go and not see her once more. He was quite mad about her, present or absent, and now the thought of her cool loveliness was too much for him. No telephone, no radio yet has served for lovers. He took the night train for Deneville.

Now Deneville itself, surely, was no citadel of romance. It lies at the lower edge of one of the Great Lakes—one of those many American cities of no great size which are the mainstay of our life as a nation. In such a community, not large, but large enough, all the comedies and tragedies of commerce and life and love go on from day to day, much as they do in any great metropolis of all the world. Comfort is the lot of the average man, opulence the reward of few. But the lines of life are somewhat narrow. Life must make up in somberness, in intensity, what it lacks in breadth and scope. As though in an old-world city founded centuries ago, Deneville folk lived cleanly and quietly, with no ripple to mark the passage of their lives, and got along without any great imaginings or hectic dreams. There were bankers in small musty buildings, grocers in large musty ones, a discreet quota of little tradesmen, fishermen, artisans, craftsmen who labored from day to day as peasants do—in short, the whole intricate tragedy and comedy of life went on here as it does all over the inhabited world; but it all was cut and dried and done for long ago.

There were six churches, all much alike, and the building locally called the cathedral. There was a section where those known as "the poorer classes" lived. There were also several streets sacred to the seats of the mighty, especially one exclusive avenue where dwelt the socially elect.

On a smug street lined with elms apparently immemorial, although really planted there by the last generation, ranged the residences owned by those who had been destined in the race of life to amass more money than their fellows. They averaged perhaps an acre or more in grounds, so that a certain air of reserve, remoteness, exclusiveness obtained. Usually there were trees scattered here or there across the expanse of green turf, across which latter a straight brick walk led from the sidewalk up the front steps of the mansion house. Here and there were clumps of shrubbery, more or less formal flower beds. The master of the house might now and then be seen attending to the mowing of the lawn, to leave which unkempt were social disgrace.

As for the houses themselves, they were for the most part uniformly, victoriously and victorianly ugly. There was small ease of line, much gingerbread of cornice or cupola or tower. No one went into these towers, none looked out thence. Yet from the summit of certain of these lofty architectural decorations one could catch a glimpse of the blue lake beyond, or sight the smoke of a boat passing far off to the north, or coming down from that upper wilderness whence originated the most part of the wealth which had built Deneville.

Within the houses were examples of funereal furniture, dark, graceless, gloomy, abominable. Carpets for the most part covered the floors to their remotest edges. There was an air of six-per-cent respectability about every house on Portland Avenue. Usually not much romance goes at six per cent.

The persons who dwelt in these abodes were for the most part Americans of the mild middle class. Some of them, of New England ancestry, had a generation earlier gone into the lake trade. Others had taken kindly to twine, and had acquired great opulence from pound nets set in the fresh-water seas, harvesting as man does gladly, where none has sown. A few had practiced law cannily. Others had erected kilns for the making of brick and tile and had reaped therefrom largely.

Among the richest were those who had garnered for a time an ever-increasing harvest from the vast pine forests of lower Michigan, acquired when that was yet an unravaged wilderness. Some were concerned in iron ore, or the manufacture of steel, or the casting of iron—not a few of these having become wealthy by reason of the activity of their fathers or grandfathers, who, with no great foresight on their part, it is true, but with great good fortune as events proved, had acquired largely of waste lands in the far northwest, later to be discovered rich in ores of copper, and iron, and standing trees; things that cost no planting.

In short, the great mother America had been kind to these, as to many others in communities of similar sort. Most of the men who had built their gloomy mansions on this gloomy thoroughfare were able to live without labor, to educate their families, and to maintain such station as seemed to them advisable. Grown rich by accident or inevitableness, they laid that to their own genius. Romance was unknown to them—even the vast romance of America.

Miracles may happen in such a spot largely because miracles may happen anywhere. The great miracle was that any one on Portland Avenue should ever wake up in the morning at all. Yet Mary Westlake set in force this miracle every day at five-thirty or six in the morning. Indeed, Mary was miracle enough in herself.

The father of Mary was not yet an old man, but was staidly wealthy and beyond the need of further commercial activity in pine and iron. It had been many years since he had built the gloomy proof of his success in life, this square, dour residence of brick, of twenty-odd rooms, a front porch and a cupola. A yea-and-nay sort of man, he had run to straight lines. It was Mary who first introduced curves in walks and flower beds—she also who set out the first and only rose garden on Portland Avenue.

Now a rose is mighty sweet when dew-wet of a morn in June. First sign of life about the place, this morning in early June, Mary paused on the wide porch for a moment, drawing a deep breath or two into her lungs, as was her morning habit. Then she passed down the great front steps—made of three-inch cork pine—a part of her father's reapings long ago—and left the moldy red brick walk with intent to diverge across the close-cut lawn of green to see her roses, touch them, scent them, taste them.

She passed on, no more than turning her head aside to look at a warbling robin which she half imitated gayly. There were lilacs, green and graceful; a bed of stiff foliage plants; but the most cherished part of her personal realm lay just a little further—her garden, full of all sorts and colors and sizes of roses, now all or most of them in bloom.

Presently she must have been lost to the view of any one standing, say, at the moldy brick walk. It might have been chapel as good as any, place good enough for a maid's morning devotions. She stood, her eyes lifted just a trifle when a bell boomed, looking at nothing visible in particular, one hand idle, the other at her bosom, her white garment showing clear against the green background.

She was twenty-four, her figure superb, her gray eyes clean and cool, none of her movements light, agitated, causeless, but all well correlated, actuated by a grave, well-poised soul. To look at her thus, you might not have guessed romanticism of her soul. But you must have thought her monstrous fair to look upon; aye, and reason enough, here in her rose garden, to hold any young man back from a desert where such a girl never yet was seen.

Mary Westlake, alert and expectant, saw her lover come up the walk. There was always about her a strange dignity, shyness, inability of self-expression, amounting almost to awkwardness in love's ways which needed now the softness of her eyes for apology. But now indeed her eyes were shining in joy of his presence. She had not seen him for three years. Now, as he stood back, his hands on her shoulders to look at her young womanliness, a moody shadow passed over his face. He was, forsooth, not a conquering hero, but a man come to ask another extension of his chance with happiness.

She seemed extremely adequate; indeed a picture of extremely beautiful, self-sufficient young womanhood. Allison looked at her hungrily, his natural ardor for her person almost subordinated by his sheer admiration of her as a type of her sex to-day.

CHAPTER II

MARY'S SECRET

WITH scarce more than monosyllables—they both were rather genuinely abashed—the two walked toward the lake front, Mary's parasol unagitated, her eyes straight ahead. Finally they came to the little strip of beaten grass and scraggly trees known as the Lake Front Park, and made their way to one of the short iron seats which served the public during the evening band performances which were given in a little wooden pagoda located midway in the park. The local band, the motion picture, the Carnegie library, the churches—these made pretty much the sum of social resources in Deneville.

They sat now, still strangely silent, staring out over the unbelievable blue of the great lake which lay before them, dotted with far smoke trails. A soft breeze stirred the lace of Mary's parasol, stirred also a long strand of her hair at a white temple, so that Allison suddenly felt half crazed to take it and press it to his lips. There were few others besides themselves about—a man who read a paper, a maid with a baby carriage. The message of the time and place was one of calm, of completion, of the finish of all impatient effort.

In no corner of the world could there have been found a more perfect example of practical workday success, of common caution and risk. Never a chance had been taken by the generation which had built Deneville. Those men had played certainties all their lives.

Seeing that her young man was too silent, that something had chilled him, Mary touched him in gentle query, a hand on his arm, to make amends, to make some sort of beginning.

In her eyes he caught her shy wish to express her love for him, since he was so slow, so embarrassed.

"I am so glad to see you, Barry," said she. "You don't know how lonesome it is here."

"Don't I, though? It is the dullest place on the surface of the earth. Don't I wish I could take you away from here!"

She checked a little sigh. He continued, turning to her half savagely.

"This time I said that you and I were going to have an understanding—or else I would call it all off between us. Time I came across with something. We can't wait forever this way—it's not right for you."

"Is it for you?" her slow smile challenged him.

"It's different for me. I can work alone all my life if I have to—of course, I would be alone. But you've only got one life to live, and ought to be a success. There'd never be any one else—it's you or no one, that is one thing sure."

"Won't it be that way for me, too?"

"It has been, yes; but a girl can't wait forever."

They sat, again silent, for a long time, but the fringe of Mary's white parasol, whose staff was steadied by her hand, trembled a little bit, though he heard her laugh.

"I had such a bad time of it yesterday," said she.

"What, my dear?" He turned his moody face toward her, his eyes devouring.

"You know my aunt's old crystal sphere—the 'scrying ball' we used to call it? I showed it to you once."

"Why, yes. Spooky sort of thing—I would not go in for crystal-gazing if I were you."

"Well, I did! I got it out yesterday for the first time, tried to use it. You know how it is done?"

"No, I don't think so."

"Well, I went into a darkened room—just a little light at one window. I covered my desk with a big piece of black velvet and put the crystal on the velvet. I sat there with my fingers on the edge and looked and looked into the crystal. Oh, I wanted to ask it all sorts of things. That was after you wired me that you were coming. I wanted to know my fortune—our fortune, you know? Well, I was frightened, of course."

"Of course. There is no good in monkeying with those things. It just upsets your nerves, that's all."

"Well, I'll say it was spooky, as you call it. I looked and looked—an hour it seemed to me—and I didn't see anything at all. I was about to quit it. Then it seemed to me I could see a kind of milky film starting down in the glass, deep, deep down. I couldn't be sure, so I went back at it again and tried once more. I looked straight into the middle of the crystal ball!"

"And you saw nothing?"

"Oh, but I did see something! As I kept on, the streaks and films seemed to grow, to come together, and I tell you, honest as I sit here, there was a picture that showed in the middle of the sphere.

"Of course, it must have been something from my subconscious mind, something that must have been within my knowledge or my thoughts, or within the reach of my possible knowledge—or yours! But it came to me just the same as if it was the picture of another world and it was so strange! The silliest thing—you know how impossible dreams are sometimes? Well, I didn't have any Mr. Freud to help me."

"Tell me about it."

"I do tell you, Barry. It was there in the crystal—a picture as real as life! It was in the mountains——"

"The mountains?"

"Yes. Maybe because you have been living out there so long. But it was not any scene in the mountains that you ever told me about or that I have ever seen. It appeared to be in a warm country—there were tropical plants, trees. Yes, it seemed to be in a warm land—palms, I thought. The trees grew down all sides of the hill into the valley."

"The valley?"

"Why, yes, the valley, Barry. But what should I say about it? It was a dream place. You will think me crazy, call me a child. I couldn't blame you. But I did see it!

"Yes, there was a sharp-walled valley, and I was looking down into it. There was a great deal of color in the valley—some birds were flying, they looked like birds of paradise. But that was not the strangest thing."

"What was it?" He leaned toward her gravely, his eyes burning.

"I suppose it is because everybody is trying to get rich—it's money, gold, in our house, all the time! Well, Barry, true as I live, across the middle of that whole valley there ran a lode, a dike, a dam, pure as solid gold! Why, I can see it as plainly as if it were out in front of me.

"It was solid gold, I tell you—and there in that dark I saw the raggedness of its walls; and sometimes there were little points of light like diamonds in the sun. And the sun was shining—it made the west ablaze, coming up all the way over the terrible shining wall that ran entirely across the valley. Oh, don't laugh at me!"

She sat, looking straight ahead, not daring to turn to him, but his voice ended her laugh.

"I am not laughing, my dear," said he. He also sat motionless now looking out across the lake.

"Mary, dear," he began again, after a long time, with a deep breath. "I don't doubt in the least that you saw just as you say! Neither do I doubt that it exists just as you describe it."

"That is so silly!"

"Indeed not, and you must not say that. On the contrary—now don't think me silly or crazy—you've seen what I have come here to tell you about. Gold? A valley? Yes, yes, yes! No more, no less. You have seen our valley—my valley!"

"Yours?"

"No, ours! I am on my way right now to go into that valley. We call it already found. Mary, my dear, my dear"—he had her hands now—"I delayed my start to get away and talk to you about that very thing."

"I'm afraid, Barry."

"And so was I. I was so afraid you would think me crazy that I almost dared not tell you. It was utterly absurd, impossible. If you wouldn't listen to me I believe I would have been obliged to set you free. Because that very valley to-day is my one chance of any sudden fortune.

"I have wasted time enough for you. We can't go on this way. Only a gamble will do. Well, my dear, that was the gamble I was going to put before you. And so you have it—you have seen it just as clearly as I ever did. More so, I think."

"Was that what I saw, Barry?"

"God help me, yes! I do so believe. You leave me scarce able to realize that we are both awake and alive to-day. But, oh, if we are right! If, indeed, my friends and I do find the Madre d'Oro!"

"Madre d'Oro!"

"I've never dared tell you before now. Let me do so—let me tell you what you truly did see in the crystal. I'll go back a bit.

"You see, during the War I was in Washington for a time, and being a mining man by profession, I used to prowl around the Congressional Library, reading all sorts of things in my line. Well, I found a dusty old book there, big as a family Bible, put out once, many years ago, by the Bureau of Mines. It was a great collection of facts and fiction and methods of the mining industry all over the world.

"Well, Mary, true as I sit here, I saw there—saw again—four years ago, the whole story of the Madre d'Oro—the mother vein of all the earth's gold. My friends and I ran across the same thing years ago at Cornell. And I was going to tell you about it—of our secret—and now you have told me! You have seen the same thing. Well, what shall we believe? Was I crazy? Are you crazy also?"

"The mother of gold!"

"Yes, my dear. A belief in it exists in every corner of the world. In Thibet there is a great cavern where a people or a whole race of men disappeared hundreds of years ago. They walked down into another world.

There is gold all through that country. Lots of it. And that is the tradition of the mother vein—and they all believe in it! The theory there is the same as all over the earth—it is the same crazy dream of all the prospectors of the earth.

"Somewhere there is a great solid vein of gold, from which all the gold of the earth comes. It comes up to the surface of the earth in places—places, shall I say? It may be also in mines!

"The ancient myths all have the same story. There is a valley hidden, known to no one. Across it runs a wall of gold. It lies between deep hills. It is open to the sun. Birds fly across it. A stream of water runs across the middle of the great lode."

"Oh, yes, yes, that is true. I saw the beautiful stream of water there."

"Precisely, my dear. And you will find that story you saw and that you describe in Peru, all through the Andes, in Colombia, in Central America—you will hear of it in Alaska, and I am told it crops up in Africa, too—that same impossible, insane dream of a great mother vein of gold, somewhere under the surface of the earth! But no man has done more than record the different phases of that dream, that tremendous myth which comes up spontaneously, independently, in every corner of the world!"

"Barry, you are talking crazily."

"Why, yes—I am. But what you saw there in your

crystal sphere is set down in type by the United States Government."

"But I don't understand what you were going to tell me just now. You were going—where? You are not going to try to find the valley of the scrying sphere?"

"Don't jeer at me, Mary. Don't talk to me. I don't dare to tell you the truth—but that is the truth!"

She only sighed, deeply.

"Listen, my darling. At this very minute there are three friends, all mining men, waiting for me at the border of Mexico, while I am talking to my sweetheart. One of them, John Palmer, has been prospecting for years in lower Mexico. I told him years ago—you see he is an early alumnus of Cornell, as I am at a later period—what I had read in Washington. He had heard the same thing a dozen times—I tell you it is in all the air of all the earth, that legend.

"Well, there are three friends of us, all mining men, who swore with John Palmer that if ever either of us found a good thing he was to call the other three together! and we four were to make the adventure as partners.

"My dear, as you know, nothing but discouragements have happened to me in Colorado—the industrial situation closed down our mine and put me out just when I was going to telegraph you to set the day.

"And only the other day came a telegram from John Palmer, naming the rendezvous. The others are in camp now waiting for me. I couldn't start without coming to see you first."

Again her sigh, deep drawn.

"Listen, my dear—John Palmer is no visionary. He started as a mining engineer and then as a prospector—but he never has played for anything but big stakes. His wire means that he has in sight the biggest stake that ever was in all the world. I know his cipher. He has located the Madre d'Oro, as I believe with all my heart and soul!

"And he knows of the valley that you have seen and of which I read—that magic valley which holds the mother gold. If that isn't magnificent, I don't know what is. And if we are not crazy, we two sitting here in the dullest town on the face of the earth—then I don't know anything at all."

"Strange things have happened in the world, Barry," he heard her voice, quiet, unagitated. "Though I won't say stranger things than this."

"No," said he moodily, "I suppose it isn't strange that by radio you can talk across the world—that by wireless you can span the Atlantic—by submarine cross under the Atlantic. I tell you, there is nothing too big, nothing too impossible. And it all is as natural and commonplace as eating breakfast, when it does come.

"Now, I'll tell you what I have been thinking, Mary—I should just as well be altogether crazy as part way. Here is the entire currency of Europe gone to pieces—

nothing under it in gold values, or anything over there normal except what is left of the British pound. But always, every time, when the world has needed a great discovery of gold, that great discovery has been made. It seems that the great mother of gold shows herself, fractionally at least, just when there is need for it.

"Well, was there ever a more terrible crisis in all the industry of the world, a more terrible crisis of all humanity of the world, than there is now? Mary, do we dare dream this way—do we dare hope?"

"Why, Barry, since we have met I have been living in a wonderful world. Is this more wonderful than that you and I are here?"

His hand lay on hers now. "Nothing is more wonderful than that, no. But I want you to feel that what we dream is known all over the world. If our little party of fools ever found the entrance to the valley—why, then you would be the queen among the queens of all the world. What couldn't we do for you?

"But I mustn't talk that way—I must only remember that you took me on when I was poor and hadn't a prospect or a chance. I am not sure that I'm better off to-day.

"Now, let me tell you some more things about your picture—and see if they are not true. The upper end of the valley is sharp rock, straight up and down."

"Yes, it was there—a straight wall."

"Of course, no one could come down it; and a stream of water falls down there. And that is the little stream which passes through the entire valley, and passes mid-way of the entire vein of gold."

"Yes, I saw that."

"But you didn't see where it went? It disappears?"

"Why, yes, I think that is true."

"You don't know where that stream of water goes?"

"No, I couldn't guess from what I saw."

"Well, I'll tell you. I learned about that in the last book; and John Palmer has brought back confirmation of what the book said.

"Of course, there are lots of mine stories scattered all though every mineral-bearing country. It does seem sometimes that these mines have actually been seen and then disappeared. Take the story of the Blue Bucket mine, up in eastern Oregon. A party of emigrants under Joe Meek as guide, who separated from a big wagon train in 1855 and tried to find a short cut across to the Willamette Valley—those people really had made a tremendous gold discovery. A woman came back with pieces of pure gold and said she could have filled her blue milk bucket. But they were lost, crazy. After they got through, twenty parties tried to find that place again—they were all for killing Meek because he would not lead them to it. And without doubt or question there had been a rich placer which was covered up with that outcrop of gold by some land slip. Now, that is what we can call straight history. The Blue Bucket placer has never been found since then. Yet they had lumps of gold from it to prove that it was there.

"Take the Pegleg mine, the Lost Cabin mine, the hundred-year-old placers, who shall say they never existed? True, the mother vein never has been found. In all our history of mining there is only one real mother lode—that is the Comstock. But the Comstock itself would prove the Madre d'Oro might be possible somewhere if only it were found. Well, who knows?

"I tell you, it is time for the Madre d'Oro! And I tell you also, it does exist. And I tell you also, John Palmer says that he has found it!

"Mary, your little valley was a hole punched down in the center of the earth. There was no way to get into it or out—only one. Your little stream of water disappeared in the side of the valley nearest to where you looked. Well, it ran directly under the mountain. It came out under the foot of the rock—and there it seemed like an original wellspring, just a spring stream starting out as so many do, later to be lost in the sands.

"Now, where this stream comes out of the rock wall there is no trace or indication that there is an entrance into any place—no one would ever dream of going up after the water, because there the water is, ready for use. But—I know it as well as if I had been there with John Palmer—a leaning rock almost covers the spring where it comes out. The aperture is shaded by heavy tropical vines and bushes. No one with his senses or without them could dream that this is the entrance to the mother of all the gold of all the world.

"There she lies, shining, waiting, I think. Waiting

for the day. I would rather say that than to say waiting for us."

"But, Barry, where is all this?"

"Mexico, my dear—Mexico—to-day. It is distinct, concrete, objective. We are not going on a wild-goose chase. We know precisely where we want to land and what we want to do.

"You know about the great gold supplies of the Aztecs down in Mexico? You know how Cortes, the original conquistador, extorted gold from Montezuma?

"Well, our history agrees that the Aztecs had some sort of tremendous supply of gold, fine, pure gold. Montezuma used that gold. Though they grilled him or pulled out his finger nails to find where it came from, he would not tell them—because he did not know himself.

"Now, that is the truth about it. Not even the king of the Aztecs knew where lay his supply of gold! If that knowledge were general how long would it have lasted?

"But it was guarded, kept as the sacred secret of the Aztec people. It is always mysterious and baffling, as is the whole history of that people.

"Now, the story tells that only three men of all the world, chiefs of the war clan of the Aztec tribe, ever had the secret of the magic valley. There were only three of them—there will be four of us!"

"Tell me all about it, Barry."

Suddenly he drew up, to think at last.

"Mary, if you and I were not one, I could not tell you anything without breaking my own oath. You know what they say about giving a secret to a woman?"

"Why, Barry!"

"True, this is too big to be a secret of two—we simply are one. And we must remember that."

"Go on!"

"Well, then, I shall. When Montezuma needed gold, he felt word at the council of the tribe that he must have it. As though he had rubbed Aladdin's lamp it came in due course. No one knew whence it came or who brought it—it was there, that was all.

"Now, the tradition, as I get it, was that no one knew the identity of any of these three owners of the secret of the Madre d'Oro. No one suspected that they even lived. It was general knowledge of the Aztecs, of course, that there were rich placers in their country; but they did not live on the same standards which we have—wealth meant little to them; they were happy in their own way. When the king needed gold he wished for it—and, being king, he got it."

"But the three men, Barry? They could not live forever."

"No. That is true. But the secret came down for a couple of centuries perhaps, and only three men at one time ever had it.

"Those three men knew the identity of each of the three guardians. So when death took one of them by war or by disease the remaining two guardians must choose a successor. Kill all three of them, and you killed the secret, of course. Well, very likely all three of the guardians were killed by the Spaniards in the fighting around in Mexico, and that was how the Madre d'Oro disappeared for these centuries since then.

"Well, say our two remaining guardians held a conference at once. They agreed that a certain man, wise and mature, of their clan, might be candidate timber. One of them went to him and made some excuse to go back into the mountains alone with them for a few days. He never could suspect what was the actual reason.

"The three of them now would camp out and talk of general things, the two guardians feeling out their candidate, whose fitness was pretty well determined in advance. Little by little they broke to him the purpose of their visit. By and by they told him outright—if they concluded he would be fit and worthy, but they killed him if they did not elect him.

"And then they sent him alone into the wilderness for a week of fasting and prayer. Patiently they waited in the wilderness for his return, purified, sanctified. If they did not accept him?—well, then he did not go back to the settlements again.

"But we'll say he was accepted as the missing one of the Three Guardians. Now he was bound by oaths, whose terribleness you and I can only guess, to protect forever, as dearer than his life, this secret of his people. So now, with the wrath of their god impending over him in case of his faithlessness, the new man came into this terrible secret."

Suddenly Barry Allison straightened up, as if smitten of his conscience. "But to-day there are four —and you would make five!"

"Don't! Barry—I think that you and I—that we are one."

"So be it then. If I never come back it is still my secret and not yours to tell."

"Finish with it, darling. You can trust me, I think—we can trust one another. Finish!"

"Very well. Now, the Three Guardians went back to the villages, the temples, back to their lives, as though nothing had happened. In all the history of the Aztec people there is no hint or trace or suspicion that one of them ever endangered the secret. And the actual history of the Spanish Conquest shows that the source of the Aztec gold never was determined.

"Neither have we ever found the great mines of Peru, where the Incas got their gold. Nor was the actual secret of El Dorado, in Colombia, ever found by Drake or the Spanish pirates. The wealth that came from Carthage never really was traced back to its source in the mountains. The whole bloody, wild history of the Carthaginians never has been followed back to its source. At that time the world was crazy for gold—and great ships brought gold to Spain, France, England, tons and tons of it; because Europe needed that gold. But no one knew the actual secret of the source.

"Is it too much to suppose that some one of those old peoples knew the outcrop of the Madre d'Oro—some place where a natural, continuous deposit of gold, deep down in the middle of the earth, rises like the writhing of a great snake, and shows itself a little at a time here or there—just enough to show that the Madre d'Oro does not forget her people?

"Well, Mary," he went on after a long silence between them, "it costs no more, since we are into this, to go on with the whole story. Suppose the Aztec king needs gold and says so in his council. No one shows a trace of having heard the message as for himself. But, silently, one man or two—never all three—stroll away from the village and disappear. If only one, he knows where the little river runs down in the sands. He follows it up slowly, and comes to the place where a spring seems to burst out from a solid rock. He knows how to push aside or to get under that leaning rock. He goes in—and the passage opens before him.

"In the pebbly valley of the stream he walks, or crawls, a long, long way, through the channel. And so at length he sees what no one but the Aztec guardians ever before have seen—that which you saw before you yesterday in your scrying glass—the face of the Madre d'Oro herself.

"My dear girl, the thought in my own mind is how John Palmer has stood at that leaning rock. He has seen the flash of the morning sun on the face of the Madre d'Oro—more. He could not handle it alone—he needed us. He came out. He sent for his three friends, as we agreed long ago, solemnly. We four—and you—are the guardians to-day. Well, am I crazy? I suppose I am.

"Yonder comes the smoke of a steamship of a man whose fortune was made in ore he mined and sold—but made by using the raw resources of the world. Well, gold is a raw resource, no better. Only, he must have it, as much as we must have youth. And there it is. There it lies, waiting.

"That is how I came," he added at length, simply. "Am I a fool?"

"Oh, glorious fool—yes, yes, you are!"

"You believe we'll find it, Mary?"

"Don't ask me that. I believe I love you; isn't that enough? Can you say so much for me?"

He choked as he turned to her. Then, forgetting even the wild vision that had burned his brain, in spite of all who might have seen, he cast an arm about her, under her great umbrella. His lips burned at her lips, his cheek lay against hers—there in the open day, looking out on the open lake where the lazy smoke told of a steamship going out for the wealth of the world, proved and sure.

Now there could be no further talk between them. The great thought of their love outweighed everything else in all the world. Youth was theirs, as was hope.

He rose at last, seemingly ten years older than when he had come to that little seat where both had talked of magic.

"Give me a year," said he. "If I don't come back, forget me. If you find another man—well, you are free—but don't tell him, ever. Part of you is mine whether I live or die; and that you must never share with another man."

Her great gray eyes looked into his strangely, questioningly, neither could have said when they actually parted. But presently she was walking back alone, advancing along a shady street of Deneville town. Her lover was gone—whither, and on what wild errand? A secret was buried in her heart, never to be told to a living soul.

CHAPTER III

THE GRINGOS

THE pink dawn of the high Chihuahua plains, again saluted by the quavering call of the coyote, drew apart the curtains for another pitiless day. The dead ashes of the little camp fire were stirred by the morning breeze. In the blanket cocoons of sleeping men sounds of life appeared, stretchings, accompanied by yawns and groans of humorous discontent. Silsby arose to his feet and spread his arms to the sun as some ancient warrior of sunworshiping days. Hallock followed with a whoop of youth and exultation. Old John Palmer sat on his bed roll pulling on his boots, silent, as was usual with him.

"Another day of loafing," began Silsby as he began his own morning duties of the camp. "Allison ought to be fined. I don't see what's wrong with him—holding us here for a week."

"Two more days, and then we start," commented John Palmer quietly. "With or without him, we start. Some things can't wait. As for the reason of his not coming, that's easy enough, I tell you."

"Oh, yes, I suppose so," rejoined Silsby. "Well, he

showed me the girl's picture once. Some looker, I'll admit. She's got a head like the goddess on the dollar."

"Hum!" rejoined Palmer. "He had better look at the dollar more and the head less. So far as this party is concerned, he can have just to-day and to-morrow for his chance. I always told you that, if there is any trouble in this game we are after, it will be because of some mix-up about a woman."

"Well, John, they are more or less prevalent all over the world." Silsby began to slice the breakfast bacon.

"They weren't prevalent in the councils of the Aztecs," rejoined Palmer. "They knew how to safeguard their little secret. Fact is, I believe it never would have gotten out at all if it hadn't been for a woman. At least, that's the way it came to me."

Pug Hallock looked up at him. "Been holding out on us, John? You never said anything about a woman so far as we were concerned."

"Well, I have learned enough about women down in here and elsewhere to know the danger of trusting young people like yourselves. I'm superstitious. There was never a chance taken of any kind in the old Aztec system. And here we are, held up when time is worth everything to us, while one of our party fiddles around with a girl two thousand miles away. For a cent I'd cut him out and start to-day. I haven't worked all the best years of my life to have this thing hang on anybody's whim, I'll tell you that."

The others caught the note of decision in the older man's voice and fell silent. Allison was known and trusted by them all, and the two younger men were unwilling to discount his loyalty or discretion. They ate breakfast rather moodily.

"Well," ventured Silsby after a while—carefully feeling at a coat pocket where lay a certain letter of his own—"wait till we hear what Allison says, if he ever does come. How'll he find this place, anyhow?"

"I gave him directions," said Palmer quietly. "If he can't find us here by compass, he doesn't belong in this country."

"Well, me, I trust him all right. He'll explain," said Silsby.

"Yes? He'll say we ought to have seen her beautiful eyes."

"Tut, tut!" rejoined Hallock. "How about your own mysterious lady down in there? You ought to see her hair, her eyes! When it comes to woman folks, least said soonest mended."

With a certain feeling of division among them they completed their simple camp duties. After that nothing remained to do except to sit in the sun and look over the wide plain. Palmer began to pace up and down nervously, a little apart, his impatience growing. From time to time he swept the horizon of the east with narrowed eyes, again with his field glasses. At length his posture showed arrested attention. He stood for a long time at gaze before he spoke.

"Boys," said he, "something is moving over there, and I don't think it's cattle."

He handed Silsby the glasses, and the latter gave a long look also.

"Narrow cloud dust," said he, "coming on steady from the direction Allison ought to come, eh?"

"Yes."

"Well, we'll have to hold our horses and not get in too big a hurry. I'll bet that's Allison. When he does come, he'll come running, that's sure."

"In half an hour we'll know," replied Palmer. "Go smother out the fire, you fellows—don't let a bit of smoke show. We can't take any chances with friends of the late Mr. Villa. We might not be able to explain to their satisfaction. They'd do what they could to put us out of trouble, eh?"

"Very likely," replied Silsby. "But all Mexico just now is enjoying quiet and security."

"I wish I could say so," grumbled Palmer. "I'll feel a lot safer when we get inside the cover of the Sierra Madre There you might hide. Here, it's plain shooting, with no place to go but up."

All three now turned toward the camp site, which was below the rim of a flat draw, so chosen that their figures might not be seen against the sky line. Mile by mile the tiny dust cloud grew upon the great plain. At length Silsby spoke.

"One man riding hard, one pack doing its best. I'll bet my clothes that's Allison!"

"Better late than never," grumbled Palmer. "He's come close to losing his share in this treasure ship. You young men have got to learn right here at the kick-off that team play is the only thing that goes. If any of you has any doubt about this fortune hunt, best say so like a man, and go back and stay back. If we are located as gringos in here, good night! These Mexicans don't love us a little bit."

Silsby again felt something crinkle as he laid his hand against his jacket pocket. How long it seemed since he had seen the girl who wrote that letter!

Presently Hallock sprang to his feet and waved his hat.

"I see him, plain!" he called. "Lord, how he's riding!"

They all sprang to the edge of the swale, signaling to the approaching rider, who apparently spurred onward the harder. At last he came in, sprang from the saddle and threw his reins down, approaching, grimy, smiling, hard-bitten, burned red by the sun. He caught the hands of each in his before he spoke.

"John!" he said at last to the oldest man. "Eight years since I saw you. This certainly is fine. You think we're on a good bet, eh?

"Fellows, I'm sorry I kept you waiting."

The long-suppressed wrath of John Palmer at length found voice. "You kept us a week. Don't you see this sort of thing can't wait? We are in danger every minute of our lives now and will be until we get out."

"Well, maybe we can do that in a year," said Allison, smiling in his frank way, his white teeth making a clean line against the brown of his face.

"A year?" queried Palmer. "It may be more or less than a year. Why a year?"

"Well, I have my own time limit, John. You see," he went on, answering the questioning gaze of John Palmer, "I told her—that is, Mary—that if I didn't come back inside of a year she could call it all off and do as she liked. Mary—you see, that's the girl in my case. Risk? Yes, I am risking my life."

Palmer stood looking at him soberly. "You didn't tell her anything! You didn't spill over anything of the business we are on? You didn't talk to a *woman*, now?"

Allison flushed a deeper red. "By Jove! I did, though," he admitted like a man. "I didn't tell her any details, because I didn't know any. Why, John, she's part of myself!" He looked at his companions, a sudden consternation at his heart. "Why, I couldn't help telling her, John," he said at length. "Why, John!"

Palmer had hastened away and sunk upon his bed roll once more, his face turned aside.

"Have I done anything wrong, John?"

"You know you have," said John Palmer at length. "You have broken our first oath—of silence. Talk to a woman! Great God! was there anything so colossally stupid in all the world!"

"But you don't know a thing about it," broke in Allison. "You don't know her. You never saw such a girl!"

"And I don't want to see her and don't want to know her! Well, she will tell the next man who makes love to her. My first concern is for your safety and that of all of us. I told you teamwork was our only hope. Tell? Why, of course she will tell.

"And so I failed!" he added slowly, breaking the heavy silence that fell. "If ever I take any partners in with me again, they're going to be men who can hold their tongues so far as women are concerned."

"John! Why, John!" began Allison yet again. "I'll go back, if you say so. I don't want you to feel that way about me at all. Come now, you really know nothing, you only suspect something. Mary and I are just the same as married. Don't you think she's in on this partnership as well as I am?"

"I don't think anything of the sort!" exclaimed Palmer.

"Great Heavens! this secret may be spread all over the world by loose-tongued people—you know how any gold story flies. You can't stop it once it starts. And it's sure to start!

"I've tried to impress on you the bigness of this whole thing. If we find the Madre d'Oro, it will change the history of the United States! It will mean an extension of her territories—it will mean perhaps war for us. That's not all. It will mean the reconstruction of the economics of the entire world. It will mean the readjustment of the currency of the entire world! There isn't a man, woman, or child anywhere on the earth's surface that won't be affected by the thing if once we pull it off. Chance? Aren't there chances enough, without adding to them? Bitter? Why, of course I feel bitter about it.

"How much did you tell her?" he demanded at length, turning squarely toward Allison.

"How much? Why, only as much as I told you before you ever started down here. Only as much as she could have found for herself in the Bureau of Mines book where I first ran across the story. Come now, I'm not going to stay along if you think I've been foolish about this. Shall I come, or stay back?"

The three looked from one to the other. "It's his first offense," said Hallock. "He can't offend again down in here."

But Palmer would not jest. "When the two priests of the war clan took the third candidate out in the mountains, either he was found fit or he stayed in the mountains. He never went back. Now, you ask me, and I tell you. We'll take you along with us because that is the safest way. Beyond that, what comes, comes; it's too late now to help it."

"Well, I hope that, as an American gentleman who has given his Aztec word to the priests," said Allison slowly, "if I ever endanger you, you can treat me as though I were not an American, but as an Aztec—as though we all were that."

"Well, let's get down to bed rock. You didn't tell her where you were going?"

"No!" exclaimed Allison. "How could I, when I didn't know myself? I didn't tell her anything which I learned from you or any one else. Oh, yes, she knew I was going to Old Mexico, guessed that, I think; but this is a wide country. I don't know even now where you are headed, John. If you want me to ride back, I can go just as fast as I came."

"No, you don't!" said Silsby. "John doesn't mean that, really. He's just wrought up. We are soldiers four, and none of us must think that anything has happened to change that. One sandstorm back of us, and all traces are lost. As to what's ahead, only John knows."

"What do you guess about it, Allison?" queried Pug Hallock with a smile.

The newcomer turned toward Palmer directly.

"Well, if I had to guess," said he, "I would say that we have got to go a long way south of here. When you study the whole ancient civilization of this country you will find that their headquarters lay far to the south, not far from where the City of Mexico is to-day. That's the Anahuac Plateau. The Toltecs held that before the Aztecs came. That seems to have been their promised land. One race after another—and now here comes our Saxon race!—from the north, like all those others. You say you are superstitious, John. So am I."

He fumbled in his pocket and drew out a tiny news cutting. It told of the discovery in Mexico, at a mentioned spot, of a vast lode of gold so rich as to run nine pounds of solid gold to the ton, and one hundred and fifty pounds of silver also—not ounces, but pounds. In short, the two lines or so of the clipping stated that such was the richness of this new-found mine that it bade fair to cause a readjustment of the currencies of the world!

"Well," said he, "I didn't put out that news myself, did I? I found that in a paper on my way here, before I crossed the line. It may be some one else has found the Madre d'Oro, John. Maybe we are too late. Anyhow, the thing is nearly ripe to break. Superstitious? Why, yes. For myself, I feel mighty small about it. Maybe we are just puppets in some great game."

Palmer nodded, silent. But Allison was not content.

"Now I'll move to the previous question," said he. "Do I go with you, or do I stay back?"

Palmer turned to the others. "The buccaneers always left it to the vote of the company," said he. He smiled. "I know how the other boys feel. You will come along with us."

"That's the talk, you old desert owl!" exclaimed Silsby. "And I'll bet Allison guessed it clean. You want to go back into the hills somewhere, two hundred miles from the City of Old Mexico? You have located the secret valley somewhere within sight of old Orizaba? You want to work where Cortes failed?"

Allison turned toward Palmer suddenly. "Don't ask me how much I told Mary Westlake. I have told you how much. But I have not told you that she already knew as much about the Madre d'Oro as I did myself. She told that to me independently."

"What do you mean by that?" demanded John Palmer. "Is this whole thing going to be in a news dispatch?"

"Oh no; not so far as I am concerned, or as she's concerned."

"But what do you mean about telling you something?"

"You have heard of the art of crystal gazing? The Scotch call it scrying. You take a crystal sphere, perfectly clear, and you look and look into it until you begin to see things. You can see in the glass things like a dream—things you couldn't possibly have known about yourself. Next to the second sight of the old Highlanders, that's the most mysterious thing in the world. But there is no getting around the facts as they actually exist.

"Well, now, Mary Westlake isn't just an ordinary girl, content with dancing and the movies. She has always thought, experimented, investigated ideas. She took up crystal gazing, using it for study, experiment, trying to see if she could explain it. She never did explain it; but she told me one thing. I'll leave it to you to explain if you can.

"I didn't feel I could go away without saying good-by to her. We have been engaged off and on over five years. I didn't think it was fair to her or fair to myself to go without seeing Mary first and telling her that this was my last hope. If I didn't win, then she must forget me, for I would never come back to her again. Well, then, after she got my wire telling her that I was coming, she took out her little crystal sphere and went into her room and began to look into it. John, she told me what she saw!"

"And what was it?" The others turned to him eagerly.

"She saw—the real Madre d'Oro! Why, you condemn me for telling her the secret—she knew the secret already.

"She described it to me. There was a deep-lying valley with its sharp walls rising all around it. There, across the entire valley, ran a great dam or dike of solid gold, with a little stream of water breaking over it in the middle. There was the whole picture as the old Book of Mines told it to me and to you. If there wasn't anything in this, how could she discover it independently and tell it to me after gazing into her crystal sphere?

"Of course, scientists would say that I had that picture in my own mind; that her mind and mine were closely attuned; that what she saw in the crystal was only what I had seen in my mind. That's very pretty? Yes. But what I am saying to you, John Palmer, is this: the girl you condemn had that secret of the Madre d'Oro before I ever spoke a word about it. Now explain it if you can! And doubt me if you can when I tell you that I impressed on her the fact that all her happiness, and mine, and the lives of all of us, rested on her secrecy. She's scared about all this as you and I are. Trust her? I would trust her with my life. Even with yours."

Again silence fell upon their little group, waifs, strangers, far out in the great desert of Chihuahua which, time out of mind, has been known as the *Llano de los Cristianos.*

"Build up the fire, fellows!" said John Palmer suddenly. "Allison's hungry. Make some coffee. We'll saddle up at once then. We'll not break our company."

Before the younger men turned away each went up to John Palmer and held out his hand. Then the four clasped hands in token of their agreement, their resolution.

Their doubts, suspicion, recriminations now set aside for a common purpose, the four partners in the desert bivouac now fell to work together. When Allison hastily had snatched a bit of breakfast at the renewed fire he joined the others in catching up the hobbled stock and making the packs. It was speedy work, for these were accomplished mountain travelers.

"How about these picks and shovels?" asked Allison

of Palmer. "If any one finds those, won't they advertise us as prospectors?"

"We'll put all that stuff on one mule," replied Palmer. "Then, if they ask us anything, we'll say we're freighting some stuff." He busied himself at another pack, knocked it open, and disclosed a half-dozen tall-spired sombreros of the Mexican pattern, and as many gaudy serapes. "If we wear these," he said, "at a distance we would be taken for Mexicans. We may evade the villages, but there are always vaqueros and shepherds who might see us. Besides, I am especially afraid of some band of the old Villastas. Those people have found that it's easier to murder than it is to work."

"Well, we all knew the risk before we went into this," replied Allison quietly. "It is little less than a miracle that could ever get us in or get us out."

"Yes. We have got to take the supernatural on trust," rejoined John Palmer.

"Tell me, John," Allison asked, smiling, as he looked straight into the gray eyes of the old mountain man who had spent his years in the waste places of his country, "how do you figure that we four men can take the rôle of conquistadores? Cortes hadn't very many men, and he burned his ships behind him; but they had armor and horses and swords, whereas the Aztecs wore cotton armor and fought on foot with bows and arrows. To-day the rifle of any moso will shoot as hard as ours. Suppose we find our valley; how would we profit by it?"

"We are all fools on this errand, of course," rejoined John Palmer, "but I have never been such a fool as to try to read all the future at once. All we can have to start with is a general plan and a readiness to pay the price of risk. If I hadn't thought over these chances, do you suppose I would take on you three young fellows and go down into this country where they would cut a throat for a dime? Probably not. But we four might not be enough. We might need some sort of allies, auxiliaries, if it ever came to any real trouble. You have heard of the Yaqui Indians, maybe?"

"Yes. I have seen some of them alive in the penitentiary at Chihuahua, waiting to be shot. The Rurales brought them in."

"Well, the Yaquis never have made peace with the Mexicans. For a hundred years the Mexicans have made them prisoners and sent them down to the hemp fields in lower Mexico, Yucatan, Honduras. But no one ever yet broke a Yaqui's pride or changed his enmity.

"Not far from the place where I have lived there's a valley full of these Yaquis—sullen, silent, resentful now as they were before they were sent down there in slavery. I have been among those people. Don't you suppose I know what they would do if they saw a chance to make a little revolution of their own?"

"So? You have done a bit of figuring on some fighting?"

"Naturally. You have been asking me how we

would get out of there if we had cause to run or fight. I know that much of the answer. I know that one man would not be enough. I wanted additional leaders, additional allies. That's why I took you boys on."

"Fair enough," smiled Allison. "I think you will find we will make good. But just one more thing, John, I'll ask about—if it's true that the valley of the Madre d'Oro lies within striking distance of the old fighting ground of the Spaniards in the Conquest, why do you come away up here, north six or seven hundred miles, and undertake a horseback journey across the entire republic of Mexico? Why don't we all jump the rattlers and ride up or down to where we want to begin our work?"

"You've a great head, young man," answered John Palmer, grimly. "Well, in the first place, I wanted to see how you young men would wear—whether you were fit to have the full details of the Madre d'Oro or not. Two or three months of saddle and camp life will show that to me well enough. In the next place, if we had traveled by rail we would have been seen and watched and followed, without a chance of escape from it. I am hoping I can get through in this way by dodging all the settlements. I know the trails. Of course, in any case, the security for life is poor, very poor, yes. But if we succeed!"

Allison nodded, the solemnity of the undertaking once more impressing him. Palmer went on.

"If we could find and utilize the Madre d'Oro, of

course we would be the richest men the world ever saw. But there is something bigger under all this. When Cortes found Mexico he unsettled the international relations of all Europe. That put England and Spain at war for a generation. Now you are asking what we would do if we found the Madre d'Oro. Why, man, that would mean war once more! It would mean the last revolution in Mexico. It would mean that the flag of our republic would move down across this republic. America then would handle the key to the wealth of all the world. You talk to me about the World War—down in here I have missed all that happened all these years. But you tell me enough, and I have read enough already since I got out to know that the world you and I knew is gone forever. There's a vast debt hanging on the world which has got to be paid. Suppose you and I could pay it—suppose the United States could really be the benefactress of the world? What, then? Sounds rather large?

"Now, listen! I have all this figured out more conclusively than you think. If we can get through and uncover the Madre d'Oro itself we probably can do so without discovery. If there should be any fighting, I shall have local allies. As to the ultimate utilization of the great vein—that is a question for our country and our flag. That flag will follow us, as surely as the flag of Spain followed Cortes. We may be forgotten as he is. That, it seems to me, is one of the least of our considerations."

"You talk in large terms, John Palmer," said Allison, gravely. "But what you say has not the sound of a foolish man's words. You are no idle man. Cast away all these years—well——"

"By a woman!" exclaimed Palmer, bitterly. "Yes. It was some woman who drove almost every prospector and wanderer out into the West when I was young. And another woman even here—even down there——"

Allison's eyes narrowed.

"Why, yes, then. We speak of Cortes and his Mariana. He could never have conquered Mexico without her any more than Lewis and Clark could have crossed the continent without the help of Sacajawea, the Indian girl. I will not deny it: it is as Silsby said—women seem rather prevalent all over the world. Let those things rest—you will know about my life the last eight years when we have got further forward with our journey. Don't ask me now."

Allison still looked at him, soberly.

"John," said he, "am I crazy? Are you?"

"Why, yes, certainly," replied the older man. "Every one is waiting for us, in my valley." He smiled grimly. "I am one of the fair gods. There is a primitive world down there which has not changed much since the time of Cortes himself. When I bring you in there—when we bring other Americans after us—well, they will only smile and say that another race has come down the old road."

"The old road?"

"Yes. If you had read your history as you ought to have done before you came down here you would know what I mean. As I told you, all the prehistoric conquistadores of Mexico have come from the far North, from some mysterious region that you and I don't know anything about.

"You ask me where we are going. I think it is enough to tell you that we are headed for the Anahuac Plateau, the dooryard of the Madre d'Oro."

"You frighten me, John," said Allison, soberly. "I don't mean that you make me afraid of the physical and personal dangers. Have the mountains put madness in you, or is all of this true? If it weren't true, what did that story in the old book mean? What did the story of the crystal sphere mean? John, I tell you I don't dare stop to think of these things or I'll get rattled!"

"If we have faith," replied John Palmer, simply, "we can move mountains. And if any one of us lacks in faith—well, then, let the rest die. Even if we die others will follow us over the Old Road. When the world needs the Madre d'Oro the doors will be thrown open once more.

"And as for you and me and our friends," he concluded, turning at last to saddle his own horse, "we must humble ourselves even as did the Sacred Three. Free agents? Why, no. You tell me about the telegraph and the wireless and the radio and the airplane—was the discoverer of any of those things a free agent of himself? No. Providence? Yes. Something which we don't know about, after its own fashion chooses the necessary agent. It might have been an idle toss of the dice in the hands of the immortal gods, laughing as they cast them. You men—some other men—what is the difference? When the time comes, the Madre d'Oro opens her doors!"

CHAPTER IV

THE OTHER MAN

"BUT, Mary! Mary, listen! I tell you they have known it all along—the whole town knows. Why shouldn't I love you—shall I be ashamed of that?"

"Perhaps not, Randall," replied Mary Westlake. "But I should be ashamed if I allowed you to go on. Yes, it is true—I have guessed for quite a time the state of——"

"—of affairs between us, yes?"

"Yes, call it so if you like. We have grown up together. It is true, as you say, that our parents have rather planned for us, without consulting us much about it—at least, not myself."

"And why not? The two greatest fortunes in this town, in this part of the state—the best two families in town! Can't you tolerate me at least? All I ask is what any man would ask when he finds he has got to wait. Won't you let me wait?"

"But I have already said no."

The two sat together, on the great veranda of the Westlake mansion house, she with a foot on the floor as she pushed back and forth the wide hammock which at times made her refuge of a summer eve. His porch chair was close to the end of the hammock. They were alone about the place. Mary Westlake's parents had departed with pretentious indifference shortly after the arrival of Randall Trent.

As to the latter, he was quite altogether the most desirable *parti* of all Deneville.

At that very moment more than one mother in Deneville entertained bitter thoughts, for they had seen Randall Trent's car drive up in the twilight, saw it now still remaining in front of the Westlake home. And Randall Trent was quite the richest young man, the most desirable young man, for any unmarried girl in Deneville; which latter community naturally held its own quota of unmarried young girls.

It was June, and Allison had been away now for a month. Since his departure Trent had come again and again, ever since he had arrived in town. Was it Allison's visit itself which had called out a new attractiveness in this stately young woman? Was it the thought of him which brought a new color to her cheek, a new light in her eyes? Did her blood still pulse the faster for his words of love, making more active her charm for another man? At least, Randall Trent suddenly had awakened to the fact that this girl, whom he lazily had regarded as sure for him when he chose to tell her, had become as once more remote and more attractive. As he saw her now she seemed to him indispensable. He found in her all any man could ask in a woman—

knew her, beside, from long acquaintance; knew her loveliness, her highness, her aloofness, her freedom of all usualness. Love her any man might, respect her any man must. And now she had said no once more.

"Yes," said he. "But women do sometimes change. I have always come back, haven't I? And I always will. I've never been accused of quitting."

"Quitting? What have you had to quit, Randall? Hasn't life been handed to you about as much ready and finished as for any one you ever knew? You were rich before you were born—richer now that things have advanced. You have success without any effort of your own. You have not had to quit any line of your business, because you have been backed for all the capital you have needed by other branches of your family. Why, pine forests and iron mines bought by your father and mine forty years ago—how could their children keep from getting rich? They did the struggling for you and me. At times it all bores me—it's so respectable. So cut and dried and commonplace that it all must lack in actual things worth while, this life here."

"I haven't found it so," replied the young man soberly. "I have always had plenty to keep me busy. As to my fortune, I haven't lost it and I'll keep it. Haven't I told you before I was just back from Mexico? I have made a million in oil down there at Tampico. I did that on my own thought and judgment. What do you find wrong with that?"

"Mexico?" She spoke dreamily. "That's pretty far off, isn't it, Randall?"

"Yes! The richest country in the world. We ought to have it. Our own lands are gone—everything is taken up now, all chances. Pine—iron—where do you find them to-day? It is well enough that our fortunes were found by men who had a different day and generation. There is no ground floor left."

"So you call it all luck to-day, Randall?" she asked him. "As though it was not always luck from the first till now."

"But you don't answer me, Mary," he went on. "Am *I* to have luck, now when I need it? They call me Lucky Trent. Myself, I don't know. What can I call myself if I fail with you? Why, the unluckiest mortal in all the world!"

"I don't think I can listen to you any more, Randall," said Mary Westlake quietly, but with decision. "There are many sweet young women in this town. Find the one you fancy—there will be many to choose from, Randall." She pointed down the street. "But not myself."

He drew back, chilled. "That means only one thing," said he.

"You guess shrewdly, sir! But isn't that just the jealousy of a man for every other man?"

She spoke slowly, looking dispassionately at him as he sat, noting his long, well clad limbs, his immaculate, scrupulously exact summer attire, his well-combed hair, his well-kept mustache, his general appearance of well-groomed prosperity, not untouched with frequent metropolitan environment. Randall Trent was indeed a very fair example of the rich and good-tempered young American, who does himself rather well and takes his life easily and gently. Not at all soft, not at all awkward, indeed, not at all unmanly; she could have said so much as that. Compared with lean, sunburned Barry Allison the latter would have suffered in the eyes of more women than one. But what Mary Westlake reflected just now—and she did compare those two—was that never in his life had Randall Trent heard the hounds at his heels; he had never in his life done the one decisive, eventful, remarkable thing.

"You were in Mexico then?" she began again tentatively, for a reason that perhaps not even she herself guessed.

"Yes, and I have to go again. My interests down there are getting heavy. The oils have made me rich and are going to make me richer. Even down there the big things are pretty well taken over now. There is little left of the big things of our country now—water power, gold, oil, energy—the world must have that to go on. But how much longer can we supply our own wants? I say, we ought to take Mexico. We need it."

"That is as far as morality goes in your mind?"

"Well, yes, since you ask it. There is no such thing as morality when it comes to commercial things. But I didn't come here to talk like Bradstreet to-night, Mary.

You know why I came. We both have health, money, education—what more is there left?"

"You make a good argument—but always it comes back to a Bradstreet basis! You're fair enough, I can say so much as that!"

He flushed a bit in spite of his self-contentment. "Well, as to the rest, you have heard it more than once. But I love you—love you more than anything else in all the world."

"Girls like to hear it," said Mary slowly.

"Well, then, I love you and always will love you."

He reached out to take the long fingers of the hand that lay idly close to the hammock edge as she swung gently. But the hand was drawn away. She avoided physical contact with him easily, steadily, unconsciously. The clasp of Barry Allison's hot fingers on that hand still lingered there.

"Mexico!" she repeated once more, dreamily. "When were you there?"

"I told you I just got back last month. I called here the second day after my return."

"You have often been there, haven't you, Randall?"

"Yes, a half dozen times or more."

"You will be going back soon?"

"Yes. Awfully hot in the summertime; but I can't help that."

"What is it like down there, Randall?"

"No place for you or me to live. A thousand years

behind to-day—but rich—rich beyond belief! No government, no energy, no race, no nothing. I tell you, it is a country just waiting to be used."

"And very rich? Very, very rich?"

"Beyond belief, Mary, as I said. Why, look here."

Suddenly he dug into a pocket and pulled out a creased newspaper clipping which he handed to her.

It was identically the same newspaper cutting which had been duplicated by Barry Allison in the Chihuahua bivouac with his friends. It went on to tell of the enormously rich discovery in Mexico of a mine which seemed fabulously impossible.

"Think of that," he commented as he saw her reading. "Nine pounds of solid gold to the ton—do you know how much that is? And, besides that, one hundred and fifty pounds of silver to each ton. Why, if we got a lode of that, there would be money enough for all the world. And so, Mary, it would unsettle the economics of this whole world—it would alter the currency of the whole world. If it's true, all the world will have to re-mark the values of its goods and chattels!"

Mary looked up at him with drawn brows.

"Why, yes," said she. "I have seen that before."

"How long ago? Where did you find it?"

"A friend sent it to me."

"And what friend?"

"Well, you ask me rather frankly, don't you Randy?"

She laughed at him, the tips of the two little incisor teeth showing as they sometimes did. "Well, it was a gentleman friend, Randy."

"Who was it?" he demanded.

Something in his dictatorial way, his half-rudeness, seemed to give her a warning. She drew back.

"Let me see whom he could have been," he began. "Was it that young man who came here three years ago—a mining engineer—Harrington, Abington, what was his name?"

"You perhaps refer to Barry Allison, Randall."

"Yes, that's the name. Cornell man, I remember now. He once asked for work in our mines back of Superior. We didn't want him. He went west—Colorado, I think. He has never showed in any big deal I ever heard of—Allison, it was he?"

"Yes. Now you know."

"But, Mary, what on earth do you mean taking up with a man like that? He hasn't been here for years—you can't have known anything about him. He can't have amounted to anything or he'd have been around here long ago."

"Well, he was here this spring. He told me—yes, he was very fair about it—how poor he was, not how rich. His people have done nothing for him and never can do anything for him. He has known hardships, yes. It has been a fight for him—and he hasn't won it yet."

He sat looking at her, lacking an immediate word. She looked down at him calmly from her hammock level. "Yes, I am engaged, Randall," said she quietly.

"Engaged—and what kind of a prospect is that?"

"I don't know. The engagement is to last for one year."

He brightened. "A year? That is a short time."

"It seems a very long time to me. But he said that if he did not come back within a year he would not come back at all. It was a dangerous thing—what he planned."

"And if he fails, what then?"

"Why, I don't know. I can't think so far ahead as that. I can't believe that he will fail. But—I can hope that possibly he will succeed."

"You were talking about Mexico," said Randall Trent keenly. "Has he gone down there?"

"Why, yes; it was Mexico."

"Where—Tampico?"

"I don't think so."

"It was oil? He is a mining engineer. Was it about some mine—some gold mine, maybe?"

"How should I know?" She began to fence.

Randall Trent drew himself back in his chair. "Well, he just wandered in here and kissed you good-by casually and said he would marry you if everything went well within a year, though he was broke and always has been broke; and he didn't tell you where he was going, or why or where?"

"You seem to think I am on the witness stand. You can't cross-examine me, Randall."

"No, but I can guess when you don't answer! Mexico, is it? By Jove! I wonder if he ever saw this clipping. You say he had that with him when he came to see you?"

"Yes, that is where I got it. As to the rest, you can do your own guessing if you like.'

"Hah! If I can strike his trail and follow him—why, he might get to be my mining engineer, isn't that so? I might take him on now and not let him go as I did when he first asked work of me?"

"I fancy he has seen a little in his time," said Mary. "I think he knows his way about by this time."

Randall smiled. "Well, suppose he ran across this very mine that is mentioned in the papers? What could he do? Where would he get his capital? Many a man has found a prospect, even found a mine—but he didn't always get anything out of it for himself. It takes capital, my dear, nowadays more than it ever did. And yet—why, listen to me, Mary! I'm not going to be bluffed out by any man, least of all one who has gone away for that length of time and left the woman he loved. I am going to be right here, as often as you will let me come. I am anxious for your happiness. I tell you I always have loved you. I would do more for you than anyone else in all the world. I'll not be gone any year—it won't take me that long to comb out all roads into Mexico. Perhaps I can tell you more about that young man than he ever has himself!"

She smiled at him slowly, amused, unmoved. He himself was radically moved. "Mary," said he suddenly, "how would you like a wedding journey down in Mexico—with me in my new airplane? We can cover the country from Juarez to Mexico City. I'll wait for a year, if you say so. When he is passing I will just be coming. Meantime, while I am here in town I will be here every day or every night if you will allow me—and every time I see you I will tell you what I am thinking, both day and night. I am thinking of marrying you sometime, Mary."

"A la bonne heure!" said Mary smiling.

The richest girl in Deneville—the richest young man in Deneville. What fortune!

"Well, thank God!" exclaimed Dan Silsby at noon of a blinding, sunlit desert day. We're in sight of the hills and at the edge of this flat country. I swear, I hate the sight of cholla. As for the famous water out of the celebrated barrel cactus, I am free to say I like even the rain barrel back home better."

Pug Hallock grinned with cracked lips as he nodded. The two were lagging a trifle back of Allison and Palmer, bringing on the pack. "Sure hot!" remarked Hallock. "Well, as near as I can figure from our map, we'll be between the two big ranges all the way south.

We have been out about a month. We've done ten, twelve, fifteen miles a day, haven't we?"

"Easily that, I should say, yes."

"Then we must be now three hundred and fifty miles from where we crossed the Rio Grande near the edge of Chihuahua. Southwest with the crows for guides over the Plain of the Christians—why they ever called it that I can't see. It's no place for any Christian faithful man to be at all."

"Horned toads!" grimaced Silsby. "Rattlers till you can't rest. Barrel cactus, organ cactus, cholla cactus, prickly pear cactus—ocatilla, Spanish bayonet, soap weed! Jack rabbits! Antelope with white tails a mile away! Yes, I am free to say I'll enjoy the mountains for a change."

"You have to hand it to old John," mused his friend. "He's one good old desert rat, if you ask me—travels as well at night as by day and carries his plan under his own bonnet. Well, it has worked so far. We haven't met anybody—and we hit the railroads square between Escalon and Jimenez—slid across at night and didn't leave a trace behind us."

He tried to look at his map as he jogged along. "We are in Durango now, I fancy," he said. "A couple of weeks will find us halfway through. So far we have dodged all the people from the placitas. As to old John's late plans I can't guess. He certainly keeps a tight mouth."

"Best way. If we were held up and asked where

we were going we couldn't tell any one. But look at the doorsteps we keep crossing—these little cross ranges as we ascend toward the high country. We are coming into the worst volcanic country in the world, I suppose. Around Orizaba peak—she has been dead for four hundred years—you could stick your finger in a dozen live volcanoes between there and the Pacific. As for the *temblor,* if they don't get one for breakfast down there they don't know what to do. Folks tell me it makes you seasick along the Pacific coast, the ground rocks up and down so much.

"That volcanic country is the natural and rational home of the Madre d'Oro. Some of the heaviest earthquakes ever known to man have torn and twisted that country all to pieces, turned it upside down. That's the very melting pot of the centuries, down there. Another three hundred miles and we'll be in another world for fair. All this country—all of the great plateau—is built only of the ashes of the past. Well, we take our chances—I have and so have you."

"My Kismet is working pretty well to-day," rejoined his friend, rubbing a forefinger across his forehead. "What is to be will be. We have enlisted for the utter and entire war, as I understand it.

"Hello!" he added. "What's up now?"

The two riders in front of them suddenly had swung aside from the trail and were coming back, bent over their saddlebows. The four now closed together rapidly. Palmer held up his hand.

"Round in the mules!" he called. "Head them toward the foothills yonder—we have to get under cover."

"What's up, old man?" asked Silsby, turning to Allison.

"There's a little pueblo right ahead, beyond the cañon mouth yonder," answered the latter. "We'll run right into it if we go ahead. Come—let's be off."

Their leader turned them into the foot of a dry arroyo whose soft sand gave little sound as they hurried their animals along. Presently they got cover in a scattered growth of piñons which reached up on the hillside between them and the cañon which they had evaded. In this way they advanced for a mile or two, until Palmer pulled up, feeling safer.

"We'll wait here for a while," he began. "If I'm not mistaken that little town is called Loma Verde. I have heard that old Pancho Villa used to come in here once in a while—one of his favorites lived here, maybe. If he should happen to blow in now it might be awkward for us. I think we'd best hold up here until night, and then try to get by. Meanwhile I think I'll go have a look-see."

"In technical language," began Pug Hallock, who had been a captain in France, "this is what is called a meeting engagement—where two forces run across each other without warning. The advantage will rest with the force best fitted to attack. The assault must be composed of three units, the attacking column, the flankers, and the reserves. That leaves about one man to hold the horses. That's not going to be myself."

"Tie all the stock fast and hobble them besides, and fix on side lines," ordered John Palmer. "If they leave us we are done for."

"One thing is sure," he added. "We have got to have some corn meal before long. Beside that, we have got to have some mule shoes. Come on, let's have a look through the glasses over the edge of the hill."

All four of them advanced under cover of the long ridge which he indicated, well scattered and each looking to his weapons as they ran, stooping, taking cover among the trees and rocks which marked the mountain side. Palmer at length turned and held up his hand, beckoning the others to join him where he lay behind a rock that gave a view of the country on ahead.

"Listen," said he. "That's a drum!"

They could hear it, a dull intermittent throb or boom from some strange instrument like a drum, struck with small interest in rhythm or regularity.

"That gets me!" whispered Palmer. "I don't know of any revolution down in here. What have they to revolute about anyhow? It's peaceful as a grave here. But look at that—one hundred and fifty of them marching off up the valley!"

The sounds of the drum seemed to recede. They moved along side by side, cautiously but eagerly, until at length the whole hidden prospect lay open before them.

Coming up from the lower levels of the Mapimi marshes—those curious highland remnants of a shrunken and forgotten ancient sea—the travelers now had reached the edge of the foothills of one of the low mountain ranges to which Hallock that very morning had called attention.

For an hour or more they had followed the faint trail which led to the opening of an abrupt passage between the hills. From their present point of observation they could see that this continued like the neck of a curved bottle. On ahead it opened out into a pleasant valley whose sides swelled equably toward the shoulders of two mountain spurs.

These lay before the explorers, an unexpected picture of trees, fences, cultivated fields. Here and there the sparkle of *acequias,* leading down from some mountain rivulet, showed where the water was conducted among these plots of green vegetation. Close at hand, just at the entrance of this valley, lay a group of low adobes, scattered as though thrown down by some careless hand. Beyond these lay the communal fields and pastures, running back a mile or so into the open range.

Over this kindly little picture of a far-off land the sun shone benignantly. It was a corner of the world where white men rarely if ever came. Even old John Palmer, traveler and dweller of interior Mexico these eight years, admitted it was new to him. He had come north across another angle of the range.

But now a half mile or more from them, they could

see long lines of persons of both sexes, mingling with groups of others, marching alongside. Most of them seemed clad in white. Their course led beyond, to one side of the valley toward a cañon which seemed to make back into the hills a mile or more away.

An exclamation escaped from John Palmer as he lay, his glasses set on the rock before him. "Well, it isn't war! On the contrary, it's peace, if religion ever does mean peace."

He handed the glasses to Allison, who studied the scene below him.

"They're in white!" he exclaimed. "They're following a man—he is carrying something. He's"—his voice fell into a whisper—"what's this, John? Have they a Passion Play in here?"

"Something like it," Palmer nodded, turning over on his back and venturing a cigarette. "Yonder is proof of the thoroughness of Cortes and his friends, the padres. That is a procession of *penitentes*. That's all.

"I've heard of those people," said Hallock. "They scourge themselves for their past sins."

"I'll say they do!" ejaculated Allison, still busy with the glasses. "What should we do?"

"Let them alone!" said old John Palmer on his back in the sunshine.

"Well, where does that leave us?" asked Silsby. "Here we are on foot, with no flour to speak of, since we lost that mule in the Mapimi marshes."

"Yes, he got off the path—the old path which a

decent mule ought to have kept to," said John Palmer. "Good old mule he was, too—and with our flour! Well, you ask what's to do now? I'll tell you—this, now I come to think of it, is about the luckiest thing that could have happened. We struck this village at precisely the right time. Give them till nine o'clock to-night and they'll all be home and happily drunk. In the dark they might take us for people of their own sort. I savvy their language all right."

"But you're not going in there, John!" Allison looked up at him suddenly. "Can't we sidetrack this outfit and get through without their knowing we are here?"

"We could, but where would be the flour and the mule shoes?"

"Mule shoes? How do you know they have any?"

"They've got to have! They've known how to shoe mules in Mexico ever since the time of Cortes, and the mines have taught people that a mule will wear his feet out on rocks if he isn't shod. Of course they have got mule shoes down in there—they need them in their own business, and we need them in ours. I'm going into that village to-night."

"I approve your general strategy," said Pug Hallock. "But I'll admit that this looks a whole lot like using fighting tactics."

Palmer only laughed at him. "We are not going to let any of these peons scare us," said he. "To-morrow we'll be on our way. To-night—well, we'll go in and have a look-see.

"Yes," he concluded. "Those must be the *Penitentes* I heard were at Loma Verde. They said that old Pancho Villa's inamorata would not have much to do with the faith or with him. In fact, I heard that she shot him in the knee one day."

"That's right," asserted Silsby. "That story was handled by the Associated Press. Villa was reported to have been wounded in battle."

"Only a little battle between one man and one woman, if I got the story straight. Well, I am willing to go in to-night for two or three different reasons. It's always a woman, no matter where you go, isn't it? Maybe we can see the lady who shot the robber prince."

CHAPTER V

THE GHOSTS OF LOMA VERDE

THE heavy purple robe of twilight fell upon the shoulders of the mountains in subtle majesty and beauty. The stars broke out, brilliant lamps in the high, clean air. By nightfall the travelers had finished the meal which they had prepared at the tiny fire now extinguished. John Palmer untied his riding horse.

None of them mounted, but led their riding animals, followed by the pack train, tied neck and tail, in single file, so that there could be no stampeding and no scattering. Slowly, silently as possible, they followed the sandy footing of the arroyo path which threaded out not far from the entrance of the little cañon.

"Come right along in," whispered Palmer. "Don't get up—follow me!"

They did so, passing finally within the wall of the cleft between the two hills, traversing the cañon for two hundred yards until it opened out at the foot of the little valley which they had seen. Carried down the cañon came the pungent smoke of piñon fires. They knew from this that the people had come back to their houses. Indeed, lights showed at windows in the little group of adobes, fully visible in the twilight.

The religious celebration had ended. Wearied, exhausted, bloodstained, the devotees had come back and cast themselves on their rude couches in the little huts. Women, some of them old, bloodstained also, moved here and there from one hut to another, vaguely seen by these invaders. They all were stiffening now under the wounds inflicted in the madness of the day's devotion.

The strangers, led by old John Palmer, came straight on in, the clatter of the led animals' hoofs partly muffled in the sand and all keeping to the shaded side of the valley entrance. Presently they reached a corral of logs and poles planted upright, lashed with rawhide to cross poles. Palmer paused and held up a hand.

"Let's tie here," said he. "Silsby, if you don't mind, you might stay here for a little while and the rest of us will go on. You will be the reserves. The rest of us will push in a little deeper."

By now the light of the marvelous southern moon had begun to irradiate the valley, which lay half in moonlight and half in the shade of the eastern hills. Palmer advanced, still in the shadows, making cautiously up to the side of the first large house.

There was a window upon the side nearest to him, a window without glass, for that was an unknown article here. He approached this aperture on tiptoe. When he turned back he seemed amused rather than frightened by what he had seen.

"About a dozen of them in there," he said. "All over the floor, tired and drunk. Two women cooking—one is a girl—I couldn't see much except that she seemed to be light-haired, not like the others. Some Andalusian blood, I suppose. Sometimes that persists in Mexico generation after generation. I have seen blue-eyed and fair-haired Mexicans in my time, plenty of them. But that isn't all. That girl is getting corn meal out of a sack near the door. And, what's more yet, there are eight mule shoes hanging on the left-hand side of the fireplace after you get in!

"Do you think your Uncle Johnny knows the habits of this country?"

"Oh, all right," admitted Hallock. "But where does that put us? We can't go in and buy anything from them, can we?"

Palmer only smiled. He felt in his pocket and drew out an old rusty nail which with prospector's thriftiness he had put there in some forgotten moment long ago. Out of another pocket he produced a piece of string which he now carefully unwound.

The others watched him, not understanding. About three or four feet from the end of his string he tied on the nail. The rest of the string he uncoiled behind him as he once more approached the window. They saw him raise his arm as though to attach the free end of the string. Then he came back, carefully overhauling the thread which he had left on the ground. He dropped down to them in the shade of the corral around which they had crawled. When he began to move his hand they heard very plainly a faint tick! tick! It was the sound of the nail as it dropped again and again against the lower edge of the window frame.

"Good old tick-tock!" said John Palmer, turning his head over his shoulder and grinning. "It would be better if they had any glass in their window. But you know how it goes—which one of us hasn't tied a black thread to a nail and scared people foolish by putting up a tick-tock? Wait, now."

All at once the voices in the adobe seemed to hush. They were listening. Then, excitedly, the inmates began to break out, shouting. Came exodus of sandaled feet. An instant and the house was empty.

John Palmer put his hand to his sides, shaking with silent laughter. "Simple trick," said he. "But sometimes the simple things work. Come on over to the house."

They got his theory now—laughed as he did at this first success. Most of the frightened people had gone into a neighboring house which, like the other, boasted a fireplace and an open window. But now the tactics of John Palmer were changed.

"Barry," said he to Allison, "go back to the horses where Silsby is and open the pack of the front mule.

Bring me all the hobbles there are—the chain hobbles only. I don't want the hide hobbles, but the old army sort."

He did not explain himself nor did the others ask it. Allison slid back in the dark. Palmer had wrenched from the corral a long slender pole and brought it along with him.

He and Hallock stood listening to the excited voices of the fugitives, their general clamorings. Through the shadow came confused conversation, ejaculations.

"*'Espiritos! Espiritos!'* That's what they're saying," whispered Palmer to Pug Hallock. "Ghosts! Wait a minute and I'll show them a ghost that'll make them sit up and take notice for fair."

They waited until Allison had returned, carrying with him a half dozen pairs of hobbles, the latter closely connected with steel chains. All of these Palmer carefully lashed to the end of his pole. Then, silently, he stood up and thrust the end of the pole, carrying its strange armament, directly through the open window. With that leverage he began to jerk the other end of the pole up and down. The chains clanked loudly in the dark. No one upon the inside could see any one on the outside. Only the noise as of fetters and shackles could be heard. This Palmer now accompanied with certain long and lugubrious groans which must be heard distinctly by the frightened inmates.

A wild and general shriek of dismay came from

within. Again the rush of sandaled feet, and in an instant this house was empty as the other.

"*Malo! Malo! Es malo!*" came back the word as they ran. And such was their firm belief that their abodes were infested by evil spirits, so assured were they that all the devotion of the day had been rendered nil by some shortcoming—that not only these inhabitants of the village but all the others, warned by their outcry, incontinently deserted their own firesides and betook themselves to the refuge of the hills.

The three invaders stood close together in the dusk when John Palmer withdrew his contrivance from the window and untied the hobbles. They did not dare laugh aloud, but slapped one another on the shoulder, ready to burst in their mirth.

"Let's go back to the horses now and get Silsby," said John Palmer. "It looks as though the road was clear to the meal and the mule shoes!"

"Well, fellows"—John was speaking aloud now—"that was easy, wasn't it? They have all flown as birds to their mountain. What?"

"We have surprised the enemy," said Pug, chuckling. "Turned his flank and broken his center. It would seem that now we might move on his supplies."

They all took turns in explaining to Silsby what had happened. He laughed as loudly as the others. "Well, John," said he, "I'll have to admit that you're a natural general. You ought to be revoluting down in here—what a team you and Pancho would have made!"

"We had better move on in and see what we can find," said Palmer, as they struck a moonlit open spot. "I don't know just how long they will stay out—probably as long as we keep hid and stay quiet. I'm a bit hungry myself for a little native cooking. The smell of that stew the señorita was fixing came out through the window mighty fine. I haven't lived under Orizaba for five years without learning to like red peppers."

They walked to the front of the house and without ceremony stepped inside. The interior, lighted only by the firelight, now fallen low, contrary to their expectations, was scrupulously neat. The walls were whitened with gypsum, the little conical fireplace in the little room also was whitewashed, and the earthen floor, trodden hard, was swept clean as though it were floored with boards. Here and there a sheepskin lay upon the floor, some stained with blood from the wounds of the devotees.

"Take that whole sack along," said John Palmer, nodding toward the meal bag of coarse flour made of the blue Mexican corn. "They will think the evil spirits took it, if they ever think at all."

By this time he had reached for his coveted mule shoes. Silsby swung the meal sack across his shoulder and stepped out into the night. By now the point of moonlight was creeping toward them as the orb edged higher above the eastern edge of the valley. Absolute silence had fallen upon the little village. Its inhabitants all were cowering somewhere, hidden out beneath the piñons, no doubt looking down in terror but dreading to visit in the dark the homes from which they had been ousted by the malicious spirit.

"Sit up now, boys," said John, when Silsby had reëntered. "Take your sheepskins and gather around, and let's have a shot at what the Greasers eat. Gee! but she smells good, looks good, and tastes good! Well, happy days—and greasy fingers!"

"Happy days!" rejoined Pug, fishing for his jack-knife. "I don't mind a little stewed mutton myself. I wonder where they left their *pulque*. I wouldn't mind a swig."

Palmer reached toward him a low, wide-mouthed jug of pottery which he found. Hallock tried it once.

"Bah!" he exclaimed. "I have tasted better in my time. These people here are primitive, very, very primitive! But the stew's all right, anyhow."

They helped themselves from the cooking pot, which they had swung off from the fire—a composition of peppers, red and green, and a sort of dumpling made of meal. As though in a home of their own they sat, trusting to the lasting success of their strategy. Health and appetite left them as comfortable as though they sat in some gilded cafe of a far-off metropolis. Once in a while one of them would step to the door and rattle the mule shoes which John Palmer had tied together; then return to take his place on the floor with his companions.

They laughed like schoolboys, far off here in a country where none lived who might not be their enemies—all these surely would have been had their real errand been suspected.

All at once John Palmer held up a hand. "Hush!" A sudden sound had come to his keen ear. They all paused, listening, each shifting his weapon into place for use.

It came nearer, the soft whisper of sandals on the hard earth of the sidewalk path outside. It hesitated, began again, came close to the corner of the house; paused there.

The men inside the house were now in a position suddenly reversed. They were lighted to the view of any one who looked through the door or window, but they themselves could see no one, even at that stage of the moonlight. They sat in their turn almost as much in consternation as had the occupants whom they themselves had frightened away.

. . . . . .

Randall Trent held to his asseverances with Mary Westlake. No day went by that she did not receive some reminder of his presence or his purpose. Flowers came regularly, not from the local florist, but bearing the name of prominent Cleveland concerns—violets, orchids, roses, more expensive though no sweeter than those of her own garden. Daily his car drove to the front of the Westlake mansion. Yet it tarried there no more than a few moments; so the watchful matrons who sat behind the curtains on Portland Avenue remained puzzled over all this question of Randall and Mary.

But much as he persisted in his open advances—and the more she repulsed him the more maddening became the very thought of her—so much the more intense became her quiet indifference, coldness. Time and again he came to the front door of the Westlake home, morning or afternoon or evening, confident that, as the father and mother still held him *persona grata,* he should see the daughter on like basis, but time and again the old house woman who answered the door would grin understandingly as she announced, "Miss Mary is not home to-day." If he demanded where she was, when she would return, he had no answer but the same understanding grin. It irritated him immeasurably. Only his devotion could have brought him back. He was the richest young man in Deneville and, moreover, much accustomed to having his own way. He had it not with Mary Westlake.

One morning when he drove up in a brand-new, one-seat roadster—which he had purposed to give Mary as earnest money on the bargain which he coveted—he was met at the front door by no less a person than Dr. Blakely, family physician for the Westlakes these many years. Blakely none the less was a modern medical man, keeping abreast of the day. He was rumored to have a considerable reputation in the columns of medical journals which no one in Deneville had ever seen.

"What's up, doctor?" demanded Trent. "Any one sick? Not Mary, surely?"

The older man grinned amiably. "Not so bad as that for you. It's her mother."

"Mrs. Westlake? It's not serious?"

The man of medicine spread out his hands. "Not so sure. She's been rather under the weather for quite a while but wouldn't give up. The old stock, the old stock! They keep house till they drop, and how're you going to stop them? Well, she had to have a rest or come to a regular breakdown. If it was a woman who didn't work we'd call it a nervous collapse. The remedy is just the same for all classes."

"And what's that, doctor?" Trent was now walking down the brick walk toward his car.

"The only way to treat a nervous collapse, my dear man, is not to treat it at all. Rest—that's everything. I call my prescription the three S's—sleep, silence, and sunshine. We can't get those things here."

"And so then?"

"I have ordered her out of town."

"But where, doctor? Canada?"

"By no means, just the other way. I told you I want warmth, sunshine, rest. I thought of North Carolina, and, of course, California. Most people think all they have to do to get well is to go to California. Some feel better out there, and, if they think so, they are."

"I know that country mighty well myself," ventured Trent. "In fact, I was just thinking about taking a little run out there before long. The golf there is the best in the country, and, as for roads—we have nothing like it anywhere else."

Dr. Blakely grinned pleasantly. "Thinking of going, too, eh? Just a coincidence. Let me feel your pulse. I'd just as well do a little business while I'm riding along with you. Yes, I think you need a trip to California.

"But, as to knowing California," he went on, "you don't know it. Anyhow you don't know the country I've got in mind. It's not California at all, but part of Mexico."

"Well, I know every place in the state or out of it that's got a decent hotel."

"But you don't know this place, and there is no hotel there at all, and there never has been. I'm referring to what these Mexicans call Baja California—Lower California, that long strip that sticks down south of San Diego. Japs and booze-runners and pearl-fishers—all that sort of thing."

"Well, do you know that country, then? I've been over the line, to Tia Juana."

"No doubt. But this is a long way south of there. It's away down and away in."

"How did you happen to go there?" demanded Trent.

"I never have been there at all. All I've done has been to write about it. You see"—he drew up a trifle importantly—"I do a paper now and then for some of the medical journals. Not often, but once in a while.

"Well, there was a member of my profession wandered down to Lower California and came back with a story which made all the medical professors of America call him crazy. He had found an old Mexican down there, Pedro Sandoval, whom he reported to be in all probability the oldest man in the world to-day. He was known to be over one hundred and forty years old and still going strong. At eighty he cut a new set of teeth. At one hundred he began life all over again—and he had the teeth and hair to show for it. He lived on red peppers and goat meat like the rest of them, and never saw a shingled house or sat on a chair in all his life. He was never known to work beyond rolling a cigarette.

"Of course you have heard of old man Shell down in Kentucky—a mere infant compared with Pedro Sandoval. A while ago the old man got married again—to a young woman under thirty, so the story was—and he is starting in to raise another family to add to the several families of his interesting past. Down there they say the men never die at all. They just dry up and stick around.

"Well, now you see that the story was so weird that a company of doctors went down there from Los Angeles. When they came back they confirmed the word of the original rumor. Ever since then doctors have been dropping down there from time to time—I know one Chicago doctor and one from California who have been there—you see, they take the steamer and go down the coast from San Diego. They are interested in seeing the oldest man in all the world.

"It ought to be pretty fairly easy to get sleep, silence, and sunshine down there in old Pedro's country. I thought I'd take my patient, or my two patients, and we'd all make a trip down in there for a few weeks at least. If my patients don't get their health back, at least I'll get a story."

"I've never been in that part of lower Mexico myself," said Randall. "I know the east side pretty well."

"The truth is, we don't know a thing about Mexico," rejoined Blakely. "It's a land of mystery. Mexico is less known than Spain right now. And yet from all I hear there are places down there which come as near to paradise as anything on the earth's surface. It isn't too hot, nor too cold, too wet nor too dry—and we don't own it and don't know anything about it."

Randall replied with much alacrity that he was of the opinion that Lower California was the very place;

that he himself would not mind taking a little trip thither himself.

"You must look out that you don't get hypnotized," was Blakely's comment. "Why should we ever come out of paradise if we found it? What have we got up here, and what does it come to? We hurry our lives out and what does all that come to? What does money do for you, for instance, Randall? You have only got the wish to make more. Hurrying and crowding, all of you, until after a while—well, I have seen some collapses in my time. Sometimes I'd ask what this or that man ever got out of his busy life. Maybe Pedro had him beat at that. The old Greeks were reported to know a good bit about living and enjoyment in their day before there was a Greek shoe parlor in America; but now all Americans are as busy as shoe-shiners—they don't know why. Sleep, silence, sunshine? We have got to go somewhere else."

"This is the first I have heard of all this," went on Trent, rather discontented.

"Mary didn't tell you? Why?"

The young man eased himself out as well as he might. "I suppose it was because her mother was so sick. I've called to inquire once or twice."

"Yes, so they say. Well, son, I don't blame you. If I were a young man and had your health and good looks and your money, I'd make it the first order of business to marry Mary Westlake, and I'd keep at it till I did."

He had a hand upon the door handle. "Whoa! Hold up! here's my office. I must get out here. Thank you, Randall."

Without much volition of his own, Trent turned back up the main thoroughfare of the better residence district of Deneville. He sent in his card this time to inquire for the health of Mrs. Westlake—and this time he had the great fortune to see Mary herself coming down the stairs, holding out her hand.

"Randall," said she, "how do you do? Come in for a moment. I think I have been rather rude for a time, but I haven't been seeing any one at all. You know that mother's ill?"

"Dr. Blakely was telling me about it," said Trent. "Tell me, why don't you all go out to California for a change—rest up, you know? I have been thinking of going out there myself, just to get freshened up a bit. It would be mighty fine if we could all go across together."

"But I thought you told me you were going into Mexico, about your oil wells."

"I've changed my plans about Tampico. But, Mary—you know why. I couldn't go away from this place, where you live. I've been here day after day. You know what I have had for my pains. Tell me, is it a crime for me to love you? If so, I am the guiltiest man in all the world. I can't help it."

"But I haven't told you where I am going," smiled Mary.

"You need not! But don't ask me to return from following after you. Is that a bargain? There's no place you can go where I can't find you!"

Suddenly she held out her hand, smiling, mindful of the hidden place of which she had heard in that far-off land. "Yes! That's a bargain," said she. "I don't think you can find us."

He was tactful enough to rise, to bend over her hand and be off. He felt as though there were some sort of secret between them and was happier than he had been for weeks.

He began to plan about wooing Mary Westlake under a moon where life and love were better understood than here. He looked at the tall columns of smoke, at the long flat barges and ore steamers out in the lake. He hated it all. He longed for the waving of palms that whispered, near some little stream, under brilliant stars. And where Mary went, there he proposed to go.

CHAPTER VI

LUISA

THE four men in the semidarkness of the adobe of Loma Verde sat silent, eyes and ears strained, each with his hand on a weapon.

The soft slither of footfalls along the walk continued, pausing, hesitating, but coming closer to the door. There was but one entrance. As to the open window, Palmer was too much of a border man to sit where he could be shot from any window. He and his friends sat under the farther wall. Each covered the single door perfectly.

The moonlight lay brilliant on all the open spaces of the huddled village, so the interior was dark as the open air was bright. But now presently the low door was filled; a figure stood there, outlined perfectly against the flooding illumination. One hand was raised to the door jamb, the other remained docile, the fingers spread.

It was a woman. Moreover, obviously it was a young woman. Her hair caught the back lighting of the moon, though her face was left wholly in darkness. With no more than this definition, with the concealment added of the drawn mantilla, the imperious presence of youth and beauty of woman, never to be concealed, made itself felt now. A sense of amazement, of sudden curiosity, came to the four watchers.

The voice of John Palmer rose distinctly, not loud, but imperative. *"Entre en la casa, señorita. Estamos amigos."*

The apparition at the door still hesitated, only a low exclamation escaping her. The next moment she stood reflected in a sudden glare of light in the darkened interior. Pug Hallock, in spite of the laughing protests of his friends, always carried with him in camp at night one of the modern little electric spark or flashlights. He found it in his pocket now and used it.

A scream of terror broke from the visitor's lips. She turned, would have fled, but feared to do so; her hands caught at her throat in sheer woman terror, whose speech is much the same all over the world. But before she could escape, the tall form of John Palmer strode across the light beam, caught her wrists and drew her into the room.

"Luisa!" he cried. "Luisa! You!—what are you doing here? Did you know I was coming? Come, tell me!"

He spoke, of course, in rapid Spanish. His friends heard a softly murmured reply. The girl was now fully within the door. Silsby hurriedly freshened the fire with dry piñon boughs.

The hint of beauty which made itself felt even

through the semidarkness now was verified. The girl was beautiful, indeed. The gracious, round, not so tall figure was Spanish truly; but for the rest she lacked the usual marks of Spain. Her eyes, even in this light, were dark and soft, but might be blue or gray. Her hair, lighted as it was now, was not black, but blonde; a perfect golden blonde. In fact, she was of that type of beauty which is found in certain parts of old Spain and in certain parts of old Mexico—the so-called Andalusian blonde. The women of this type, even as they resemble, always differ in contour from their golden sisters of the far north. They have no rivals even in lower Mexico, a land of beautiful women.

As for this young woman, even clad as she was, even present as she was in this little hovel, she owned a strange air of loftiness, hauteur, dignity—what we call class, for want of a better word. This was true even though she showed sheer terror, caught as she now was, unprotected, in this room with four men who must be enemies, not friends.

But she knew this man, John Palmer—spoke to him directly in full recognition. Palmer's friends looked on, puzzled. What did it mean? How came she here in the darkness of this adventurous night? How should she know John Palmer? Why should he call her Luisa, as though she were his daughter, sister?

He turned at length to them. "Boys, I know this señorita! I know her people, her sister. She's three hundred miles from where she ought to be. She doesn't belong here. Can you guess now why Pancho Villa came to Loma Verde?"

He turned again, began rapid questions. The young men found themselves waiting for her replies, so soft, so low in the dimness, spoken with low voice and sweet, an excellent thing in woman in any land.

There was not a chair, not even a box, in the whole apartment. At Palmer's request, the young woman seated herself apart, on a sheepskin on the floor, easily, graciously, as though it were a throne. She drew her mantilla halfway across her face modestly, for the Mexican woman is one of the most modest women in the world.

Palmer seemed to have forgotten them all, went on for some moments in his conversation before he again accosted his friends.

"Yes, I know this girl, and know her family. That's why I am here, and that's why I sent out to my own country for you others. She has a sister down below —I can't tell you about all these things just now. But if we ever get out of here, I'll tell you more, sometime. It was down there—through this girl's people—that I learned some of the things which bring us all here on our errand!"

"She knows why we've come?" demanded Allison of his friend. "I thought you had said that no woman knew the secret."

"This girl's family is acquainted with some of the old traditions," replied Palmer, coldly. "Beyond that, it may be very fortunate that she's met us here.

"The young lady is Señorita Luisa Martinez. Her people have lived for generations in Lower California. I met them there years ago, before I went to southern Mexico.

"You see, I drifted south from San Diego down the Camino Real, hundreds of miles through the mountains. I was trailing south, I didn't know where, trying to get away from myself and certain things—traveling just to see and to admire. Well, down in that country I found the Martinez family—and the sister of Luisa. Luisa herself was then little more than a child. She went—with us—when I moved out to the coast. I can't explain everything now. I was younger then." His voice half broke as he went on after a time. "Well, at last I had found the one woman in the world! Each of us does, you know. You ask me about secret traditions? Because of the way in which I made these friends I came to know about that great secret, that great tradition. It's time now for me to tell you that I lived for a time in the middle of Lower California.

"They came from Spain generations ago by way of Vera Cruz—this family Martinez. They seemed to have tried to get as deep into the wilderness as they could—even as you and I. Well, there wasn't any place much farther off than California Baja. They crossed the gulf on some mission of their own, a few centuries ago. They made that desert blossom like a rose. And roses grew there. Luisa is like her sister, yes. Fair as a rose."

"But, John!" the voice of Barry Allison ventured once more. "We're not headed for Lower California."

"No! Nor was I headed for that country when I found it. But then I didn't know that presently I would pull up in sight of old Orizaba, a thousand miles from there. I didn't know then that I ever would be within touch of the valley of the Great Mother.

"Well, you may begin now to ask whether or not I am a fitting guide for you. I tell you, to make all this short, that for five years I've lived within thirty miles of the mouth of the valley of the Mother of Gold herself!"

"But that's two hundred miles, three hundred, below here," broke in Pug Hallock, his eyes still fastened upon the figure of the beautiful apparition of the night. "How does this young lady come here?"

"She's just told me," answered Palmer. "Oh, yes, I have known her—I have seen her grow up while I was dreaming the years away down in there. She grew up under my roof . . . I've ceased to dream. The woman who took me there, this girl's sister, died there more than a year ago."

"Yet she's here!" the resonant voice of Hallock broke in. Silsby felt the rattle of paper under his hand in the hidden pocket. Allison had in his mind the picture of a tall American girl.

"Why did she come here?" Palmer went on. "Listen, I'll tell you. You have heard me say that there was a rumor Francisco Villa came to see a favorite of his own, a very beautiful girl. Well, that last part is true—she was beautiful! This is the girl herself! This is the girl who shot the Honorable Pancho in the knee—gave him the wound which the press said he received in battle! She's been here a prisoner for months. I didn't know where she was, though I did know that Villa made a raid south with some of his bands, looking for help in the lower country among the Zapatistas. You see, the Honorable Pancho had ambitions to be president of the Republic of Mexico. Well, Mexico might have done worse—I don't know.

"But in town the Honorable Pancho saw this girl, Luisa Martinez. He took her prisoner, carried her north, and dropped her in this hole in the mountains, where no one would ever see her again. But for some reason or other that ruffian did not pursue his usual tactics with Luisa Martinez. That much I do know. She would have killed him if she could; she meant to do so. Pancho never resented the wound she gave him. He only laughed at her and promised to come back again some time when she felt more amicable. Now, my friends, we are going to take this girl back home with us. She doesn't belong here. It may mean the end of all our chances for personal safety. What do you say?"

The gaze of young Hallock was riveted upon the face of the girl before him. He could not draw back from regarding her. Her beauty fell upon him like an actual spell. Indeed, in any Garden, woman must be.

"Why do you ask that question of us?" demanded Hallock quietly.

No one spoke for some time, but at length Palmer laughed gently.

"Poor old Pancho seems to have had some sort of reverence for Luisa Martinez. It's well he had. He had chosen her for his consort. 'She will make me hidalgo some time'—that's the way he spoke to her, so she tells me. He was going to have her teach him to read and write. Oh, yes, it's quite possible Pancho would follow us if he knew—even her villagers may follow us, who knows?

"There is no prouder, cleaner blood in the world than that of the Martinez family, my friends. This girl was rich one time, could be now. There was no reason in the world why the whole family should not grow rich.

"Luisa!" He turned to the girl, whose eyes had been following him, perplexed, as he spoke. "*Querida,* you don't know what I have been saying in my own language to these others? I have been telling them that you would go back with us."

"When?" demanded the young girl eagerly, still using the Spanish.

"To-night—now!"

"You have others—you have a force with you?"

"We are an army of four, that's all."

Her eyes were wide, her lips trembled as she turned to him once more. "Can that be, señor? Can you dare?"

"Boys," said Palmer, "she asks if we dare take her away from this place." Then rose the Tartar laugh of these invaders, the laugh in front of danger. The girl understood then, even without Palmer's added words.

"Oh, yes, they'll follow us, I presume," he went on. "Come, Luisa! It's women that make all the trouble in the world. No, we can't leave her here after what she's told me. Still, I told you fair enough that we'd have enough trouble every foot of the way. Now look out for trouble!"

"Tell her that we are going to take care of her," said the deep voice of Hallock. "She shall go with us!"

"Well, that's settled then," said Palmer, beginning to get the odds and ends of his present belongings together. "She's got an old woman with her—old Serafina, a servant of her family. Villa let her bring a woman. They have a little house of their own up the street. Luisa just came back because she has more courage than these others, not being a half-blood herself. She heard something in our spirit business at the window yonder which made her suspect that there were Americans about. Well, there were.

"Yes, we're Americans. The actual conquerors of this country will not come from the south. Doniphan knew that in 1847."

"But no one ever knew a thing about the Madre d'Oro in those times," protested Allison.

"The very old town of Guanajuato was rich beyond belief—is rich beyond belief now. They had mine after mine, all through these hills, so many they could afford to go away and leave them if they felt like it. The Spaniards always knew where the gold was—always, except in regard to the mother of all the gold. That valley has not yet been found by them.

"So this girl goes with us—she and her woman. It may very well happen that she may be of great aid to us in what we have to do. You see, she's known down below—Oxaca, Jalisco. Not that her people ever loved me. We may be running into complications of more sorts than one. But we take her with us?"

The clearing of throats, unspoken words, made all the renewed answer he needed.

The young woman now broke out in a torrent of rapid Spanish, which Palmer understood sufficiently well. He turned, interpreting.

"She says we ought to pull out just as soon as we can. Says that she knows where the horses and mules are corraled and will be ready in three minutes to go with us. She thinks Villa is expected down in here again—he is getting tired of being a farmer where he is. Says we have to get up and ride as far as we can. Of course, we all know that when her people come back they will have to sit down and pass resolutions and talk before they can follow us. Maybe we can get over the next range and make a run for it. They'll only get about so far before they get tired, anyhow. What do you say to it, fellows?"

"There is no argument about it," replied Allison, and the others nodded. Allison was fingering over some dust of tobacco in the side pocket of his coat. Absorbed in the situation before them, he absent mindedly cast a pinch of the dust from him into the fire. It puffed up, broke out into a blaze, and gave a little cloud of white smoke.

"What's that?" demanded Palmer, suddenly turning.

Allison laughed. "By George!" he said. "That's some of that flashlight powder I spilled in my pocket. I was doing some vein photographing up in Colorado—some spilled out in my pocket, I suppose. I didn't know any powder was there."

Palmer turned toward him eagerly. "Is there any more of it?"

"Maybe so," replied Allison. "I think I have got an ounce or two of it in my war bag. I used to carry it around when I was making photographs of the drifts for my company."

"Go get it, quick!" said the older man. "Bring it here! Sit still, the rest of you! I've got an idea!"

Allison, without asking for any explanation, strode out of the door and across the open space to the place where the pack animals were tied to the corral fence. He had little difficulty in slipping his hand into his personal pack, which was placed near the top of the one-mule load. He returned and without comment handed over the little paper of chemicals to their leader. The latter spoke rapidly to their visitor. She rose and passed out swiftly.

"I told her to hurry and get her horse saddled, and to bring Serafina at once. When those two women come, all of you but Hallock go on down the cañon with them. I don't want to lose our caballada, so you go down the trail a half mile, where you can't hear much or see much.

"You see why I want this powder? You have to understand the mental processes of these people. I'm going to throw a spirit scare into these folks which will make them think of anything else but following us."

Hallock broke out into a gust of laughter. "By Jove!" he said. "We'll touch her off outside."

"Exactly! We'll disappear in a pillar of fire and a cloud of smoke by night. If I'm any guesser, that'll hold them for a time. Now, Allison, you and Silsby set the packs and cinch up all the saddles. We don't want to stop, once we do get started. There's quite some country between here and Orizaba peak—three hundred miles or so at least."

Hallock was least anxious to mount and ride. Instead he sat down, leaning against the adobe wall. "I'll just wait along with you, John," said he. "I'll take the women on down."

Palmer laughed. "Oh, all right!" said he. "It's too bad you can't speak Spanish."

"Some day," said Hallock. "Some day—who knows?"

"Quien sabe?" Palmer still smiled. "Well, I'm going to give these people a Fourth of July which they'll remember as long as they live."

He scraped together a little pile of dust from the hard earth, hollowed it slightly on top, and into this receptacle poured his flashlight powder. He and Hallock stood listening to the lessening footfalls of the animals as they passed rapidly down the cañon. A few moments and they heard hoofbeats coming from the upper portion of the plazita. Luisa rode a side saddle, evidently from the lower country. Serafina, her serving woman, was seated after any fashion on top of an easy-footed mule.

Hallock rose, removing his hat as he stepped up to the bridle rein of the foremost rider. "Tell her not to be afraid, John," he said. "Tell her I am going to take them down to where the others are waiting."

Light-hearted, boyish, he hummed to himself a carefree air of his college days. "Around her neck she wore a purple ribbon!" Then, unconsciously, he hummed the refrain, "Far away! Far away! She wore it for her lover, who was far, far away!"

"Hush!" said Palmer. "Don't be silly, Hallock! Go get me that old door hanging against the house there. We'll prop it up against this new fireplace so I won't get my legs burned when she goes off. I'll take a chance now. You two get out of here, fast as you can! I'll wait until you get around the corner."

A moment later old John was left alone in the center of the deserted village of Loma Verde. He paused until he heard no sound of hoofbeat from the cañon mouth. Neither did he hear any sound from the surrounding hills into which the population had scuttled and lay hidden. At length he stooped over, a lighted match in his hand. His hand reached out above the top of the sheltering plank. He dropped the match—sprang back.

There came a roar, a vast, blinding flash. A tall pillar of white smoke rose up into the mountain moonlight. It was a thing inexplicable, not to be dreamed of by these ignorant observers hidden in the surrounding fringe of trees. To them it must have seemed a thing of terror.

Palmer turned back, laughing like a child, and ran as fast as he could down the cañon.

"She's good powder, boys!" he exclaimed, when he came up to them. "I'd like to have a few more pounds of it along."

The others, hidden in the defile, could only guess at

what had happened. He explained. "That ought to explain to them, if we haven't proved it already, that spirits are abroad to-night. I'll bet a thousand dollars that's the worst scared bunch of *pelones* in all Mexico right now."

"Far away! Far away!" The others cheerily broke into the old college refrain which Hallock had started.

"What is it that the young gentlemen sing?" asked Luisa, close at Palmer's elbow. "I don't know the English."

"Rest easy, my dear," replied John Palmer, in her own tongue. "This young gentleman is only singing that he is thinking of his loved one, far, far away."

"Indeed?"

"Yes. And she wears around her neck a purple ribbon, my dear."

"A ribbon of purple? And she is far away?"

The voice of Luisa was low and sweet, even if now a trifle contemptuous. They passed out into the night of the cañon walls.

It is a wild and unknown country, mystic, mysterious, strange, old, that long peninsula which lies just under our lower borders in the far southwest—one which we held under our own flag for a little time, and abandoned as worthless. Spain originally held it, if it could be said ever to have been in any human holding. Its original inhabitants were the wolves and the antelope, the wild deer of the wastes, the small foxes, the reptiles of its deserts, the wild, horned things of its dry mountains—these were the first and fit peopling of that strange, fascinating, yet forbidding land.

Always men have dreamed of treasure there, and some have found it; others have lost it. Against the few and scattered natives who once dwelt here hundreds of years ago, the bands of Spaniards sent out by Cortes waged war for sake of treasure. These natives dwell to-day as they did then, in the little valleys, around the water holes, in isolated settlements, infrequent, inconsequent.

Should you travel the trails which reach inward from the sea, you might come upon strange valleys; or you might find some of the little bays where vessels have been coming for years. Gold, pearls, the fur of otter and of seal—all these things and many others called the adventurers of earlier years.

In this land time is not noted. There are almost no instruments known for the measurement of time. Life flows on in one vast, steady stream. There are men here so old that they do not know when first they looked on life. There is no reason why life should be here, or why death should come here. Sometimes death forgets to come.

Now it was this last fact to which Dr. Blakely, physician for Mary Westlake's mother, had adverted. The story of old Pedro Sandoval, the Spanish centenarian, had brought its own hysteric publicity of to-day; and now to-day was bent on tearing asunder a great and splendid yesterday.

It was long ago the rumor came up to the California cities—of an old Mexican said to have passed a century and a half of life. Surely he was far above a hundred years of age, as could be proved. This man, as Blakely said, had cut his second set of teeth at eighty years of age, and was past a hundred years of age when he married one more young wife and set himself seriously about the business of beginning once more the establishment of a household. Thereafter he added largely to his already large flock of children, who lived about him in the sun and sand.

It was the strange case of this old Mexican—nameless, not famous in any way—which first attracted the attention of medical men to this far-off country. Had old Pedro not lived on so stubbornly or apathetically, forgetting much to concern himself with life, forgetting even to die at the appointed time, Doctor Blakely could never have learned of the strange little valley where dwelt the white man Father Ernesto, in his own unknown Ranch of Good Hope.

Father Ernesto—as he was known long as any can remember—did not care for mines or flocks or herds, seal fur or pearls or sugar lands. He devoted his life to the good of others. Provided apparently with some little means of his own, he had established himself in one of the rare and beautiful little valleys far back from the seacoast. Here he had built for himself, on ancient foundations, a comfortable home of rock and sun-dried brick, adding to his adobe structures from time to time as he had need or wish. Not accredited to any church, none the less he had builded himself a little church! He had some flocks and herds, some servants who live on in tenure of one sort or the other, and who raised for him sufficient to supply his table.

It was Father Ernesto, strange recluse, who sent out to his own country, a Saxon world, the story of old Pedro and his second youth, his many marriages, his carelessness as to dying, his renewal of his youth many times. One or two parties of medical men came down by coastwise steamer, combining medicine and pearls, working inland later. Sometimes parties came down mule back, overland, passing for this or that reason across the unknown country. They all were welcomed at the home of Father Ernesto, the Ranch of Good Hope!

When the little party of medical men, of whom Blakely was one, found themselves in Father Ernesto's company one time in San Diego, something of fellowship sprang up between them. Blakely, keen soul that he was, knew without speech that here was a man who spoke no evil.

"About this old man, father," said Blakely, "what of him?"

"He is one of very many," said Father Ernesto.

"People do not die there. I read sometimes, though you may not think it. It seems there is talk of what you call germs, bacilli? Very well, we do not have them."

"How far back is old Pedro's country from you, then?"

"Thirty miles, perhaps—inside of ten or twenty miles you will be in a wilderness, in a desert. It is high, but always warm. There are very few diseases known there. They bring in men to me who have been wounded, hurt in accidents. Surgery is possible here which would be fatal in your cities—though I am but an amateur surgeon. I only take the place my people give me. It pleases them best to call me Padre. They can understand that."

Blakely answered soberly. "You have here a splendid dream, the dream of a great man, a good man."

"Wholly a dream! My piles of rock are the houses of God. My lanes between the desert streets are the streets of God. The stars of God are above them. Here and there the water of God comes up for us. There a man can forget, and be forgotten, and can learn. Do I not know?

"For instance, there was the American, John Palmer, a good man, who came to me years ago. A good man, but young . . . Well, the woman was beautiful! So, together, they went out into the world, hand in hand, not yet ready to forget. But I have seen many people go away. Myself, I remain."

"How came you there?" demanded Blakely suddenly.

"I cannot tell you that."

"They call you Father——"

"Perhaps they do well," answered Father Ernesto.

"I ask you a hundred pardons, Father."

"Some day I shall be as old as old Pedro! He is a man of tradition, Aztec beyond doubt, and of pure blood. Yet he was slave of the Spanish family of Martinez.

"That was her name, the young woman whom John Palmer loved. And they never dared return. I do not know what became of them. A man of mine, babbling, told me old Pedro had told them of an ancient treasure."

So now it was here, far back in the unknown interior that one day came a strange cavalcade, belonging here not at all—the party of Dr. Blakely and his patient, Mrs. Westlake; Mary, the daughter; their servants.

Then Father Ernesto felt his heart sink. White men, or one, at least, he had welcomed here. But this was the invasion from the north. He knew now that his own day was done. But as his life long since had been devoted not to his own happiness but to the good of others—for the sake of what he knew he owed by his own ancient fault, not yet expiated—he welcomed them; and with him, in quiet and in comfort, Mary Westlake, her mother, her physician, found temporary home.

CHAPTER VII

RANDALL TRENT AGAIN

WHEN these new travelers advanced along the descending trail into Father Ernesto's valley, presently they reached a low wall of stone, flung out to make a sort of inclosure, a few acres in extent. Its rear was fenced by the shoulder of a hill that jutted out into the lower levels. Within this inclosure stood the ranch buildings of stone or adobe, small affairs, with beams projecting from beneath their dirt roofs, the front very clean, the walls white with gypsum wash. Native hands cared for the Padre as though this were Mexico centuries ago.

At the head of the inclosures, where a rock ledge thrust out from the foot of the mountain, there sprang a spring of clear, sweet water, unceasing, very beautiful indeed in so dry a land as this. The waters of this fountain were led all about the inclosure, serving to give life to much verdure, to tall date palms, many strange plants.

Hard by, built about a palm-lined patio, stood the house of Father Ernesto, its roof, extended out on heavy beams, forming a shady cover on all edges of the patio save that where the entrance gate led in.

Under this roof was a continuous floor of wide and heavy flagstones. The adobe walls were heavy, the embrasures of the windows three feet or more in depth. The native whitewash had made all neat, and where a glance passed through a door toward the rear of any of these rooms, all of which opened upon the inner court, the floor might have been seen to be scrupulously clean, though it was no more than clay, packed hard, sometimes sprinkled with water, and regularly swept.

Some signs of comfort, though not of luxury, were visible near the window and door of a suite or apartment at the farther corner of the patio—a canary in a cage, a parrot in yet another cage, a cat lying on the floor. Mary Westlake, advance agent of the party now, caught this, and reflected how like it was to the home she had known far away, with its touch of repose—she smiled in a sudden feeling of comfort.

It was from this door that there had emerged, when he heard the tinkling of the mule bells, the patron of this place—Father Ernesto, a stranger to these newcomers.

As though a figure of some old-world picture, he advanced to them, his hands outstretched, a tall and singular figure. He was clad in a long, brown robe, caught about the waist with a plaited leather thong. On his feet were sandals. His head had no cover, his hair was long and white, his beard, strong and full, also white. His eye, the sort once wont to shine with the light of battle or the flame of love, now was calm, hid deep beneath bushy brows of gray. He had taken no orders, had known only the great vow of renunciation, but you must have thought him indeed a member of some holy order, such was the fashion of his dress, his kindliness, his fatherliness, as now he greeted his visitors.

"You have come, my friends?" said he. "I have expected you since the doctor wrote. This is the end of your road."

He reached out and took the hand of Mary Westlake.

"My daughter," said he, looking at her keenly, "the doctor wrote of you. You have wept. Why? You are young, not ill of body. You are only weary, you are only worn in mind? Come, it soon will be well with you. You are welcome here."

He turned now gravely toward the interior of the patio, beckoning them all to follow him, as they did, abashed into silence. Presently all were shown places where they were to sleep; and ere long they were led to a low-ceiled room which might have been a refectory of some old European monastery, with its clothless tables, its floors of earth packed hard, its walls of stone or earth, whitewashed with the all-prevalent native lime.

One or two silent native women passed here and there, bearing food to the newcomers. Father Ernesto also passed among them, speaking kindly to them. "Eat, my friends," said he, in his quaint way of speech, "the trail brings good appetite. These fowls are ours, and the eggs are from our own yard here. Our mutton is of the best, and perhaps you may like the peppers which we fancy here. You see, we have fruits. Our bread is ground from the corn we raise. Tea we do not often have, but coffee we sometimes get from the ports, and this sugar you see we make here in the country. Oh, we make out to live in this country, rude as it must look to you.

"You, my sister"—he turned to Mrs. Westlake—"you must eat or you cannot thrive."

A certain light came in the depths of the somber eyes of this middle-aged woman, into whose life so little of romance had ever come. Swift, unbidden tears welled quietly to her eyes.

"You are a good man, you are kind, Father," said she. He smiled at this. "You are not a Spaniard, Father," she added.

"Oh, no. I speak the language and love it very much—speak in its idiom, I fear, for I think in that speech now. But I was once American. I came from your country. That was very many years ago. I would not know it now. They call me now the Father of the Ranch of Good Hope. I am not good enough to be really of any church, though it is supposed I am. For my people here I have built a church, and sometimes holy fathers worthy the name come here and preach for us, hold mass, accept the confessions of these poor people—who have sinned little enough, it seems to me.

Sometimes also I have had Protestant ministers of the gospel from the towns far above, and have asked them to speak here also in my church. Sometimes I have argued with them all the night through as to what was religion. I do not as yet know. I have found a strange world down here. But sometimes there have been good men here. He is a good man, the doctor who brought you here, what I call a brother. To bring hope to others—that is religion."

"You are a strange man," said Mrs. Westlake, her mind struggling to understand what all seemed to her like some odd dream.

"Why do you say that?"

"Because of your charities——"

"It is not charity, it is hospitality."

"That is religion, yes!" said Mrs. Westlake.

He smiled. "It is religion enough for me, and success enough. Sixty years ago I came to this country. Forty years I lived in the hills, and taught myself to learn calm. Then I saw that it might be given me to do something wider than that, something for others as well as for myself. For twenty years I have tried as best I might to do what I could to make my peace. I prayed for ten years, madam. I am very happy, I am but paying a debt, a heavy one, one which perhaps in the eyes of God never will be paid.

"But I cannot talk of myself." He turned aside, his face showing some strange emotion which she could not fathom.

"Believe me, madam," he added, turning back, "the desert does wondrous things. Face to face, wandering in the hills, there, perhaps, one may meet—one's self!"

His voice, slow, gentle, giving almost biblical words of comfort and hope, ceased. Mary Westlake had heard much of what was said to her mother. She found herself standing alone in the dusk, on the hard swept earth before the door. A servant came and showed her with lighted candle to the room where she was to pass the night. There was no bed save a thin mattress on the floor.

There came through the door of the little room, through the entry gate of the courtyard, the sound of a tiny bell, tinkling some summons. A sort of rustle, a hush as of the evening settling down, went on all about her, as she felt insensibly. A calm came upon her mind, some sort of relaxation to her body.

"At least, Barry," she said to herself, "I'm closer to you here! Ah, where are you? Have you indeed gone? Could I ever forget?"

Mrs. Westlake, never demonstrative, did not much change her habits even in scenes so new and striking as those of the Ranch of Good Hope. Much to her physician's pleasure, she took readily to the doctrine of *dolce far niente,* which for the most part ruled thereabouts, and quietly settled down to the enjoyment of the soft air, the blue sky, and gentle mountain breezes. To her daughter alone did she express any opinions as to her personal status. "I declare, Mary, it don't seem right to me not to do any work at all. I wonder how your pa is getting on back home?"

Dr. Blakely advised her that she need give herself no concern over her absent husband, but should settle herself down to the full enjoyment of the greatest place in the world for a rest cure, as he expressed it. "You have not a thing in the world to worry over," said he. "This is a simply wonderful place. Look at the sky!"

Mary Westlake needed not this injunction. She did look at the sky, at the environing rim of the valley. Her gaze instinctively turned toward the east. She was wondering where, in the far-off land of Mexico, might at that time be wandering the feet of the man she loved.

No word had come out from Barry Allison, nor could any come. He did not know that she was here in Lower California, no more than she could guess where at the time he himself might be. The more she stopped to reason, the more convinced she became that her lover had departed upon an errand wholly chimerical.

One day, yielding with a certain shame, as a drug addict does to his chosen potion, Mary Westlake found herself alone in her little room, in her hand the crystal sphere which, for some reason that she could not explain, she had brought with her to this far-off country. Almost blushing in deprecation of her folly, once more she placed the little ball upon the bare table top, sat looking at it intently, ashamed of her fatuousness, yet hoping that once more her senses might be deceived.

And as she sat, once more there came to her eyes the same picture she had seen back yonder in her home —the picture of the deep, shut-in valley, with a stream of water flowing through, and across it a great bar shining in some unreal yellow light. The valley of the Madre d'Oro!

How long the girl sat looking at this strange revelation of her subconscious mind or that of another, she could not tell. But once more there came to her the comforting feeling that there was, or perhaps might be, something of reality in yonder figment product of unknown and imponderable forces. Yonder somewhere lay the valley of gold. And yonder, somewhere, was her lover seeking for it.

Always methodical in her habits, and realizing that here in Lower California she was closer to Barry Allison than at her home in the far north, she began to look about the ranch for some sort of map of this lower country. Telling Father Ernesto of her wishes, he smiled.

"My dear," said he, "we have no maps here; that is to say, no modern maps, for we retain small interest in what the outside world may do or be. But a map of old Spain—old, very old—that I can show you if you like."

He fetched for her an ancient parchment, placed it upon the table of the central room. "See," said he. "It shows no railroads, for the railroad was not then known. But few of the old sailing routes are given here, and almost no points of this old peninsula. Here, below, you see the pearl fisheries marked—rich, always rich, they have been."

"Yes, I know," said the girl, bending over the parchment with him. "Our friend, Mr. Trent, Randall Trent, of our town, has told me of that place, La Paz, isn't it?"

"Yes. You know our country? Does he?"

"I know nothing at all of it myself," she replied. "But Mr. Trent has been in different parts of Mexico. He is interested in oil wells over on the east side. He travels a great deal. Some men, you see, are always looking for a place to make money."

"Yes!" The face of the old man clouded somewhat. "They come more and more, that sort. We cannot forever keep them out. Yes, progress is hard at our heels now, after all. The richness of this country cannot be denied, cannot be concealed.

"The old Spaniards no more than scratched it!" he went on. "But still they had the instinct for riches of any country. See now, here is the old trade route from Cathay to Spain. Yonder, east of the Gulf of California, is where the galleons from Manila landed. Here at San Blas or at Acapulco they disembarked their cargoes for freighting mule back across to Vera

Cruz, over the old Spanish road. Bold days they must have been, my dear, when the mule trains went across. Silks and spices and gold, pearls and gems and precious stuffs of every sort—that was when Spain gained her wealth, when Europe did. Here was the treasure house of the world, my dear—here, under our fingers on the old map."

"Treasure house?" Her eyes turned upon him. In response he looked at her as keenly.

"Yes, the treasure house of the world!" said he. "Of course, you know of a great many of the old legends. Did you never hear of the great mother vein of gold in Mexico yonder? Some said that was where Spain got more gold than anywhere else of all her possessions.

"You have heard of that, perhaps—a sort of superstition?

"Perhaps more than a superstition. At least some men have thought it more. Did I never tell you of one John Palmer, who lived with us here in this valley, and was one of us for years back? We thought him settled here—he was living at the great Martinez Rancho, deep toward the interior of the peninsula."

"John Palmer!" A faint recollection came to the girl's mind. She had heard Barry Allison mention that very name!

"Yes, we called him that—or Juan Palmero. We thought that he would be happy here. For a time he said he had put the world behind him. Some woman, perhaps? We do not ask of those things. But what I know is that there was one woman here. For sake of that which we call superstition John Palmer perhaps ruined the happiness of as sweet and beautiful a girl as ever lived—Dolores Martinez was the most beautiful young woman these eyes of mine have ever seen. Well, Dolores and her little sister, Luisa—but a child she was then—went away with John Palmer when he himself left our country! Why did he go? I can tell you that. He went to see if he could find the Madre d'Oro!"

He saw the girl before him start, flush.

"You have never heard of the Madre d'Oro? You do not know the superstition of the great valley full of gold—the origin of all the gold in this country? Well, John Palmer and I talked over that.

"You see, he lived close to the home of old Pedro, that very old man whom Dr. Blakely has come down here to see. He is so old that he is of interest to science, Pedro. Well, John Palmer lived with Pedro, talked with him. And I say to you, John Palmer left with Dolores Martinez to find the Madre d'Oro!

"True, he took the maid with him to save her life and his. They were married here at the Ranch of Good Hope. Well, who should say them nay? Palmer was not a man ever to be balked of what he wished. But that thing he did because of what Pedro, the very old man, had said to him. Pedro came here long ago with the great Martinez family, from the rich country of Mexico beyond. What Pedro knew—well, why should I inquire? I am done with gold—and life!"

Again Mary Westlake looked at him keenly, endeavoring to remain on her guard. She must not talk, must not divulge anything of the secret which her lover had given her. She did not tell him that John Palmer's name was one that she had heard before. Only she felt her heart thumping at the thought that now the trails of human lives of which she knew began to converge, as though toward some magnet point of interest.

"But look here!" she said, suddenly startled out of her own attempt at poise, her finger at one point on the old map. "Look at that!"

"Yes," said the old man, quietly. "I know all about that. This point is close to a portion of the old Spanish road which once ran from Vera Cruz and Guadalajara, San Blas, and Acapulco—the old treasure road of Spain. They knew something of the Madre d'Oro, although they were not sure. See—here is what they wrote—I will translate for you: 'The supposition is that here lies the great lost mine known as the Madre d'Oro.'

"Not even the Spaniards were sure. They never have been sure. But they knew that somewhere in those mountains over yonder there was a valley tremendously rich in gold. They never found it. Not even Alvarado with all his cruelties could ever wring from the ancient peoples knowledge of the actual site of the Madre d'Oro. So they guessed at it and marked it down—so that yet others may disturb their minds regarding it, I presume.

"Well, it may be that John Palmer went somewhere in that direction. I know that he landed at San Blas when he sailed from here. Then he disappeared down the ancient road of Spain. He and his wife—that beautiful girl whom I loved and whom all loved who ever knew her—never have been heard of from that time till now. My dear, that is tragedy. They found the ancient curse of the Madre d'Oro."

Something about his senses, keen from their long-continued disuse, caught some sort of agitation in the girl's mind. His keen eyes narrowed. "What have you heard, my dear?" said he, quietly.

She turned to him frankly. "As much as the next, perhaps, Father Ernesto. History, you see, has always been the favorite study with me. I have read an old book or so—naturally they were interesting.

"But this Pedro of whom you speak, Father, what do you suppose he knew to tell your friend John Palmer?"

Father Ernesto shrugged. "How should I know? It might be natural for one so old to bring up the stories of his childhood. No doubt he and Palmer discussed the old superstitions of the land where he first saw the light of day. Oh yes, Pedro has talked to me from time to time. For twenty years, thirty, he has told me some things which no doubt he told John Palmer."

"What was that, Father Ernesto?" Her eye was innocent, though her heart was thumping in her bosom.

"My dear, his talk to me was of a hidden valley filled with gold, which lay somewhere in the mountains."

"Was that all, father?"

Again he looked at her keenly and then smiled. "No, that was not all," said he. "He told me that the Aztecs actually knew the location of that valley; that they guarded the secret with the most extraordinary precautions. Of course, you have never heard that tale."

"Tell it to me!" Her eyes, wide with surprise, were turned full upon him.

Father Ernesto spread out his hands, and then, to her amazement, her half terror, he went on to tell her what old Pedro again and again had given to him as truth—the full story of the Sacred Three, guardians of the Madre d'Oro; the method of selection of a survivor in case of the death of one of the guardians—in short, the whole detail of the Madre d'Oro legend precisely as Barry Allison had given it to her, and precisely as a document of the United States government had given it to him!

"He is very old, this man Pedro," mused Father Ernesto. "Yet never have I known him to vary an iota in his story. It is written on his mind ineradicably, that's sure. A strange man, Pedro. He had few friends, seemed to be suspected by every one on account of his great age and his great vitality. With John Palmer he talked—with me also.

"But what use have I for all the gold in the world? It could bring me nothing. What has it brought to Pedro? Some day he must die, and will talk no more of the valley within sight of the top of Orizaba. What will it bring to John Palmer? Gold—that great secret? What could it bring to me except new unhappiness?"

"Come with me," he said. He took her hand in his and led her to the far end of the shaded patio where stood two great rosebushes full of countless blooms. Between them lay a heavy slab of stone, upon it no inscription.

"You see this spot, my dear," said the old man gently. "I have shown it to no other person these many years. Under that stone for many, many years has lain the only thing in life that ever seemed to me worth having. That was the woman who brought me here. In every man's life there is a woman, my dear. You know that? You have heard that? Well, this is a sacred secret to be kept also.

"For reason of what went on between this woman and myself, for reason that all toil and danger and trouble of this world, long since ended for her—for reason that once I loved and never could love again, I say I have given up all thought of the world and of those things which interest most of the persons who live in that world which I long since abandoned. Ask me no more, my dear; but now you know why I am indifferent to all this secret of great wealth. The Spaniards at length became indifferent. Long since, I became indifferent. The Madre d'Oro? It may be—why should I care? What could it buy for me if I owned it all to-day? Ah, *Mea culpa! Mea culpa! Mea culpa maxima!*"

"Then you, too, have a story, father?" Her voice was gentle.

"None may ask me," he replied, half fiercely. "I once saw the procession of the days, as other men. Now I have seen the world go by here, day by day and year by year. We have seen it bring us a great change. When the day comes I must die. Well, so must old Pedro yonder—our work will have been done. Yet once I loved life. Once I drank to the last drop the draught of all that life had to give. But to-day—gold? Not at all! I would not sail across yonder gulf to find the Madre d'Oro."

"You speak like some old player of the morality plays!"

"I don't know what you mean. I am Ernesto. Father Ernesto they call me now, although I am no priest and never have claimed to be. Simply I have tried to do what good I could among people simple and innocent. I have set the world aside—fled from it as far as I could go. What has gone on in the world since I forgot it—that I cannot say.

"But John Palmer had not lived through all the drama when last I saw him. The woman who loved him went with him as his wife. Well, his story is his own story. Those who go out of our life need not come back to it again—they go into the world; and here the world has not yet come."

"May I see old Pedro?" demanded Mary Westlake, turning to him suddenly.

"That could be done. He is up two days' journey inland from here. But why should you undertake it? What do you wish of Pedro?"

The girl looked at him with straight eyes, her features firm. "You are a man with whom one speaks the truth. I want to ask old Pedro what he knows of the Madre d'Oro!"

"Why should you ask him?"

"I wish to know more about John Palmer."

"Why should you wish that? Have you ever heard of John Palmer before I told you this?"

"Yes, I have heard of him. I knew who he was."

The face of the old man clouded. "My dear," said he, "you do not know what you are asking. You are treading on dangerous ground."

Mary Westlake said nothing further about her desire to interview old Pedro, although the desire, the intention to do so, remained none the less keen. For three weeks, while her mother slowly recuperated, improved, under the kindly influences of this far-off valley, she and Dr. Blakely passed their time idling, reading, dreaming, making short excursions into the country that lay about them—it took but a step to carry them into the wilderness.

And then, at the end of three weeks, came an occurrence which Mary almost expected, not with happiness, but with something of dread. Randall Trent, none less, appeared at the Ranch of Good Hope, unannounced and yet apparently confident of his reception!

He did not come overland down the long trail from the southern border, but had found mule transport at a seaport on the western coast of the peninsula. Immaculate, florid, well turned out in his sport clothes, apparently free even of the dust of the trail, he dismounted at the entrance of the Ranch of Good Hope as keenly and confidently as though he had been a bridegroom.

Blakely met him, explained his coming to Father Ernesto, saying he hoped to have the privilege of joining this newcomer to their party, since he had come from their town and was a friend of the Westlakes.

Trent lost no time in finding his way to the side of Mary Westlake. He explained his presence easily.

"Of course, I knew where you had gone," said he. "I might just as well admit that I came out to California because I knew you were coming. I've been down the coast—of course, I've known about the pearl fisheries of La Paz, and lately I have heard that pearls were getting low. Two or three of us formed a little company to go down there and buy up a few bays and start a little fishery of our own. See now, I have brought something for you."

He held out his hand, in whose palm lay a half dozen magnificent pearls—black, pink, cream; the best of the marvelous product of La Paz fisheries, never surpassed in any part of the world.

"For you, my dear!" said he. And he looked at her as though he felt the same sense of ownership in her that he had in the pearls themselves. She declined to receive them from his hand.

"But you're glad to see me?" he went on, not wholly abashed. "You might know I would come! Mary, I'll follow you to the last end of the world. Sometime I hope you will let me have these pearls made up for you."

"I didn't expect you, no," said she. "I didn't ask you."

"Not in so many words. I told Blakely I was coming down."

He was poking at the pearls with a finger as he held them. "See this big black one!" he broke out. "Isn't it a beauty? We'll get it made into a ring for you. And I say! how perfectly stunning you look—you don't know how beautiful you are. I declare, the tan improves you. Isn't it a wonderful climate here?"

"It's good for those who want rest and quiet."

"It's good for anybody," he rejoined. "I may come down here often. I can see plenty of easy money all over Mexico—oil, gold, silver, even these pearls; and some men, you know, pick up money wherever they go. They tell me I'm one of those. I hope so. I would like to bring all the world and lay it at your feet. Maybe you would listen, then!"

"Is that all?" she asked, smiling almost indifferently.

It was evening now and the vast purple shadows were coming from the hills. They too had walked a little apart from the entrance to the ancient ranch house. The rim of the pale moon began to show above the distant hills. Near by came the tinkle of water among the stones, the soft shining of silver on the fronds of palm trees. They both were young; he surely was not an unmanly nor an unsuccessful man. Yes, he had succeeded, after all. And this was a world apparently made for love alone. She did not altogether check him as he spoke of love.

"You still want time, don't you, my dear?" said he, after a silence. There was a certain diffidence, delicacy, in his tone, the best weapon he could have used in his assault upon her heart.

"Yes, I still want time. My year isn't up."

"A year! How absolutely absurd! Time passes for all of us. Each year is a year gone out of our lives—so much taken out of our happiness. A year? I can't wait a year."

"Hush! You must not say such things," rejoined the girl. "If you keep on in this way I must leave you."

"Ah! You're free of all this!" He waved a hand around him, at such setting for a scene of love alone.

"I swear, I don't see how you can be so cold as you are!" He cast back his shoulders, not ashamed of himself at all.

"I did not ask you here and do not ask you to continue here. I've told you not to talk of any of these things."

"You ask water not to flow downhill!"

"You go too far. No man is ever going to compel me to do anything."

"Then you never will be happy, my dear."

"I'll take my chances. Besides, I'm going away to-morrow morning."

CHAPTER VIII

OLD PEDRO KEEPS HIS SECRET

"WHERE? Back home?" Trent was aggressive at once.

"No," said Mary. "Only on a little journey inland; perhaps thirty miles or so. Father Ernesto, who knows the place, has been so good as to tell me he would send over some servants to show Dr. Blakely and me the road, take care of us on our way."

"Is Blakely going along? Is your mother going?"

"No, my mother would not be able to take such a ride. But old Anita, one of the women of the place, will do for a chaperon for me. Mother didn't object to my going with Dr. Blakely and Anita. We're to have mules and everything! It may be we'll have to camp out a night or two. I thought it would be a lark. So you'll have to excuse me for a few days, Mr. Trent."

"You think so? Not in the least! That sounds interesting to me also. I would like to see the inside of this country a little bit myself. What's the great idea about your going, anyhow?"

"Dr. Blakely wants to go over there to see old Pedro, the man in whom he is so much interested, you know—

said to be about the oldest man in the world. He lives over in there, thirty or forty miles, near the Martinez ranch. I understand that is quite a place—rich people and a good family. It's an odd world, isn't it?"

"Yes, a strange world and strange people in it. You're one of the strangest. You're beautiful and you don't know it! You're wonderful and you don't know it! Pearls—they aren't good enough for you! What shall I find for you next, my dear?"

"If you could find my peace of mind!" she exclaimed; "could make me contented to swing in the hammock here as mother does—that would be something!"

"But what's on your mind, Mary? Why should you be stirred up? Isn't everything in the world just as it ought to be?"

"If only it were!"

"But as to your going with us," she went on—"you can't go unless you promise me."

"I'll promise anything to be near you. Do you really think I care so little? Why have I come this far? Do you suppose I can sit here alone and have you ride off into the hills for a week or so? No; I'm sorry, my dear, but I'll have to go along! I may find a mine or something over in there!"

"It always comes to that—money?"

"It certainly does, Mary—it always comes to a question of money, one way or other."

Suddenly she turned, striking her hands together,

her head bowed, and left him alone in the twilight. A sudden sense of the pitifulness of the condition of that other man, wanderer, adventurer, a gambler with fortune, came to her so strongly that she could no longer abide in the presence of this man, so tall, full, florid, successful, and so contented with his own success.

None the less, on the following morning so earnestly did Trent plead his cause with Dr. Blakely and Mrs. Westlake that eventually he was one of the party which rode out from the Ranch of Good Hope along the trail eastward beyond the point where the gate of the mountains closed together.

It was understood that the purpose of the journey was to interview old Pedro and to learn of his present condition of health and welfare. Dr. Blakely promised himself great things. Mary Westlake promised herself little at all, save a vague hope that she could see something connected with the enterprise which Barry Allison had put before her. The very fact of this strange coincidence, hearing of the Madre d'Oro; hearing of John Palmer, Barry Allison's friend, in a part of the country Barry had never seen or dreamed of, pulled together her emotions, somewhat vague and weak of late. Where she had doubted, now she began to hope; and found in the very thought of endeavor more comfort than she had known for days.

With them rode old Anita and yet another woman, Magdalena, also of the ranch, who went along as cooks and aids. Two mozos brought up the rear, caretakers for the horses and mules. In advance rode Blakely and Mary. Randall Trent saw to it that after they had left the foreyard of the ranch his place also was at Mary Westlake's side.

Their journey into the interior, eastward of the Ranch of Good Hope, seemed at first some nightmare voyage into a land of dread. The shrubs and trees seemed always driven by some terror, distorted by some agony. Their branches were for the most part naked and bare save for the bright flame of red flowers here and there, which seemed to voice a transient triumph, a defiance of death and torment. As they rode onward and upward into the higher regions, where the blue and cloudless dome arched over and above the desert, always they were among anguished, flame-tipped trees. As they left the tender green of the cultivated valley and began to ascend the hills beyond there came to Mary again the feeling that all this was only some strange dream.

They were now, forsooth, in the heart of that extraordinary region bounded by the two seas of the far southwest. The landscape was dotted with clumps of aloes, yuccas, the myriad forms of the cacti, the naked ocatilla, more rarely the giant columnar cacti, fluted shafts a hundred feet in height. Occasionally arose the pale yellow boles of the cirio, tapering upward toward the yellow crown of flowers which rose above armed clumps of thorny branches. Once the trail wound through a great group of prone, huge forms which seemed like some prehistoric monster sprawled upon the ground—the devil cacti, repulsive, haired, caterpillar-like shapes, monstrous, twisted about upon the ground—a family of plants springing from a common center, covering perhaps fifty yards on either side of the parent shoot. And again, almost unbelievable, once in a while where it seemed that only sand and rock had ever been, but where hidden water was, there arose fair groups of little fronded palms, airy and delicate and graceful beyond belief in this cheerless spot.

Cheerless, did one say? The desert was not so. It was a land of its own, possessing its own sinister beauty.

They passed upward on their march, rising steadily into the high, dry regions of the upper desert. As they ascended they could see yet wider landscapes, heat-kissed, wavering, lying above and beyond them. In the lower regions they were leaving there still were streaks of green where water left its mark oozing out from beneath the rocks; back of them they still could see the squares of green and gray where the ranch lay. But all around them now stood always the extraordinary vegetation of the desert—tall groups of the ocatilla, flame-tipped; giant cholla cacti; gnarled and dwarfed trees, suffering, craving comfort.

"Myra—*los dos caminos*!" exclaimed the old woman, Anita, at last, pointing ahead. They could see that they were approaching the fork of their narrow path, one arm of which went up a flat valley, reaching back to the high and dry region beyond; the other, that to the left, soon lost in a ruder and more precipitous ascent. The tongue of a high ridge came down and divided the two valleys. The little procession halted.

Old Anita motioned for them to dismount. Near by was a strange, grotesque plant known as the elephant wood, its limbs large and shapeless as those of its namesake. It sprawled out, grossly, its branches naked. Anita pointed to a slight darkness of the soil beyond this desert tree, a little tinge of green near it. There was a little spring here in the desert, which crept out from beneath the foot of a rock ledge, smaller yet not dissimilar from that which made life for the Ranch of Good Hope far below.

About the precious water were evidences of earlier human occupancy. Far up on the slope of the hill—where once perhaps this spring had emerged—there were terraces of rock, where some unknown, forgotten hand had endeavored to establish surfaces of soil fit for cultivation. These terraces now were in ruins. Lying at a level with the lower spring, there seemed to be a different configuration in the heaped-up rocks. The rude wall here had, in short, been a part of something formerly called a human dwelling place.

The wall of this abandoned hovel followed something the same contour as that inclosing the spring of the Ranch of Good Hope. There had been a sort of cave reaching back under the outcrop of the rock, and the last desert dweller, whoever or whatever he had been or was, had merely thrown up a rough wall at the front of his cave, leaving therein an opening for an entrance, undoored, unhinged, and offering no protection. It was rather a bivouac place than a house.

The water had enabled human tenancy to endure here for some indefinite, immemorial time. The elements are kind in these high, dry altitudes. Whether a decade or century had gone by since men first had lived here, none might say. But old Anita pointed to the cave and smiled *"Esta es la Casa de Pedro!"*

So! This, then, was the home of Pedro the Old! They approached and peered over the little wall which hedged off its front. There seemed nothing left within except a clean-swept floor, tracked here and there by the little feet of desert animals where the dust had blown in after the last sweeping.

"Sure!" said Blakely. "I remember the place. This is where he lives. Swell mansion, eh? Wonder where he is? Out gallivanting around somewhere, I suppose —he's only a hundred years old, or two! Well, he'll be along. Let's move in and wait."

The native women busied themselves in bringing certain packages, which they bestowed upon the floor of the cave. Old Anita pointed to two scant blankets of native wool which she bestowed in a corner of the cave. Then she took them apart and showed them how to find light wood among the bayonet plants and the yucca, showed them how a certain nourishment could be found in the pulpy leaves of the cactus, showed them how the thorns of the cactus might be burned away. Mary was overjoyed to find buzzing about cheerily among the desert flowers, quite a colony of bees such as she had known in her earlier home. They delighted her, seeming to link her to the past, seeming to give her cheer as they went on about their well ordered ways of life.

It was now mid-afternoon, and the heat of the day was at its greatest intensity, the sun beating down savagely. They were glad to find refuge in the cave house of Pedro the Old. Questions in broken Spanish led Anita to declare that *papa mia* would be back that evening. "*Su casal*—your house—" she repeated; then, smiling, "*mi casa, tambien.*"

"By Jove!" said Blakely, "I believe she means she was born here! Seventy years ago! Well, I can't say that the real estate values have advanced very much since then. But if old Father Ernesto ever takes my advice and sets up his sanitarium I'll bet here's the place for it! It's impossible to die. This water surely is the Ponce de Leon spring of youth!"

They made themselves as comfortable as they could and spent what time remained before evening in preparing for the night. And, as the sun dropped low, there came to them the sound apparently awaited by Anita—the tinkle of a little bell.

Down the left-hand fork of the mountain trail came old Pedro, no other, in straw sombrero and worn serape, in sandals and cotton trousers, if his negligent nether garments might be called trousers.

Anita went out to meet him, took his bridle rein, and led in the little burro he bestrode. Rapid speech told Pedro of his visitors and their need to spend the night. He made no comment.

An old, old man he seemed, when he came up, his small black eyes sunken, his cheeks like leather, his figure gaunt. Yet, in spite of all, he stepped alert, active.

He did not smile. All things were one to him. He had no pride that, as he stood, he was perhaps the oldest living human being on all the surface of the earth; surely the oldest known at any time of actual history.

"My God! just look at him," exclaimed Randall. "Like a mummy! I declare, he makes me nervous!"

Mary in her turn looked at the strange figure of the centenarian. What did he know? What could he tell if so he cared to tell? What could he say to her, Mary Westlake, having what bearing on her life, her hope, her despair, her happiness?

Blakely, having a little Spanish of a sort, did his best to engage the old man in light conversation. But the face of Pedro gave no sign. He was gray, dour, aloof, as though he had no interest in these others who accosted him. Trent, with the fatuousness of the Saxon, smiled at his own inability to speak the language of an inferior race, but tried out some of his recent linguistic acquirements picked up on his journey to La Paz. But if Pedro heard any of these he made no sign—did not even lift his battered hat to the señorita, although his keen eye flashed across to them as they drew up to the entrance of the cave which made his home.

"I say, doctor! Where is his family you have been telling about? You said he had been married. I don't see any signs of housekeeping here."

It is likely that Anita understood him in part. "*Bastante agua poco mas arriba,*" she remarked. She meant that there was plenty of water further up the valley; and water, of course, meant human tenure thereabouts.

Blakely ventured to interpret liberally for her. "She means that the old man comes down here once in a while to do his heavy thinking. I suppose he takes up his bed and walks when his new family gets too talkative for him. He's always had his own ways of living, I suppose—maybe that's why he has lived so long—when he gets bored he just gets up and leaves. I take it that this cave here is his club, where he flocks alone."

Trent made advances with his cigarette case, but the old man still looked at him unmoved. Blakely, more versed in his preference, presented a little sack of tobacco. A muttered "*Gracias!*" came from the thin, tight-set lips of the old man. Pedro found a corn-husk somewhere inside his serape and rolled a cigarette in his own fashion. But still he kept aside, his eyes looking out across the hills, unmindful of any about him. He seemed a thing apart in life. He was old, old, very old.

"I don't think he wants us to go further toward his valley than this," said Blakely, after a time. "No use trying to get him to go with us down to the ranch. Neither do I think he wants us to go up beyond this place—I suppose he has his own notion of propriety and doesn't want to make any show of his family and his little home. The native women down here are as shy as deer—we would never get to see his wife even if we kept on to the Martinez properties where they live. But, after all, it's Pedro we wish to see.

"I can say one thing, the old man hasn't changed a whit since the doctors were here five years ago. I wish I could talk his language a little bit better."

Mary, to the surprise of them all at this point ventured a word. "I had Spanish for four years when I was in school. Of course, it was book Spanish. I don't know whether he could understand it. After I left school I was in government work, in the translation service, in New York, the time of the war."

"Try it!" said Dr. Blakely. "Like enough he talks Aztec, but it won't hurt to tackle him in Castilian."

But by this time the old man, keener of sense than they guessed, turned quickly, his little black eye glowing like a coal, looking keenly at Mary Westlake.

"*Habla usted Español?*" he demanded suddenly. His voice sounded as though far off.

"*O, si, poquito—no mas,*" replied the girl pleasantly. "I speak it a very little, yes." From that time they two were friends. As to the others, Pedro apparently regarded them as barbarians and beneath his notice. He seemed disgruntled that the party had taken possession of his cave before he had had time to offer it to them.

For a time the old man relapsed into himself, his eyes still staring straight ahead. But after a time, without warning, he broke into a flood of rapid Spanish which required all of Mary's book learning to understand. Now and again she halted him, demanded, asked him to repeat. Eagerly, kindly, friendly, she approached him, took him by the hand, drew him a little bit apart so that he might not feel the awkwardness of talking in the presence of others.

These others looked at them, looked at one another in amazement. Old Pedro and the young American girl had struck up some strange acquaintance all at once. Why had he so suddenly come to life? Why his keen animation, his rapid gestures of thin, brown hands? What moved him so deeply?—for something certainly had stirred him.

"Oh, he's a foreigner!" said Randall conclusively. "All foreigners are strange. They have to throw fits or they couldn't talk at all."

But a sudden resolution had come to the tall young woman. She faced him squarely, determined to find out the truth of the question which had been pressing upon her—the truth of the crystal sphere—the truth of the old Spanish maps—the truth of the stories of Barry Allison—the truth of what Ernesto had said about John Palmer. Now she felt suddenly an abiding hope. A strange feeling came to her that she was coming close to the traces of the truth.

"Señor Pedro!" Her wide, gray eyes looked quietly into his sunken black ones. "You are old."

"Yes, lady, I am old. It is the truth."

"But you remember things that happened long ago?"

"Yes. As well as I ever did. My mind holds the old things. I knew many things long ago—that is the truth."

"What were some of those old things, Pedro? You know the old country over yonder—Mexico, the old land, the rich land?"

"Oh, yes. It was there I lived when I was young. Here I came later."

"With this very family?"

"Yes, the family of Don Luis Martinez, who lives beyond and above here where the water turns toward the eastern sea. I have lived there with Señor Martinez many years, lady. Yes, I knew their parents, and theirs yet again, yes."

"You came from lower Mexico?"

"Yes."

"Perhaps near the old Spanish Road?"

"Not far from the old Spanish Road, yes, lady. Where it runs from Vera Cruz to the great city on the plains of Anahuac. But you do not know that country."

"Not so well, Pedro. But listen. You knew many of the secrets of that far land—was not that once true?"

"It is the truth. I knew them, yes."

"Pedro!"—she turned to him suddenly as one of authority, as though administering some inquisition—"Tell me, why is it that you have so long concealed the place of the Madre d'Oro?"

The old man started, dropped back as though he had sustained a rifle shot. They saw him sit down, saw him crumple weakly, a hand raised as though to ward off something of evil.

His voice trembled when at length he could answer this tall young woman of America who had asked him that astonishing question. She had knowledge or part knowledge which did not belong to her or to any woman.

"In the name of the saints, what is it that you would do? Do you wish to be killed? Do you wish to kill me? You have spoken the sacred word! What do you know? Why do you ask that of me? What is it that you have done? Oh, Santa Maria!"

His voice, which till now had sounded somewhat thin, rose almost into a shriek. The others of the party who heard him thought him in anger, but when they would have approached Mary waved them back.

"No!" she said. "It's quite all right!"

"But what were you asking him?" demanded Blakely suspiciously, rather jealously.

"He will answer! Please let me talk alone with him." Her eyes were bright, shining.

But Pedro would talk no more! At length he rose and approached the two old women, his daughters, whom he accosted violently in a tongue which the others did not understand. Actually he drove them away from the spot. They must have guessed that he knew they might understand words never meant for them to hear —words which said something regarding the Madre d'Oro!

He beckoned Mary to come with him. They stepped aside. He turned towards her a face almost ghastly, a mummy face, old, old, and now drawn unspeakably. But the girl had no mercy on his evident agitation. Her love was carrying her away.

"Pedro," she said, her voice high and clear, "I come from the north. I came to see you. I came to learn from you the truth about the Madre d'Oro! Of whom *then shall I learn if not of the last of the Sacred Three?*"

The old man flung himself upon the ground, his serape drawn over his face. It was long before he stirred. At last he rose upon an elbow, looked at her as a wounded animal looks upon its destroyer.

"Was it for you, young, beginning life, to end my life for me? Do you think that it was for myself alone that I have lived so long in this land? Would you end my life now? Is it not also sweet to me? I look at you and you seem kind, yet you are as one who wields a knife of glass upon the heart of a prisoner. I didn't ask you here. Why did you come?"

"Pedro, listen," she went on. "You need have no fear. I have had a dream of you, that is all. It is true, I know about the great Mother Vein, which lies in the hidden valley—not all about it, but something I know it is not far from Orizaba. I know that it is not far from the old Spanish Road. And I know that the Spaniards never found it, the Madre d'Oro, not even Alvarado for all of his tortures."

"He tortured, yes!" groaned Pedro. "He who carries that secret knows torture. Many lives ago, that was. But as the war priests guarded the secret, even so it must be to-day. Why should I deny, since you know? Father Ernesto has perhaps told you?"

"No, Father Ernesto did not tell me so much. But he showed me a map marking the Valley of the Madre d'Oro as close as the old Spaniards ever knew it."

"Spain never knew—not even Alvarado. Not even Mariana, the traitress of her people, ever knew it. She only knew part of the old story. Cortes never knew, nor any Spaniard. No, nor do you know now! Neither you nor any Alvarado of to-day can torture the truth out of me! I tell you no more! Well, I have lived long."

"But suppose the secret died with you, Pedro. Suppose that the last guardian were dead."

"That is not true."

"But about Juan Palmero, whom you knew? Why did he take Dolores away with him, these years ago? Was he only guessing? Or did old Pedro, the Third Man, finding himself as he thought about to die, tell Juan Palmero some things about the ancient secret? Are there not now two men living—yourself and Juan Palmero—who know where lies the valley of the Madre d'Oro? I can tell you, Pedro. Juan Palmero has stood at the gate of the Madre d'Oro itself! He has been in the valley. He has seen the sacred vein of gold. He knows the secret—I know that he knows it!"

"God of my fathers! has he told you? Has he, too, been traitor? Is there no faith left in all the world?"

"No, Pedro, he has not told me. I never saw Juan Palmero—would not know him if I saw him now. It was another who told me, and he himself only guessed."

"And what other? The holy saints defend us!"

"The man whom I love, Pedro—the man whom I shall one day marry—told me this."

"You mean that other señor who came with you?"

"No, it is not that one."

"He does not know the truth?" The old man's voice was trembling now.

"He knows nothing. He may guess, but he knows nothing. The man I am to marry is not here. He is with Juan Palmero now. If Juan died and if you died, Pedro, there would be the man who ought to be next in turn to know the great secret."

"Yes, yes. But my day has not yet come. Who are you, a woman, to ask a secret that never should be hinted to any woman?"

"Pedro, listen to me! I have looked into the round glass ball. It is the world. I have seen its spirit. I have asked of this spirit, to what end does that Madre d'Oro exist? Why may not the story one day be told, Pedro? If it were not for the good of the people, if the time were indeed come, why should not that secret at last be known? For what purpose did the old priests hold it safe?"

"It was for the Sacred Saints!" replied the old man.

"What saints, Pedro? That was before the day of saints. Was there not to be the day of the Fair God? Was he not to come from the north, not from the east? Pedro, if he has come at last, why then should you or I complain?"

The old man's eyes blazed red in somber fury. "You I ought to kill!" said he, "so that you may never tell!"

"Very well, Pedro, do so. I am not afraid! But if you do, others would guess and they might guess too close. Would it not be better that only three in all the world should know that secret—three who would be wise?"

"No woman is wise! You are but a woman!"

"That is true. And yet, but for a woman, this secret must have died long ago. Always life has been. Every secret which has come down from the past we owe to women, is it not true?"

"It is true," said the old man. "But still a woman is no more than woman."

"You would not tell me, Pedro, the place where the great valley lies? You cannot trust me to tell one other man, to establish once more the Sacred Three? Who knows the secret here? Not Anita, not Magdalena, not one of your sons. You came here to live and die—but you alone knew of the Madre d'Oro."

"He who wins the Madre d'Oro must say good-by to love."

"You will not tell me then, Pedro?"

"I die! I do not tell! You do not know!"

"Does Juan Palmero know?"

"It is for you to learn. I am old."

"But I do know that somewhere there is the great Madre d'Oro, the sacred mother of all the gold. Is not that true, Pedro? For the man I love, will you not tell me?"

Sheer scorn wreathed the old and wrinkled lips.

"What could you give me that I should tell you that? What gain is there in all the world for me?"

"None, nothing in all the world, Pedro! Only, when you die, you could feel that you had done your duty, that you had lived to be old in order that you could be sure to find the right man to share the secret. Surely you know that the Madre d'Oro cannot be hidden forever! At the end of the great cycle, at the time of the need of the world, Pedro—then all the war priests of all the tribes of all the centuries—then they would give their consent! Would not you?"

He did not answer her.

"Then you do not tell me, you never will? Why? Is there to be no one else to hand down this secret which has been kept so splendidly all these many years?"

But he made no answer to her this time. The staff upon which he leaned supported him no longer. He dropped to the ground, straightened again and leaned back against the rock wall near where she stood. His eyes stared straight ahead, wide open; and in them was a look of horror.

"Pedro! *Pedro*!" She touched his arm, shaking him by the bony shoulder covered with the faded serape which he wore. But Pedro did not move.

Again she called to him: "Pedro! What is it?" But still he did not move.

She rose, stood near him, looking down. The movement of her hand on his shoulder had caused him to drop over a little sidewise. His eyes still gazed out straight ahead.

But what the eyes of Pedro the Old now saw no man, no woman, ever would know.

"Dr. Blakely, come quick!" The girl's voice rose

high. "I have killed him! He is dead! My God, he is sitting here, dead, right now!"

Blakely sprang swiftly to her side. "What's up?" he demanded. "Is he sick? You don't mean he has fainted?"

A sudden consternation seized upon him as he thrust a hand under the old serape, straightened out the crumpled figure.

But he felt no heart beat now. He drew back. "He is gone!" said Blakely. "He is dead! The oldest man in all the world—he is dead right here, right now!"

He drew a blanket over Pedro's face, chagrin, horror, humiliation on his own face, not so much over the passing of a human life as that this human life no longer could remain an object of scientific inquiry.

And now came the two old women, daughters of Pedro the Old, blood of his blood, race of his race. Their wailing broke forth on the air. It was the old wail, the old protest against the great secret which remained unknown.

CHAPTER IX

NOCHE TRISTE

BACK of the elephant wood trees, whose heavy branches made a sort of screen, had stood the two daughters of Pedro the Old, Anita and Magdalena. Of these, Anita, the elder, could have understood, in part at least, the nature of the conversation that passed between her father and the young woman from the north. In truth, she had listened—had gathered, it may have been, some little additional inkling regarding the matter of which she had some vague earlier knowledge. The eyes of Pedro at length had seen the eavesdropper. The shock at seeing the dissipation of his whole life work had done evil for the old man.

Now came the really guilty person, the eavesdropper Anita. She shrieked out in her native Spanish, native Indian, halfway English. "*Mi papa! Lo mataran!* He is killed! He is killed!" She cast herself upon the limp body of the old man as it leaned against the rock. Then she turned to the white woman with fury and vented upon her a torrent of vindictive execration which none but the native could have followed.

The others came up hurrying. Blakely felt for pulse, for respiration. He turned away.

"We came too late," said he. "He's gone! The oldest man in all the world is dead at last!"

"What did it, do you think?" he demanded of Mary Westlake, who stood weeping, pale. "I ought to have all the facts. I shall have to report the end of the longest life known in many centuries. Tell me, what did it!"

"I don't know," said Mary. "He fell over when I was talking to him. He sank down and leaned back. That's all I saw."

"Shock of some sort, of course," said Blakely. "What were you saying to him? How did it all come about? You never had seen him before."

"She's accursed, that young woman!" broke out the ancient daughter of Pedro the Old. "She called spirits down on *mi papa.* She is a witch! She has evil knowledge—I heard her. She means to ruin us all. She spoke of the great valley of gold!"

"What did she mean by that? A valley of gold?" demanded Randall Trent, who had pushed forward.

"She knows what it means!" screamed Anita. "She was talking to *mi papa,* I heard her. She asked him where lies the valley of the Madre d'Oro! It is a word never mentioned. *Mi papa* thought she knew, so he died. She is a witch! Let me kill her! She has killed the last man who knew the secret!"

"Then you also knew that he was one of the Sacred

Three!" Mary turned upon her, tried to lead her aside. But Anita was well-nigh crazed.

"No! I do not! I know nothing!" she screamed. "If I knew I would not tell. But he is dead! What have you done? Who guards now, tell me that? Ah, my God! The Good Saints! That such a wrong should be done to one who had not earned it!"

Something of this came to the ears of the others, who all turned, puzzled.

"What does she mean by Madre d'Oro?" again demanded Trent.

"The Madre d'Oro?" began Blakely. "I have heard old Father Ernesto say something about that—it is marked on the old Spanish map he has got in the hall."

"Madre d'Oro!" exclaimed Trent. "That means 'mother of gold,' doesn't it? What's that she's saying about the secret valley? What does she mean?"

But the agitated girl whom he addressed stood before him now scarce possessed of her own reason. With horror she began to reflect on the possible spreading of this knowledge, or partial knowledge, regarding the great treasure. Surely Anita had gained some knowledge, and now here were these others asking questions. Father Ernesto himself knew at least something of this same mysterious secret. What, then, would be the end of it all? Her reason gave her no answer to that question, but there did grow in her mind a stronger conviction that what Barry Allison had told her was true and more than true.

Under Blakely's instructions the old man's daughters did what they could for him—eased his body down, covered it with his ragged serape. Huddled, shrunken, the piteous figure there lay before them—the last man of the ancient war clan of the Aztecs, who alone ever knew the actual secret of the Madre d'Oro.

"This is rather hard," said Blakely. "It is an awful thing. We came to see him because he had put off death so long. Well, it seems to come at last. I suppose we white people bring the curse with us. We've killed him—just by our coming, I suppose!"

He commanded them to bring additional blankets. "We'll wrap him up and put him in his cave yonder. I'll have men back from the ranch and seal it up forever. The oldest man in all the world!"

"I can't stay here!" broke out Mary Westlake, almost hysterical now. "Let me go back home! I'm afraid to stay here!"

"But we must spend the night here in some way," said Blakely, who practically was the leader of the party. "We'll leave the old man here and ride back in the morning. To-night you and the two women can sleep inside the cave. It will be the last time it ever will be used by living human beings, I suppose. Well, I'll try to get a fire and see if we can cook a little something, as soon as we can quiet down."

"I'll not go into that cave with Anita yonder!" said Mary. "She'll kill me, surely!"

Blakely turned towards her, still puzzled. "All this

is mighty curious to me. What's that woman mean by all this hullabaloo? Madre d'Oro? Why should those words kill Pedro? Why should they make a potential murderess out of Pedro's daughter? There are some things here I confess I don't understand—do you?"

"No!" replied the weeping girl. "I wish I had never heard those words!"

Shaking his head, Blakely turned away.

As for Mary, when the soft twilight came down, adding its terrors to the weird surroundings, she drew apart and sat huddled. A great sense of fault, of indiscretion, came to her mind. She felt that she herself had now created new dangers for Barry Allison. Barry had counseled her never to mention these very things which now were publicly discussed.

Somewhere, perhaps far to the south, farther from his own home than they were here, Barry Allison and his friends, of whom one knew the secret of the valley, now no doubt were fighting their way on to the climax of all their risks. That was in Mexico, the unknown country, far to the east. Had theirs not been risk enough at best? And now here were more seeking to learn what should have been concealed—the knowledge of the Madre d'Oro. If the news of it got out, if curiosity regarding it now went afoot, who could tell what evil might develop?

She began to think in still more concrete terms. Here was Trent, alert, keen, unscrupulous, used to following trails of gold after his own fashion. Had he not shown that he had some curiosity, perhaps some inkling, of the existence of a rich mine worth seeking? Her own confused remarks, the hysterical exclamation of Anita, Father Ernesto's naïve talk—all these things would make Randall the more eager. She knew him well enough to be sure he would not stop, if once he laid out a plan. She saw his eyes now following Anita curiously.

Of all these—the Mexican woman, Trent, Blakely, Father Ernesto—which would be the most dangerous to her? She felt her heart sink deep. In her conscience she felt that she had done a wrong, not more to her lover and to herself than to the ancient and sacred secret of the Madre d'Oro. She had disregarded the solemn adjuration of her lover. What good could come of that?

Blakely and Trent, unused to mountain going, assured themselves it would be unsafe to undertake to travel down the insecure trail by night. So, as best they could, shivering in the mountain cold, too unhappy to eat and having but little food at best, they passed a wretched night, sleepless, until morning came.

The old women, rendered almost worthless through their night-long mourning over the dead man, made shift to gather a little wood and build a wastrel fire, but breakfast had little taste for any of them. As soon as possible they had the mozos catch up the horses. Then, carrying the shrunken body of old Pedro into the cave which was to be his last home, they mounted and rode down the trail. It had indeed been *noche triste,* without hope or solace to any of them. To their strained senses every sound of the hills was full of whisperings, of warnings.

As for Mary, suddenly it seemed to her that all the world was leagued against her. What could she do?

Somewhere in its mystic valley far to the southward, without question the Madre d'Oro lay smiling at the furies, the hopes, the disappointments of men, their avarice, their restless greed. A thousand times these past centuries the foot of man in search of gold had passed by her door. The time had not yet come.

In the great valley lay peace and the dream of time.

Now, converging in a wholly unconcerted way, there existed two columns of attack upon the peace and calm of the ancient valley. That the visitors at the Ranch of Good Hope, fired by partial knowledge, stirred by the usual avarice of man, would make some attempt to solve an enigma of such fascinating interest to them, easily might be guessed.

Meantime, the definitely organized men led by John Palmer were pushing on southward, these many weeks, holding always to their general course, gaining a little distance every day. And now they began to approach the crux of their adventurous game.

They had kept as far away from the railroads and

the more beaten trails as they could, sometimes losing distance to gain that end. It was not always possible to avoid meeting with human beings or wholly to evade the trails upon which the inhabitants of the country traveled, by horse or mule or on foot, carrying their scant produce to this or that city for such meager gains as chance might bring them; but, thus far, everything had favored them. They either had passed for natives themselves or had met natives so apathetic and indifferent as not to care to note or question them.

John Palmer, leader of this little band of invaders, rode in silence, always pushing on as fast as the animals could go. Through the hilly country that lay below the village of Loma Verde, where the party had made so spectacular an entry and escape, they rapidly put many miles behind them all through the night.

Palmer was not happy. One thought came ever to his mind—here again was woman! At his very side rode an example of that sex traditionally held outside all knowledge of the Magic Valley. What might it mean? True, Luisa Martinez and her sister had made their home with him these years; almost at the gate of the Valley itself. But neither of these nor any other woman ever actually had seen the entrance. No woman knew precisely where it lay. He reflected grimly as he rode that he at least had kept the ancient law, had not been traitor to the oath of the tribal clan. He, almost alone—altogether alone thus far—had held guardianship of the gate of the valley.

And yet even as he rode thus grimly, self-proved, John Palmer knew that but for one other woman whom he had met years ago over yonder in the mountains of the unknown peninsula, he himself never would have known even of the existence of the secret, could never have found the gate of the great valley. And now here, in need of succor, was that woman's sister.

Close at the side of that sister, herself beautiful as woman often grows to be, rode three young men. True, they might have ties far back in the country they had left. But that was far away, and Luisa was here, beautiful and alluring, always to be reckoned with. What would be the result of all this?

Palmer felt uneasiness every time he heard the voice of Hallock, who rode closer to the side of Luisa than either of his friends—in fact was rarely ever out of sight of her since first he had laid eyes upon her. Well, such things happened, yes, reasoned John Palmer, but they did not happen well in any party of men bound on an enterprise of danger where absolute concentration of purpose and unity of action were requisites of success. John Palmer had his doubts. Never before now had his courage run so low.

They had good animals, the packs carried by great Spanish mules, best of all transportation in the mountains, hardy, used to dry food and infrequent water. It was not probable that the villagers back of them, in case they cared to pursue, could muster animals as good as these. Palmer counted also upon the fading away of any purpose they might for a boastful moment entertain. He doubted if they ever would gain courage to pursue at all. None the less, he took every precaution for his own safety and that of his party.

"Which way, John?" asked Barry Allison, upon a pause they made at dawn, by the side of a clear rivulet which came down from the hills. "We're striking rather low altitude again, aren't we?"

Palmer nodded, "Yes, I want to get into the flat country. Maybe we'll strike a cattle range where our trail will be wiped out more or less. What we need is to leave not a trace behind—we have got to keep up our record as vanishing spirits. At the first fault of our trail our friends yonder will be glad enough to throw up the chase. We may break back deeper into the mountains later on.

"We've done thirty-five miles, I figure, since we left Loma Verde. Good enough for a moonlit night, eh? I don't suppose those people came back out of the hills until daybreak. It will take them some time to get ready to start, and then they'll change their minds; and then when they find our trail is hard, they may quit—I surely hope so."

"Well, we've got to eat or we can't travel," he added, slipping out of the saddle." I'm more afraid of Pancho Villa starting something than I am of anything else. But there's as good a chance that he was not coming to Loma Verde as that he was. Let's eat, and let's hope. Off saddle and unpack, boys. We'll take our chances. Anyhow, we must give the stock some rest!"

The alert, methodical way in which they went about their camp duties interested Luisa, not unskilled in matters of the sort. She could not avoid admiration for these men, adventurers as they were. She saw the slender strength of Silsby, the easy power of Barry Allison, as they swung off the packs; but always her eyes seemed to seek out once more the vigorous form of this other man, of the light hair and blue eye, who always had ridden close to her throughout the night. She seemed always to hear his voice calling, to be about to answer some question he was going to ask her. A dozen times she caught his eyes turned her way. A dozen times she saw him look when he himself hardly knew that he had done so. Trust the maid of Spain to know! Her mother had told her to marry among her own people—Andalusians, fair of skin and hair—and this man from the north certainly was Goth, as her ancestors in ancient Spain also had been. Was it like blood to like that spoke now? Who may answer questions such as these?

"You'd all better spread out for a little nap," said Palmer, after they finished their hurried breakfast of bacon, coffee, and flapjacks. "We can't stop anywhere long."

They spread down some blankets for the women, and propped up one for a sort of shade. Luisa did her best to compose herself in sleep—a thing she could not accomplish.

Palmer himself did not sleep. Always on foot and alert, he walked about the camp. He stopped curiously at a low, wall-like ridge of earth near where they had tossed their packs and saddles. Barry Allison joined him, himself also on *qui vive.*

A good-sized lizard, abroad for the first rays of the sun, scuttled away from them and took refuge in a crack which showed in the bank, or wall. Allison's eyes followed it curiously. He knocked aside the overhanging dirt and bared what apparently was a wall of stones, laid one upon the other with regularity. It was as though some one long ago had built or begun a residence here by the water of the little rivulet.

"Hello, what's this!" said Allison. "I thought that beggar was too big to get into the little hole. Look here! Here's where he went. And here's a regular wall!"

He strolled over to one of the packs and came back with pick and shovel. Sticking the head of the pick deep between the rocks, he gave a heave. It was with difficulty he could start one stone from the other, such had been the uncanny skill of the unknown builder in their fitting.

The builder? What builder? This was not the work of any man of modern times. That feeling, conviction, came to both Allison and Palmer as they attempted to open the wall face. But, stone by stone, the younger man persisted in his purpose. He drove in the pick once more, heaved stoutly. Some of the pieces gave way. A little cavern opened beyond—a rectangular sort of cavern, evidently wholly formed by the hands of man. The overhanging of earth and vegetation had been a matter of chance and time; how much time, what man might say?

The cavity was not much larger than a grave, but grave apparently it had not been, so far as they could tell. It held no trace of calcined or oxidized bones, no shred of human clothing. No skull grinned at them. But, at the center of the cavity, as though abandoned there by some hand that had flung it down, sat a flat bowl of pottery, not unlike that of later native ware. In it were two small pieces of sculpture, little graven images, a few inches in length, no more.

Yet each was large enough to show distinctly the lines of the old Maya sculpture, done in the hard trachyte, which that race so often used. The pieces no doubt had some religious significance, may have been idols of a sort. They showed the rolled hair, the full eye, the strongly projecting chin which so many of the Mayas' gods, so-called, displayed. There was some curious carving of the legs and arms—as though these were an after-thought, and pinned on upon the main body by the workman who had carved them; the upper thighs and the upper arms showing clearly the outline where they had been applied—a thing distinctive in Maya sculpture of the human body.

"Old, old, very old!" said Barry, as he picked up one of the ancient relics. "I've seen pictures of things like these—seen the things themselves in museums. I wonder—but that's all we can do; just wonder!"

John Palmer was looking still farther into the little rectangular cavern which they had opened. All at once he uttered a quick exclamation, drew back, looking down at two additional objects which he held in his hand.

"While you're wondering, Allison," said he, "take a look at these."

Allison did so. His shout brought up both Silsby and Hallock, running. They stood, exclamations of surprise breaking from them as they also inspected the curious objects which John Palmer had in his hands.

Images they were, almost duplicates of the little stone gods which they had found. But they were not of stone! The undying color was here—the color of gold! And here was the indestructibility of gold; for which reason we call it the most precious metal of them all. Gold does not die.

"Gold, by the Lord!" exclaimed Silsby. "And what a place!"

They stood in silence, looking around them, uneasy, sweeping the low horizon of the hills, lest they were noted now, at this moment.

"Great heavens, John!" said Barry. "There's gold all through this country, isn't there? What kind of people are these? Who made these things—who put them here?"

"You ask," said Palmer. "It would take some wiser man than myself to answer. It's plain that one race had followed another drifting down from the far north. Look at these things—they are oriental, Egyptian, if you please. Where did they come from? Who made the sculptures down in Yucatan? Read them, if you like.

"In all your reading, in all your observation—no matter how many museums you have examined—you never saw or heard of anything like these. These are of gold; and they are solid gold."

"But where did they get it?" demanded Silsby. "Is there a mine above here?"

"Like enough. There may be placers somewhere up this very river. Who knows? This has been a country both rich enough and lazy enough to forget many things. But here's what I want you to see. Then you can wonder all you like—for I confess it's got me guessing."

He held out the little images, inscrutable, smiling, for the others to examine. Yes, they were solid gold.

"They are not placer gold," said John Palmer, "nor quartz gold. The gold was never melted and poured into any mold. They are solid, I tell you—just as solid as this piece of trachyte. The man that made one made the other. How he worked, none of us may know, because they didn't have steel at that time—the

Spaniards found no trace of iron or steel in any of this country. These things were done before Spain was born.

"These pieces were cut out of some great block of solid gold, my friends! They were worked out by tools, exactly the same as hard stone was worked. You don't see a hammer mark, do you? If a chisel made these things, we can't prove it, can we? All we know is that here is gold—solid gold—and that it must have been cut from some great piece of gold far larger than any of these!

"And yet you ask me, is it just a dream about the existence of a mother vein of gold, somewhere in this strange country. Here's proof of it, right now! There is and can be no doubt at all that the existence of a great body of solid gold was known somewhere down in this country. The Aztecs or Toltecs knew it. They traded in gold, scattered it. That drove Spain crazy. But the secret of the source of this gold never got out.

"The artist who made these things seemed to have valued this gold just about as much as he did the hard rock out of which he made his other images. But why they put them here and sealed them up—well, let some one else guess that; I can't.

"Yes, we've all seen pictures of just such objects as these. I suppose they have seemed curious to most of us. I swear, it's something more than curious now to me. These things are prophetic. Take them, boys, and put them in your packs. Maybe they belong to us, I don't know. Maybe the time has come."

"But, John, you have told us we've still a long distance to go," said Silsby, with another glance at the hills around him, which might hold their own secrets of rich mines.

"So we have. It's far from here. We may never see the place."

"Oh, pshaw!" broke in Hallock. "Let's be cheerful for once in a way. This is a good beginning. For my part I'm going to keep one of these little stone gods for my good-luck piece—going to put it in my war bag. You're the pirate chief, John, so you take the gold ones."

"One will do me," said Palmer, "if you wish it so. You others can draw cuts for choice."

It so fell that Silsby and Allison drew the stone pieces and Hallock fell heir to the other golden image.

When, after a time, they saw Hallock stroll off to the spot where Luisa sat, Palmer broke into a laugh. "It won't be his for long," said he. "Well, there's not much choice in gifts in this country—there are no shops. I suppose Luisa Martinez will be feeling that she belongs to our party before long."

In truth, Hallock did not rest long with his much-prized possession. "At your disposition, señorita!" said he, using her language as best he might. He held out the little gold god.

The girl flushed scarlet, drew back at this presumption on his part; but in spite of herself could not suppress a smile, revealing a row of brilliant teeth under a curved upper lip. She made some reply which Hallock did not understand, but the color on his face matched that of hers.

"That's doing pretty well," ruminated Palmer. "You must know that the ladies in this country don't work quite as fast as they do up north. It isn't the thing for them to take gifts from strangers—at least from strangers they haven't known more than twenty-four hours. But Hallock seems to have a way with him, eh?"

Presently he strolled over to where the two young people were endeavoring to converse, offered his own services as interpreter, smiling as he did so.

"She says she would not like to rob you of an article so valuable as this," he said to Hallock, after a while. "Says she doesn't feel free to accept it in this way. Says she doesn't wish to offend you, since you wish well. Says she'll give the nugget to her own woman, Serafina, to keep safely, while she considers what it is and who made it."

"What have you said to him, Don Juan?" demanded the girl, noting the smile on Hallock's face, his embarrassed coloring.

"I said to him, my dear child, that this that he gives you is of no consequence; that presently we shall come to a place where we shall find much more gold—so much that a small piece like this will seem to have little value to us. Therefore, I say you may take it with free will."

Luisa took the little golden image into her little hand and looked at it earnestly; looked shyly up to the face of the young man who stood, florid, vigorous, strong.

They had not done so ill. It had not yet been twenty-four hours.

"You may tell him, Don Juan," said Luisa, after a while, "that though I take this for safekeeping, if you like, I cannot wear it because it is too heavy—and because I have no purple ribbon!"

CHAPTER X

THE SPREADING NEWS

IT was a sad and self-reproachful Mary Westlake who reappeared at the Ranch of Good Hope after the tragic journey into the interior. The death of old Pedro still appeared to her as due in some sense to fault of her own. The thought of that gave her great self-recrimination. She felt that she ought not to have urged the old man, ought not to have let him know of her own partial knowledge of the secret which he had guarded literally with his life.

Dr. Blakely himself could not conceal his professional chagrin and disappointment in this denouement of what he had planned as a triumphal scientific tour. Indeed, he frowned even as he declared politely, professionally, to Mary Westlake that she was entirely guiltless, that the old man's time had come, and all that. He remained lukewarm regarding any further tarrying in Lower California; announced that he himself would be quite willing to return to the States.

The latter resolution fitted well enough with Mary's sudden plans.

"Mother! Mother!" she exclaimed, when the two found themselves alone after her return to the ranch.

"Take me away from here! Let's go home! I feel as though something were after me—everything seems to conspire. I can't explain—I want to go back home!"

Her mother was none too happy at the separation from her home and the lifelong companionship of her somewhat dour lord and master, from whose bedside she had not previously been absent in forty years of wedlock. Fretting somewhat over the strange ways of life hereabouts, she was willing enough to agree with Dr. Blakely that the condition of her health now would warrant her return. She also felt, uneasily, unconsciously, the strained tenseness of the atmosphere which suddenly seemed to envelop them all.

Randall Trent had turned mysterious. His was the nose for affairs, not for scientific investigations. He intended to turn these late events to his own interest so far as that might be possible. The little vesper bell, on the first evening of their return, brought him to the side of the young woman who had spent most of the day in tears. He persuaded her to walk with him again, away from the house, to the shade of the great tree near the little murmuring stream.

"Mary," he began, "I've got something to say to you to-night!"

"Yes?" She spoke wearily. She knew what he wished to say. It bored her, irritated her.

"Oh, well we'll waive the usual question," Trent went on. "You know perfectly well how I feel about that. But what I want to say is, it's plain there's something rather deep under all this situation here. I don't think you have told me everything."

"Well, and why should I? Am I under bond to do that?"

"Certainly not. But you leave me to guess at things. Well, I may say I've not done so badly at that."

"Guessing is a free and open privilege. Yes?" She did not smile, did not even ask him what he had guessed. He went on.

"Well, I've guessed why you were so willing to come down here with your mother—this outlandish place. It was because that man, the one you say you're waiting for, Allison, is somewhere down in this part of the country. He's in old Mexico, I suppose?"

"I never denied that, did I?"

"No. But why is he there? He is a mining engineer. There's a big gold strike that is being hidden down there somewhere. The press dispatches had that news months ago. I've been figuring out a few things."

"Marvelous, Randall! Marvelous!"

He did not wince.

"Yes. The gold game is one at which more than one man can play. Well, I've run across the cold truth down here—where we have been."

"Indeed!"

"Yes! I knew you never would argue that way with old Pedro except for one reason. And it was for that other man. So then I figured that Pedro and Barry

Allison and the missing mine all come together somewhere, in some way."

"That's very wonderful, Randall!"

He frowned this time.

"Well, I felt out old Anita. I knew she had heard something and would translate for us both. She had something on her mind. She certainly connected what you said, in some way, with her father's death. I got the old man here, Father Ernesto, to translate, make it plain for me."

"And what did you find?" The girl's voice showed her endeavor at calm.

"You've seen the big map in the dining room inside?"

"I had not noticed it."

"Well, it's a couple of hundred years old or so. It was brought here by old Pedro himself, Gods knows how long ago. Father Ernesto has always kept it as a sort of curiosity.

"Well, that map shows all the old mines of that period of the Spanish occupation. It shows the old sailing routes around the foot of Lower California, to the western seaports of Mexico. It shows most of the old trails, especially the old Spanish Road, which ran from Vera Cruz to Guadalajara, and forked there for San Blas and Acapulco.

"But that's not all," he went on, watching her as he spoke. "On the map there is marked—sort of question mark it is—the Spanish words which mean 'Supposed situation of the Madre d'Oro.' "

She started at that word in spite of herself—the last word she cared to hear from his mouth. He noted it.

"Oh, you begin to follow me? Well, that word in print sort of struck me in the face. That was the word which Anita said she had heard you using with her father, old Pedro. She said you accused Pedro of knowing something or doing something about the Madre d'Oro. What was it?"

"I shall never tell you, Randall. You have no rights in any eavesdropping proposition. Beside that, old Pedro is dead."

"Yes, and with him died some big secret! You make me guess what that was? Well, I guess your trouble with Pedro was over the Madre d'Oro and over Barry Allison! Am I a thousand miles off the truth? That word, 'Madre d'Oro,' on the old map, is what got me going. And you know something about the Madre d'Oro; because you were talking about it with Pedro. You can't deny that.

"There are times when a thing is so keen that it sharpens up a man's own ability in reasoning, guessing, whatever you care to call it. Now, I believe you think Barry Allison knows where the Madre d'Oro is to-day. I don't really even know what the Madre d'Oro is—it is some sort of a lost mine, of course. The Spaniards seem to have lost it. The newspaper clippings which I have been seeing seem to indicate that it has been found again, or something just as good. Now, what I am wondering is whether the old Spanish mine is the same thing which the newspapers mean."

"You're in the wrong business, Randall. You ought to be in Scotland Yard!"

"Well, I have got more than that to go on. I have heard all about a certain John Palmer, who used to live in here on the Martinez ranch, where old Pedro lived, and who disappeared toward the southeast a few years ago. Well, he took with him the beautiful daughter of the rich Martinez family. Old Pedro used to live on that estate—the owner is Enrico Martinez. His family came there from old Mexico, God knows how long ago. He is rich and proud, Enrico Martinez. Well, John Palmer broke his pride. He stole his daughter. Did you ever hear of John Palmer?"

"Why should I tell you? But surely I have never met him."

"Never heard the name—never heard Barry Allison mention it?"

"What could it mean to you? And am I under cross-examination here? What is it to you, that you ask me these questions?"

"Then you won't tell me?"

"Certainly not. I'll say nothing one way or the other. Go on with your guessing, but please don't trouble me with these matters."

He smiled at this. "Well, Anita and Father Ernesto helped me more than you did. They told me that John Palmer and his beautiful bride, Dolores Martinez—

they were married before they left this country—disappeared somewhere on the west coast of this peninsula. They took ship there, and then they disappeared, that is to say. Father Ernesto knows that old Pedro talked with John Palmer about the old lost Spanish mine. He knows that John Palmer had seen this old map many a time. He thinks old Pedro told Palmer something which he never told you or any one else.

"Now, that's the big secret which is not yet uncovered. You say I should belong in Scotland Yard? Suppose I did solve that riddle for you? What would it mean for you if I did? Would you give me my chance? Come, my dear, will you let me play this game? Will you make my chance equal with his? Will you give me a year, say, to come back to you, win or lose, on the proposition of finding out what all this means?"

He turned a few steps away, excitedly, hands in pockets, before he went on. "Besides, my dear," he added, "if I found that old mine we'd only be richer. I don't need to find it in order to be rich enough. The other fellow does."

Pale, unhappy, the girl stood twisting the fingers of her hands. It seemed more than ever as though all the world were conspiring to tear the veil of secrecy from her plans, herself, her heart and soul. The practical, commonplace tones of Randall Trent still came to her ears.

"Yes, we think John Palmer, some years ago, learned

enough from old Pedro, from the old map, to start out on a little treasure hunt of his own. As you know, I have reason to think that it was on precisely that same hunt that Barry Allison also has started."

"You have been at much pains, sir!" Scorn wreathed her lips now.

"It was only my right. If a man loves a woman he has his rights. And I'm not thinking of myself alone."

"What, then?"

"I am thinking of you also."

"I thank you very much."

"What you don't see is that, if we found that old mine down there, you would be the richest woman in the world. That is to say, provided that we found it through my own work. There is little law or order down there. For a poor man with no influence or no money to stumble on riches in a foreign country like that might mean little or nothing to him. With my connections, with my own money, it would mean, I say, that you would be the richest woman in the world. Yes, that's true, if half of what I think is true.

"Come, now. Suppose you take me in on the gamble as well as the other man. Give me a year—give him his year, and let my own year end on the same day as his. He's got as good a start as I have. Give me my year."

She shook her head, looked out across the little valley toward the great moon rising above the rim of the eastern hills.

"Mary Westlake, your people never despised me. Your mother doesn't, though her daughter does. You don't answer."

"I would be willing to promise you almost anything if you would all go away and leave me. I'm very weary. I'm almost worn out with all this. Have you no respect for personal honor? Haven't I told you that when a girl has given her word to a man she ought to keep it? You ask for a year. How can I give a year to more than one man? That's not my idea of honor."

"Listen to me, Mary Westlake! To a man and woman only one law runs—it is the law of selection. All is fair in love, my dear; and all I'm asking is an even break. If we two men have the same scent and something of the same start, let's see who finishes first. I'm satisfied that he has some knowledge—that you have more knowledge—about the Madre d'Oro than I can claim. All right, I'll take that handicap. At the same time I'm sure you're keeping back something from me—you were talking of that with old Pedro. You two knew some secret."

"A fine secret it is, if all the world knows it! If Anita and Father Ernesto and everybody else knows what the secret is, including yourself, why should any of us trouble over it?"

Trent flung himself into the little rustic seat and leaned back, immaculate in his modern clothing, debonair, sure of himself as always. "I don't doubt that ultimately I shall know all there is of the secret, lock, stock, and barrel," said he. "If you will not tell me I will have all the more zest in finding it out for myself. Yet it might be the best thing in the world for you if you did tell me."

"You're thinking of the gold, the money of it? Is that the greatest thing in the world?"

"Well, the two greatest things in the world run together hand in hand—money and love, my dear! They work out mighty well together in partnership. Put it out of your mind that there is only one man in the world for any one woman in the world. For you—you could choose among the best. It's no more wrong for you to marry the right man, or some man, than it is for water to run downhill."

"Well, then, Randall, that's all settled. You feel very safe about it. I've always known something of the profound content you have felt with yourself." Still he did not wince at the thrust.

"I don't play any game to lose it, that's true," said he; "in business or anything else. But I'll get back to my old question. About this lost mine, will you give me an equal chance with the other man? Come, that's fair."

"The world is before you both," replied the girl, sighing.

"What reward, when I have found that mine!"

"Your extreme virtue, Mr. Randall Trent, ought to be your own reward! Oh, yes, I'm sure it will be no trouble for you to stroll over and find that lost mine. But why bother about me? There are many more beautiful women in the world. If you come out with all the riches which you're holding up before my eyes, would you have any trouble, according to your sort of philosophy, in having the pick of the women in the world? Couldn't you try again, Randall? Wouldn't water run downhill in your case the same as mine? Wouldn't you marry some one else? I think you would. But what I know is that Barry Allison will never marry any one else—and that I never will. You see, a girl does know some things, feel some things, surely. Have you no consideration at all, since these things are true?"

"Not so much," said he, setting his teeth together. "I don't play any game to lose it. And I swear, I love you so much, so awfully much, that sometimes I think I would rather have you for my wife than to find all the lost mines in the world."

"Why, thank you, Randall! That's fine of you! That sounds like a bank settlement to me. Yes, I'll say you're fair—very fair, very frank."

She rose; would have left him sitting there. The sight of her tall goodliness did indeed almost drive him mad, the spell of the evening and their youth conspiring. He would have caught at her hand. She evaded his grasp, went on speaking, slowly, wearily.

"I have nothing more to say about it, Randall. I can't change my own soul, whatever you may feel about it.

But one thing you must remember. There is nothing I know about the Madre d'Oro that I'll ever tell you—not one stiver, not one iota!"

Now he broke out in rage. "But what you knew you told him—what he knew, he told you!"

"As you like! I'll say you have tortured me about enough. I'm going into the house now. To-morrow we're going back home."

He fell sullen all at once. "All right. You can go that way. You couldn't go where I'm going, anyhow, that's sure."

She tried a little dissimulation with him. "Nonsense, you're going nowhere! You would not be so foolish as to go off on a wild-goose chase like that, with nothing certain whatever."

"I'll report when I come back," he rejoined sullenly. "One thing sure, if I make any find I can do something with it. I can put the United States government, the United States army back of anything I do. I can put all the money I own back of anything I want."

"What do you mean?"

"Well, since you ask, I'll tell you just a little. Over at Magdalena, on the west coast, there are two or three army planes come down for maneuvers. It may be I can travel quite as fast as anybody else—travel by map at that! It won't take so long. I may be back in Deneville long before the other man."

Mary Westlake felt her heart grow cold within her bosom. Something in the aggressive objectiveness of the man before her gave her a feeling of awe, of fear. He represented the apotheosis of material success—of what men sometimes call good luck, good fortune. Romance, imagination—excepting imagination shown in material achievement—he did not own. And yet she could not avoid comparing this man's methods with those imposed upon her lover by his own want of the material means of success. In her mind she could see Barry Allison, gaunt, weary, fainting, traveling afoot across the interminable leagues, over the desert sands, under the desert sun. She heard this other man's voice go on, hard, metallic.

"And when I do come back to Deneville, I hope you will see the truth. You accuse me of eavesdropping? No, it was the old Mexican woman who did the listening in. She says that what you told Pedro killed him. She says she knows very little about the great mine, but that she thinks her father knew a great deal more. Of course, her tale seemed a little bit wild to me. Old Aztec priests, for instance, don't go running around in sandals and serape to-day, like old Pedro. That doesn't happen, my dear. Well, Anita and Ernesto together have put me pretty wise. I wouldn't say I had no chance. Would you?"

Now a sudden feeling of helplessness came upon the girl. She dropped her face in her hands, moved her head from side to side in bitter self-reproach. She had betrayed her lover! She had betrayed the sacred thing which she ought to have reverenced absolutely, religiously. She had proved unworthy of the trust which had been placed in her. If everything failed now, it would be her fault! Did that mean that another man would win where Barry Allison must fail? The mere dread of that, suspicion, fear, left her a-tremble from sheer misery.

"Oh, I say!" began Trent, clumsily, "I wouldn't feel so cut up about it. You know I wouldn't hurt you for worlds."

"But you have! But you did! Suppose I were the means of helping you and holding him back—I mean——"

"Then you do admit that he's down there!"

"Yes! I do admit it!"

"So? Very well!"

"He has more at stake than you have, and less to win with. Well, we'll let him take his chances. I think he can take care of himself no matter what comes."

"He has none the best of me at that, I fancy," Trent smiled.

"Very well, so be it! Go where you like, Randall. I shall hold to the faith of my fathers. I shall keep my word."

"Of course," she went on, "I don't thank you for following us down in here. I wish you had not. I can't hold you back from doing as you like, going where you please. Do then as you like—and may God defend the right, as the old knights used to say. That's all I can say to any one. Good-by!"

She was gone. He sat alone. In the cool suave air of the night rose the fragrance of a very excellent cigar. Randall Trent was not much agitated. It was his way to see himself successful.

The four adventurers who had taken upon themselves the solution of a problem old almost as the hills through which they traveled met with better fortune than they had reason to expect. If pursuit had been made by any of the inhabitants of Loma Verde, no evidences of that fact yet had appeared.

They pushed on, along the edge of the great mountain range, in and out of the foothills which thrust forward across the plains, day after day until their steady travel had carried them deeper and deeper into the mysterious interior of old Mexico.

It would have been impossible for them to escape all touch with the native population. At times they could not avoid the solitary riders of the plains, could not avoid little *placitas* huddled here or there under the shadows of the hills; but thus far they had been able to escape actual detection. Their own costume, their silence and reticence, the acquaintance of John Palmer with the native tongue, and, above all, the inescapable identification of Luisa and her woman with the native population, all conspired to serve as passport for them.

They were not held up in any way for almost two months' travel south of the great Chihuahua plateau where first they made their rendezvous. Their path, perforce sinuous at times, had covered perhaps seven hundred miles. Now they had approached within reaching distance of the great Anahuac plateau.

Close at hand there lay the ancient focus of all the old civilizations of that strange land. Here once had been the center of the first Spanish invasion, as also it had been the center of the aboriginal population. The marvelous capital city of the Mexican republic lay not so far ahead.

Now indeed these travelers must use every care. Here was modern civilization, built upon more than one ancient civilization. Each of these had been merciless in its day to any man who presumed too much. All these four travelers knew they were no longer in their own country. Here the game was touch and go.

The nature of the vegetation by now had changed somewhat. They encamped one night in the shelter of a grove of trees whose rich luxuriance showed the climate of the Tierra Templada of Mexico, one in which nature is most lavish of her gifts. Before them tinkled a little stream coming down from high hills. The cover of the forest concealed their tiny cooking fire. The animals, hobbled close at hand, found abundant grazing. They still were well to the northward of the Old Spanish Road, but not so far to their westward lay the rich and well-settled mining regions, crossed by many modern railroads. The little glade in which they lay had been discovered by the mountaineer instinct of old John Palmer, who had broken away from the faint trail they were following to the south, and followed his suspicion that here, among the foothills, they would find a more unfrequented spot.

By this time they all were gaunt, and sunblacked almost as natives. Their horse furniture was wholly Mexican and much worn, their costumes Mexican and more than much worn. A passing traveler, even discovering them now in their little encampment, might well have mistaken them for natives wandering through. Perhaps they might have wondered at the presence of Luisa and her woman; but certainly they, too, could have created no suspicion among strangers as to the nationality of the party.

This evening old John Palmer was peculiarly moody as he sat apart, his head dropped, twisting to pieces between his fingers a twig which he had broken from a bush. As he sat now on his bed roll, the pocket of his coat swung low. He took from it a heavy object which he held and sat regarding studiously for a time, as though demanding of it an answer to some question to which it could make reply if so it liked. But the strange, half-smiling face of the ancient image made him no answer at all. It had smiled thus for centuries —a smile carved in solid gold, covering the secret of centuries.

Barry Allison passed by on his way to the horses, and saw the older man sitting thus.

"Well, John," he said. "What do you make of it! An odd little image, isn't it?"

"I don't make so much of it," replied John Palmer, slowly, "beyond what we all talked of before. It shows that these people must have known of some great deposit of free gold. This didn't come out of quartz—it's clean, solid, an integer in itself."

"Well, that's not so impossible, is it, John, after all you have told us, all we have read? There would be room enough in the Madre d'Oro for a good many pieces like that, would there not?"

John Palmer nodded, his sunken eyes grave. "Yes, I know that," said he.

"You've never doubted it at all, have you, John?"

"No. How could I?"

"Well, you've never told any of us exactly how much you knew."

The old man looked at him soberly for a time before he answered. "I wouldn't need to tell you much, would I?"

He held up the little image in his hand. "Sometimes in the old copper mines they found a block of pure copper that was too big to be profitable. Do you suppose we have found too much gold?"

Barry Allison looked at him in silence. He went on after a time in his slow fashion.

"You know I have lived on the little Rio La Luz that comes out of the big valley? I have told you that?"

Allison nodded.

"Well, we'll be getting down there before long now.

A few more weeks will put us through. Yonder was my home for several years. I can't stay away from it now, though home it is no longer. There lies the cause, the reason for my first going down into that country. I reckon I need not talk any more of that.

"Well, old Pedro, back in the peninsula, told me once what I later found to be true—no prospector ever found the color of gold in the Rio La Luz. I suppose the lower river has been prospected in its time—every stream in the Rockies and the Cordilleras has been. But I'm a miner myself, and I tell you there isn't a color of gold in the whole valley of La Luz. And yet——"

"Yes, John?"

"And yet that's the outlet of the richest valley in all the world, my boy! I am going to tell you now about these things, try to give you some more reasons, so that you won't think me entirely crazy in this matter.

"I'm trying to show you how it can be possible that a mine of gold big enough to admit the carving out of things like this"—again he held up the image in his hand—"could have existed so long, could have been suspected so long, and yet never have been found.

"You see, they did find the color of gold in other streams—followed it up and found great placers, great mines. They located quartz mines of gold and silver both. But it was this extreme richness of the country, the great success that all the early adventurers had in finding rich mines, that kept quiet the secret of this other mine, the richest of them all. So you see, what you have thought meant improbability really meant absolute possibility.

"More than that—it meant the truth. I know the truth. For years, I tell you, I have lived within touch of the Madre d'Oro. I tell you I have put my hand on the gate of the great valley itself. I can tell you more—I can tell you all. Yes, I think that now I am safe in telling you all. Go get the other men."

Allison beckoned to Silsby and Hallock. They all sat or stood, silent, close to the little fire, near old John Palmer as he sat upon his bed roll, the little image of gold still balanced in his hand.

"Friends," said John Palmer. "We have been together now for nearly a month. On the trail, men learn to know each other. I think I know you now. I have trusted you from the start, or I never would have called for you. I feel now, I know, that you have been tested. You're the pure article—like this—" Again he held up the little golden image.

"Yes, I think I can tell you now all the rest, all I know about the Madre d'Oro. If anything happens to one of us, the others must carry the thing on through. I had reason not to talk too soon. The secret of the Madre d'Oro has never been guarded on a basis of friendship, but on a basis of absolute and inviolate secrecy. Only three men until now ever have known it. We are four. We may not always be four. So it is time we all should know.

"I have told you that for reasons of my own I lived down in that little valley which has been my home. There I was lost to the world, absolutely, year after year. I was contented. Everything I asked of life I had there.

"I tell you, I lived for eight years within arm's length of immeasurable riches. I did not need them. I had found more than that, outside the valley of the Madre d'Oro!

"But then"—his lean face was drawn a trifle, spasmodically—"I lost all that I had. The woman whom I loved, the woman who brought old Pedro to trust me and to tell me all he knew about the Madre d'Oro—the woman who led me to the valley of La Luz—died. She's down there now, at what once was my home.

"Well, when that happened, I felt alone in the world. I was frightened. Then all at once I went American again. I wanted my own friends, men of my blood, in whom I could trust absolutely. How should I know? I remembered our old promise years ago, when you were boys. I sent for you. Then I wondered if I had been safe in sending. Now, after many days, I have concluded I was safe. I have found you open and clean. I trust you as much as I do myself.

"Do you, then, all of you, feel willing to take on the rest of this knowledge, and the burden of this secret, with all it means. You don't need to. You can draw back yet, if you have any feeling that it is not wise to go farther."

"I stick!" said Barry Allison, sharply. The others nodded. Old John Palmer nodded also.

"Gentlemen, I got the secret of the Madre d'Oro from old Pedro Sandoval, peon of Enrico Martinez, the rich Spaniard, who lives in the heart of the peninsula of Lower California. He trusted me because he knew I loved—Dolores Martinez.

"That old man, old Pedro, was then the oldest man in the world in all likelihood. He must certainly have been above one hundred and fifty. He may have been above two hundred years of age—no one can tell. But he told me, and I believe it was the truth, that he was the last man to whom the secret of the Three Guardians ever had been imparted. He said that the other two guardians were killed. When he left this country and went far off with the Martinez family, across the Gulf of California, he gave up all thought of ever telling any human being what he knew about the secret. He said he would let it die.

"He did not let it die. I tell you, it was the love of a man and woman which opened old Pedro's lips to me. It was he who sent that woman and myself down into this very country below us here—into the Valley of La Luz. And I can tell you now, in case I should die—find the Rio La Luz, follow it up—and then you come to the gate of the Madre d'Oro!

"Whether Pedro is alive to-day, I don't know. I

doubt it. For the last few days I have been feeling as though he must have died—I can't explain that. But, meantime, you and I have been getting acquainted. So, whether Pedro lives or dies, I think it right and fitting that you should know as much as I do. So, I repeat—find La Luz and follow it up. You cannot fail. La Luz is hidden in the volcanic foothills of Orizaba. We'll come to it after a time, if we all live."

Silsby was moistening his lips, finding it hard to talk, so great had been his intentness. "But, John!" he broke out at last, "She—that is to say—your wife——"

"You would ask if she knew the secret also? She never did. She was content never to know it. I never knew her to inquire for it, though suspicion she must have had. We were happy enough. That was all she asked. She was wise. But she did know that the secret of the Madre d'Oro itself was in the possession of her family. And she knew, of course, since we had come all the way down in this country on that purpose, that where we set our stake must be close to the Madre d'Oro. We were so happy, I say, that she never wanted anything more. She never knew whether or not I actually knew the last detail of the secret of the great vein. We never discussed it."

He looked up at the three brown young faces about him, eager, gaunt, hollow-eyed, and he saw a question in their eyes.

"But did I myself know the last item? Did I myself

prove the truth? Have I myself seen? That is what you want to know?

"Yes! Yes! If we live, I can lead you to it directly. If I die, you can go there yourselves. Now, since we are within reaching distance of the end of this trail, and since I feel you are safely to be trusted, and to be joined to the long list of the guardians of the Madre d'Oro, I have told you what I have."

He sat silent for a long time. His eye was moody as he resumed.

"Yes, my friends, I have seen that thing which we seek. Eyes have never seen the like. Words cannot picture it. The imagination cannot measure it. If it is a great thing, it is a terrible thing. It draws us! We cannot turn back now!"

CHAPTER XI

THE PURSUIT

FOR a time Palmer sat moody, disturbed, kicking together the embers of the breakfast fire.

"Well," he said, "we're partners now, the only men who know the secret, unless it is one other—old Pedro. He may or may not be alive to-day. So we might as well make a little map, in case anything should happen to me. We have got to share our knowledge from this time on, and the closer we come to the place the greater will be the danger.

"Bring me that manta, Allison," said he. "Maybe it will do for our little sketch."

Allison brought the pack cover of heavy canvas, its inner surface still bearing traces of its original whiteness. Palmer spread it down and began to trace with a piece of charcoal which he picked up at the edge of the fire.

"This is where we are now," said he. "We've only a few more days to go, and we can take it easy. Off this way is a little village which they call Dos Pasos—that's near the old Spanish Road.

"But on ahead, east of where we are now, is one valley which the Spaniards overlooked. They knew they were missing something, but the great mines into the northwest were so rich they couldn't stop to hunt for Madre d'Oro. They sensed the richness of the Aztec people. All the time they knew something about the old legend of Madre d'Oro—that's true without a doubt or question in the world. Mariana, the Tlascalan sweetheart of Cortes, Mariana the traitress—she knew, perhaps she told. But because the country was so rich otherwise the Spaniards never really made a scientific hunt for Madre d'Oro.

"Of course, you and I know the secret valley is a volcanic rent in the rocks. To-morrow we'll see the peak of old Orizaba—dead these centuries, but once mighty active. If you want the real secret of Madre d'Oro, ask Orizaba."

He pushed up the brim of his hat as he looked up from his work, slapping the heavy object in his pocket. "That gold which our old workmen here found was melted gold, volcanic gold! Somewhere down among the big forces the veins of the mountains must have melted, must have run fluid gold. I suppose that melted mass ran into a cocoon, a great mold, just as you would pour custard into a mold, or ice cream. Now, how deep that was I do not know. But after a while old Orizaba—assisted by Mr. Temblor, his working side partner—took another heave or two at this country. They ripped a rent, tore open a valley. And maybe from down below, close to the everlasting fires, there thrust up this mold of solid gold. I am telling you, it was more than a quarter of a mile long.

"Then, just to be fair about it, they broke off the top of that mold—Orizaba and his ally—and left the yellow gold shining there in the sun—shining and shining—a century, a dozen centuries, twenty, a hundred centuries, thousands of centuries, for all that any man may know. These trees came and these hills were made all over again. And the silence came and the sky looked down on the valley. And the gold—the solid, pure gold, my friends—lay there undiscovered."

His friends fell silent. The older man for a time did not go on. At length, however, he resumed the half-idle markings with his charcoal point. "Now I am putting in, away down here," he went on, "the Valley of La Luz. That little river runs out of the Valley of Madre d'Oro. As I have told you, I lived on the upper waters of La Luz for almost ten years. I have told you what I saw there. I have explained to you why that country never was known—they didn't run their sheep and cattle in there from below because there was a loco weed, or something, which poisoned them. That's one way to look at it. Another is that there may be a sort of superstition that has kept the natives away from there—I don't know and don't pretend to say.

"But here's your little river of La Luz, making off southeast toward the great gulf—and never getting there. Now, here we come to the Spanish Road. That's easy, for we just follow up this little creek where we are now. We jog down the Spanish Road a few hours until we strike a place where we jump straight south into the wilderness. Now you see this tall mountain, and back of us there will be a niche between two tall peaks. When we reach that cross line—there's where we jump south into the country Orizaba made.

"You face at a right angle on that line, less one degree, and you sight south by your compass—I am marking that now. You will see back of you the top of a long, low, black ridge, through which we will have gone by that time. There isn't any good landmark to sight by in there, hence the need of the compass, setting off almost a right angle to the south.

"Now look here—follow out your compass line and you see a low notch to the south. That's the only place you can get through those mountains. It's a day's march from here to where our first cross lines meet. But if you strike that notch the rest is easy. That's the last landmark this side of La Luz. All you have to do is to go down that slope from the little notch in the rim, and you can't help striking La Luz. You will then be just below my house.

"We shall stop at my house, gentlemen, if it still is there."

A cloud came over the old man's face.

"Not so happy a place. But you might almost call

that the end of our journey. There we are within a day's ride of the head of La Luz. And when you get to the head of that little stream you're at the end of the world and at the beginning of time!

"Under a little scooped-out place in the face of the mountain a wellspring comes out. There's a big leaning rock against the face of the mountain, but it fits as tight as though a mason had put it there. You don't try to move that rock. On the contrary, in order to get into the valley you have got to lie down in the bed of the stream itself—take your chances of getting smothered.

"Now you need heart. Push in under the face of that rock. Follow the thread of the water. You pass through the very bowels of the mountain itself.

"And so only can you do what I have done—and so only can you go where I have been—and so only can you see what I have seen.

"And that sight, gentlemen, is one which the eyes of man never yet have equaled from the dawn of time till now!

"You see, don't you, the need of putting the secret in the hands of men who are fit? The Aztecs were wise in their day and generation, whoever they were and wherever they may have come from."

John Palmer cast his charred stick into the ashes ana pushed the piece of canvas back toward Allison.

"Another thing we ought to do," he added, presently. "We must write down the names and addresses of all of us, and the names and addresses of any friends or relatives outside. That's only a wise precaution. Write them down. I know, Silsby, that you want word sent to Sally Catherwood of Denver when you make your fortune."

Silsby nodded, his white teeth showing in the tan of his face.

"You, Allison—that's Mary Westlake, Deneville, Ohio.' And Allison nodded gravely.

"Hallock?"

The blue eyes of the last of their party turned unconsciously toward the edge of the little encampment, where Luisa Martinez sat in the shade, her eyes fixed out across the distant mountains.

"I don't know my address," said he, at length. "I'm pretty much alone in the world. General Delivery, San Diego, California, used to catch me—but it never will again."

"Her sister was as beautiful as she is," said old John, quietly. Hallock flushed.

"So be it, then. The address of any of us thirty days from now may be hard to guess. We're ready for the last lap of our journey. Let's pull out."

The treasure seekers left their bivouac while the sun still was low in the east. It was a gentle world that lay about them, seemingly holding no trace of toil, danger, turmoil. The rich green of the valley bespoke a gentle climate. Flowers, half-tropic shrubs, tall strange trees were on every hand.

John Palmer, when they were ready for the morning line of march, did not turn back to the trail which led to the distant plain. He followed an opposite course, directly up into the foothills, the babbling of the little stream still accompanying them. The scene became half-tropic. Green parrots flashed across the path—other birds of vivid plumage. The feel of the world was gay, light. They passed as though in some comedy, some gentle drama, meant for the allurement of the senses. A strange world this for these men fresh from the north.

They rode in silence, and each man now had both rifle and revolver loose and ready for work, although they made no warlike front with their little cavalcade. Upon two of their pack animals, lightened by the disappearance of their original loads, they had put pack loads of short wood, as though they were *pielados* passing to market. In garb they all were poor, in demeanor ready to give way to their superiors. Three of them, at least, spoke Spanish as natives. All were unshaven, burned dark. The women were shaded by their *rebosos.* Taken in detail, the party was not one to attract attention on any road where many similar parties passed. It was their hope to shuffle through without being halted by any authority or any idle curiosity.

Thus far they had found the presence of Luisa and

her woman, Serafina, no handicap, indeed, rather of actual service. When their scanty larder had need of replenishment it had been the custom to send Serafina on alone into this or that little *placita,* where she could do her bargaining or marketing like some native woman and bring back her purchases mule back. On the whole, it would have been difficult, even with keen examination of their little train, to have suspected them of being anything but innocent travelers, native to the country. But at length they must abandon furtive methods and little known trails and trust all their fortunes to the open road, where surely they could not escape meeting many strangers. Palmer explained this to them.

Before the morning was spent they broke down from the forest fringe of the hills and swung out, as though stepping from a door, into the great, gray, dusty and broken thoroughfare of the old Spanish Road, a highway whose glory long since had departed.

Weary as they were, having lived as they had on fare none so rich these many days, they hardly needed to assume the native apathy as they jogged along, straw sombreros pulled over their eyes, their serapes high above their chins. Other cavalcades of like sort passed them by, natives with burros heavily laden, foot passengers still more heavily laden, bearing their cheap wares to some distant market. Many passed them at a speed greater than they thought advisable. Their cue was not to show any haste, but to blend into the landscape of the country and its customs as best they might. Had they been peaceful Americans openly traveling by rail they would have been safer than Americans thus in disguise.

The great highway upon which they found themselves had its long history. Repairs it seemed not to have known in many years. In places the ancient paving remained, for the old Spaniards built it well and truly in their day, but the flagging in many places long ago had vanished, and long stretches remained where the road, broad as it was, lay nothing better than a dust heap. None the less, winding in stately curves among the mountains, for the most part steadily descending, it lay in a certain proud disdain of time and its ravages, one of the great roads of the world even to-day.

Around distant curves, hidden by trees that flanked the way, now and again could be heard the tinkle of a bell, the sound of travelers chanting. Clouds of dust would announce the coming of any party from either direction. A sort of dreamy calm lay over everything. Had these men been animated otherwise they must have found all this an experience not failing in charm.

For hours they advanced, for the most part to the southeast and along the highway, and no untoward incident occurred to break their growing content with the manner in which fortune was handling their affairs. It was almost noon and they were thinking of leaving the trail for rest when they heard behind them the sound of rapid riding and the clink of steel, soon followed by rude and sharp commands. Some party of authority was coming, surely.

Respectfully they drew aside to the outer edge of the roadway, as those who would allow nobility to pass. But nobility proved to be a band of riders in the half uniform of the Mexican Rurales. They all were armed, well mounted, and under the command of an officer, and all were bent on some well-recognized errand down the road.

Their leader, a dark, middle aged man, attired in the full *charro* costume of the well-to-do Mexican—short leather jacket, bright trousers, high sombrero and billowy shirt—pulled up across the way, ahead of them, the others following him.

The Americans were surrounded, nor did one of them dare draw a weapon. Indeed, each of them knew that safety lay only in the ability to make a peace parley.

Cuidado!" called out the low voice of Palmer, not trusting himself to any English. They understood his command for silence. No one had any opportunity to explain, to make any movement in defense or offense, although the hand of each of the Americans was ready to his weapons.

"You are of this district?" demanded the leader, who spoke in Spanish, addressing Palmer, whom he suspected to be the leader, since he pushed forward. The latter answered in the same language.

"So it please your excellency," said he. "Travelers to Espinosa, below, with humble forage, as you see."

"From what village do you come?" demanded the officer. "We have not heard of your party within the last three hours. We have ridden hard, two leagues to the hour."

"That would be sure with horses so good as those of the capitan and his men. Would that we could do so well. No, excellency, we came into the road horseback, from the country to the north of here. We are poor. The men of our party are obliged to ride very far to obtain a few *claquos.*"

"But why so many of you to guard a burro load or two of wood?"

His keen eye was noting the details of the little cavalcade. He saw hung over Serafina's mule a long string of eggs—she had wrapped each in a corn husk and tied them to a line, transporting these after the native fashion. This and other details about the equipment seemed to give the suspicious leader a certain pause. He returned to his accusation none the less.

"Why do you ride with arms—pistols and Winchesters, American weapons? You say you are poor—how come you to buy such arms as these? Well, it's all the same; we shall take them from you. Ourselves, we don't have weapons so good. Yet we are officers of the Rurales and we need arms of the best. We thank you, Señor Pelado." He grinned sardonically.

John Palmer turned his head over his shoulder. *"Cuidado!"* his men heard him whisper once again. But he turned toward the officer.

"In the name of the saints, we would live in this state in safety, capitan," said he, "but the capitan knows that for generations we who farm have lost all we had—and he knows that weapons may be had in certain service. Is it not true? The revolucionistas, the patriotas, the bandidos—they take all we have. And when shall one not meet one of these? It is necessary that we be armed—as necessary that we have rifles as that we have plows."

"But where did you get these weapons?" insisted the leader. "Don't tell me that you bought them. You lie."

"Last spring we worked at the mines near Guanajuato, señor capitan. There were Americanos there at the mine, very rich. They gave us these for our own, saying they were going home and would need them no more. That's well. In this country of ours we need no gringos!"

"You say that well," rejoined the leader, grimly. "How comes it that you yourselves all have light hair and eyes of blue? That is not common, certainly not among the peons from whom you claim to come, my friend!"

"Hah! You speak well, señor capitan. We were

not always poor. It is the revolutions that have broken us. Once we had lands. See this lady—her woman—she once had property as well as we. We all came originally from Guadalajara. You know the Andalusians there—one finds there the blue eyes and light hair. Rare, yes, señor capitan; but it is God who gives hair and eyes, and those matters are as they may be. Now we are poor people, may the saints be pleased!"

"Uncover this woman!" suddenly demanded the harsh voice of the leader.

Then there must have been trouble; but with one motion of her hand Luisa swept off the *reboso,* turned eyes of wrathful pride upon the leader. It was a bold act, a brave one, yet unfortunate. The next moment her face went pale.

The laugh of the partisan leader rose high and exultant. "So!" he exclaimed. "You are poor people, but you have with you a high-born lady! I should know this señorita here. She is the very one whom we have been seeking! The saints be rewarded for their goodness—we have found her by accident at last!

"Listen now, you fellow!" he went on, turning to John Palmer. "We have been traveling for days. We do what Pancho Villa wants, the great chieftain, though he is not now at war. This is his woman—he took this girl from down below here. Espinosa, you said? Yes! He suspected she might be going back. He sent us after her. So we find her—and you others. Poor—yes, very poor! You're peons going to market, yes, yes, sure, it is true! Well, one does not disappoint the general."

Palmer, as though by accident, drew his horse across the road between the leader and the horrified woman who heard his words. "But the señor capitan will be sure first? He will easily know that we are but chance travelers whom this lady overtook."

"You said you came, all of you, from Guadalajara."

"It is true, señor capitan, but in Guadalajara are many who do not know one another. But the good saints forbid that any of us should cause a tear to fall from the eyes of any woman. She is fair to look upon —is not that the truth?"

"The general found her so! And when he has found a woman so, that woman never escapes from him, no matter where she travels. Come now—I know where this girl comes from. We're after her—never mind you others. We'll take her back with us. She must travel north this day."

A sudden note of strength came into the voice of John Palmer; his head rose, his face hardened. "Whose has been the crime, señor capitan?" he said, imperiously. "You ride as officers of the government of the Republic of Mexico. With what warrant do you pick up a lady on the road? If we were criminals, if we were Apaches, law-breakers, fugitives—that would be different. But, by God, if this woman be guilty of any crime we do not know it!"

The captain of the Rurales laid back his head and

uttered a roar of laughter, in which all his men joined. They felt perfectly safe; were accustomed to their way wherever they rode. "Crime!" he exclaimed at length. "A crime? Why, it is a crime that one so fair of face should be hid from view! Come now, we have gone far enough and waited long enough. Unbuckle your rifle scabbards and drop them. Loose your pistol belts! If you've any money with you, you had better let us know. If you will be peaceable, we'll take the girl and let you go. If you make trouble—" A sign, a gesture, told the rest.

Palmer turned the head of his horse just a little, his right hand away from the man who spoke. He tried to get humility in his voice. "But señor capitan," said he, "we have not yet reached the market place." And what his own men heard as he jerked his face aside was, "Get ready!"

"What was that!" exclaimed the leader, pausing to roll a cigarette. "What was that you said—that was not in our language!"

"You must pardon me," said John Palmer, suavely. "A word or two of English I learned from the Americanos at the mine. I asked my men if they had any silver among them. I ask your pardon."

All this time John Palmer's horse was being turned slowly, a little bit more and more to the right. A sudden tenseness came into the air. By some fatality the leader of the Rurales did not yet act; went on talking.

"I have come for this señorita," said he, at length. "I have ridden far. It is of concern to you to do as I tell you. The girl we take with us, that's sure. For you—what do you wish? Unbuckle your weapons, I tell you, and let them drop!"

Still John Palmer's hand remained lightly poised; he made no move. His voice tried to wheedle.

"These weapons are worth so much, señor capitan! We need them so much—we can never buy others to replace them. Surely the señor capitan is only irritated with us, his poor friends.

"I am not irritated—I do not trouble with such as you. You may, perhaps, live, if you don't irritate me or my men. The Rurales never argue."

In cool insolence he went on with the manufacture of his cigarette, his men lolling securely in their saddles, grouped loosely around him, back of him. Perhaps they all had concluded that the girl had bribed these natives to ride along with them.

But Luisa knew the truth. She knew the issue here could not be avoided. Suddenly her voice sounded high and clear.

"Say to him," she cried, as though she would not condescend to speak to the leader himself, "that I will go with him! You must not follow, any of you. Leave me! It is for me alone! *Adios! Adios!*"

The swarthy face of the leader turned to her with a leering smile. "So, then, the lady gives you good advice, gentlemen! She returns with us! They always do when the general sends! Yes, she returns with us!"

But it was not thus that the four Americans rated their duty in these circumstances. Before the side swing of Hallock's body could have been noticed as he reached for his revolver, the hand of John Palmer rose almost in the face of the partisan leader. The latter fell, shot dead in his saddle.

Then a group of plunging horses, the bright sunlight, and a quick cloud of pale, pungent smoke.

From the first instant all the Americans had known they must fire; whereas the Rurales, bandits, ruffians, whoever they were—and that was hard to say in Mexico at the day and place—had felt so safe and sure that they were not keyed up to the actual break which every one of the men before them knew must come. This gave the Americans that fraction of a second of advantage in time which makes the difference between life and death in an affair such as this.

The horse of the fallen leader plunged back against that of the man next to him, jarring his hand even as he reached for his carbine butt. That was his doom. A second shot of Palmer's heavy automatic caught him through the neck, and the shock of the heavy blunt ball dispatched him before he ever raised his hand at all.

By now the weapons of the other Americans were working; those of the Rurales as well. Of the latter it could not be said that they lacked courage or skill at arms, for they had seen other days in bandit warfare and the smell of smoke was not new to them. But the better condition and higher spirit of their animals made now a handicap. Their horses rearing and plunging, needed attention; into them came the fire of the four Americans, each a master of his weapon.

Hallock had managed to jerk out from the saddle scabbard the short, high-powered rifle which he carried. The stock came to his face by instinct, the finger lever dropped once, twice, three times. Each man struck at this short range with the soft-nosed bullet was nearly cut in two by the impact. Silsby and Allison were firing with automatic pistols. What seemed to require minutes really asked only for instants. Plan or purpose could not exist. Silsby saw a man, crowded to one side, try to catch the rein of Luisa's horse. He made a quick flirt and snap shot of his automatic and cut him down. Yet another tried, and Hallock killed him with a fourth shot of the carbine. Three to one, the Rurales were beaten before they ever got into action.

Suddenly one of them threw up a hand. "Have done! It is over! We surrender!"

Palmer's revolver remained half-dropped, at forty-five degrees in the air above his shoulder. Now, for the first time, he dared look around. Silsby sat swaying in his saddle, his hand against his side.

"I wish," said he; "I think—I think—"

But what was on his mind to say they never knew. He tried to swing out of the saddle, his foot slipped and he fell, stumbling forward, and gently lay down in the dust to die.

The sight of that enraged Hallock. He fired once more into the bunched figures ahead of him, would have kept on firing so long as one remained but that the hammer of his weapon snapped again and again above an empty magazine. Palmer called out to him, swung his horse straight toward the few remaining members of the posse of Rurales. They all held up their hands, more or less indifferently, in truth, for the sight of a dead man or so was nothing new to them. They expected nothing but death.

"Look to Silsby, Allison!" cried out Palmer. "Come here, Hallock! We'll watch these men. Don't shoot again!"

Allison dismounted, put his hand under the body of his friend. Under his fingers he felt between the folds the crinkle of paper, as though of some letter resting in an inner pocket. It was a letter—the one Silsby's sweetheart had written to him. He had read it almost every night since then. Allison carried him to the shade of a tree at one side of the road, laid him down, pulled his hat across his eyes, and went back to join the others. He motioned to Luisa to ride a little way apart.

"What shall we do with these men?" demanded Allison. "Silsby's gone!"

"We ought to kill the last of them!" shrilled Hallock. "That boy was my friend. If we let these people go they'll follow us, sure as hell.

"Let me be!"

By this time he had refilled the magazine of his rifle, and perhaps, enraged as he was, he would have shot down the last of the Rurales as they stood.

But Palmer raised his hand. "Let me talk!" said he. "Yes, they may follow us. But if we send them back thoroughly cowed that may be better than if we killed them. Maybe they'll tell others to let us alone.

"Now, listen to me, you dogs!" he called out in their own tongue to the huddled group. "We told you we were innocent people, guilty of no crime, just passing through the country. You began this thing. Your blood be on your own heads.

"Oh, we shall spare you—so that you can carry back the news. You have met no innocent *pelados* here, you dogs, but Zapatistas, friends and allies of that Pancho Villa whom you say you represent. You have made enemies of us, and you have made him your enemy. Go back, now then, and report to him. See what he says to you. Make one move and we'll kill the last of you. Go back to the general—perhaps he will do the same service to you all!

"Yes, you listen to me? Go tell the general that you found four stupid travelers, that you killed one of them and had eight of your own men killed. Tell the *jefe politico* in the nearest town that you have met *patriotas,* savage men, whom you had better left alone. The crosses will show where we fought you. Tell them that if we are followed there will be more crosses should we meet.

"Now, you ruffians, dig graves for your own people! We brought shovels for such as you!"

He motioned to Hallock, who loosened a pair of long-handled shovels from the pack, under its strings of onions and egg encasements. By good fortune, no travelers had come upon the spot from either direction, because at this hour of the day most of them were resting after the noonday meal. Palmer obliged his prisoners to loosen their pistol belts, to leave their carbines at their saddles. Sullen, surprised that they were left to live, perhaps supposing that they would fill the graves they were now digging, the beaten Rurales went to work under their new master.

And so now, after a little time, there were new crosses of lashed sticks erected by the side of the old Spanish Road, marking so many more shallow graves. Upon the opposite side of the road they laid poor Silsby, wrapped in his blanket, with everything done for him which now might be done by his friends.

"Now go, you people!" commanded the hard voice of John Palmer, when this work had been finished. "Go tell the general you didn't bring the woman, and that no man ever will."

He stood, weapon in hand, commanding the weaponless men to mount again and turn back on their trail;

watched them until they were out of sight. They rode humbly enough, not unused, perhaps, to the misadventures of guerrilla warfare.

When their dust cloud had turned the corner Palmer had done with inaction. "Quick, now!" said he. "Get up, all of you. We've got to ride. They know who we are now. We'll have to make a run for it."

What remained for them to do at this place required but a moment longer. They threw the discarded weapons of the Rurales into the thicket alongside the road, saving only a belt or two of ammunition which they might need. The horses they tied bridle to bridle, cast bridles over saddle pommels, and left them standing huddled near the bloody spot in the road. A few moments and their own dust cloud was lessening down the highway. The scene spoke of peace once more. Birds, gently singing, perched near-by.

The two mules, with loads of wood and the bulkiest of camp equipage, fell far behind and were abandoned. "We can't wait for anything," said Palmer. "Come on down the road. Maybe we can make it through before it is too late."

All the time his eye was scanning eagerly the landscape on either side of the highway. At length he drew rein, threw up his hand.

"Wait!" he called, "here's where we're going to leave the road."

He showed them now, spreading out his arms wide to serve as sighting lines, the point which he had kept in mind as marking the place of departure from the old Spanish Road and their definite plunge into the wildness that lay below it.

"Come on, now; we'll see if you're riders."

A little distance from the rocky set-off where he really intended to leave the trail Palmer began to back his horse, setting him back a few feet at a time steadily, seeing that he did not swerve, the others following as best they could. Surely the tracks left in the dust of the old road must have been puzzling to any one who tried to follow them out, even had there been suspicion of their actual departure from the road.

Palmer at length whirled and pushed up the rocky slope which lay upon the southern edge of the road. Always he kept to the hard going, drew off to the right, following across the slide rock of a bald hill that lay there. There was no definite or easy trail left by the animals. He trusted to their own speed to throw off the track any pursuer, who must lose time in puzzling out their trail, if indeed it could be followed at all by the average man.

At the end of an hour Palmer once more pulled up his horse, facing to the southward. "Yonder is our country," said he. "One ridge and one mountain after another. That's the Orizaba wilderness, all volcanic, on ahead. The Valley of La Luz is what we must find."

Tired, dusty, worn, haggard from the scenes which they had passed through but now, the little party was grouped around the leader. The cheeks of Luisa still were wet with tears, the wrinkled face of old Serafina more than usually drawn, as though she, too, would have wept had not her eyes long been dry.

"What have you said, Señor Juan?" demanded the Spanish girl. "What is it that we are to see on ahead there?"

The old man turned to her, smiling in his gentle way. "Be not alarmed, my sister," said he. "You have seen us care for you? So far as we are able, to the last of us now remaining, we still will care for you and hold you safe. You understand?"

"I understand, Señor Juan! But I am afraid. I am frightened. You are but three."

John Palmer turned his face to his friends. "We are but the remaining three to-day," said he.

They spurred on, following at an angle the steep slope of the long mountain side. Save for an occasional stone clinking under hoof, there was no sound. They had left the last touch or trace of civilization behind them and were threading into the lower half-tropic wilderness, below the shoulder of Orizaba. Around them lay the dead land which Orizaba herself had created—green now and sprinkled with many flowers; a land of many secrets.

CHAPTER XII

THE WILDERNESS

THE little band pressed on at such speed as they could manage after their first plunge into the broken country off the highway. As they knew, every hour now counted, and the first hours were the most valuable. Clinging to the rocky ledges as best they could, they employed all the artifices of good mountain men who did not lack in scouting knowledge of their own. They all knew well enough that should they be pursued and found in this country, hundreds of miles below their own border line, they would, even if not charged with the killing of the Rurales on the road, be unable to explain their presence. That meant but one thing. The wilderness offered them their one hope of safety.

The two women, not unused to mountain travel, kept up well with the others, their sure-footed Spanish mules knowing what was expected of them. All rode in silence, for Palmer thought no further explanation of the route was necessary beyond the general description which he had given his companions.

For different reasons, perhaps one of superstition, perhaps from the fact that better country existed elsewhere, and closer to the main trail, this lower volcanic country, rich as it was, held no settlements at all. The landscape was broken by a series of deep ridges. There was no trend, no contour, no water-shed system at all to the country. The mountains seemed thrown down carelessly together. True, it was rich, but under the soft vegetation there lay a flooding savagery. They were leaving all the old trails back of them, advancing into a region which certainly was not inviting, not welcoming, even, although they must depend upon it absolutely for such protection as they might claim.

Luisa, as she rode, looked now and again, even through her tears, at the stern alertness, the activity and strength of these men, whose keen faces never had blanched in fear, who seemed so self-reliant, even here, with everything against them. Hallock, from time to time, much of the time, rode at her side or close at hand. They rarely spoke. Sometimes their eyes met silently.

Evening came, after their first long, hard push below the road. A little pool of water, caught in the rocks, offered what they most needed. They threw off packs, made ready their simple preparations for the night. They had come into a sort of flattening in the broken short hills, where a gentle *savanna* lay spread before them, in the manner of a primordial amphitheater, set down here among the hills and long ago forgotten. Once the stream might have run elsewhere, now the summer sun had somewhat shrunk it. The whole little picture, veiled in the twilight, surrounded by the purple hills, made a scene wild and fascinating enough for any not driven as were these who now occupied it.

"You have been here before, John?" asked Barry Allison.

Palmer nodded. "I know where I am, precisely. Once I came back here out of La Luz. I was trying to get in back of the big valley which we're after—I lost that trail—indeed, there was no trail at all. I couldn't do it. There is no definite contour to this country. It is all broken volcanic land, don't you see? But I know very well where I am and where we're going to come out.

"Even so," he continued, smiling. "We're not the first to find this spot."

"What do you mean?" inquired Allison. "Not the first?"

"No—the Aztecs knew it. The Mayas, I suppose. Come with me."

They walked a little way apart, toward the upper edge of the *savanna.* There was no sign of house or human habitation. No, and yet there had been human habitation here at one time in the history of the world. Straight up from the sloping surface of the earth, half hidden by the flood of vegetation, there stood before them one of the great prehistoric monuments which we ascribe to the mysterious Mayas; a tall shaft of the hard trachyte, sculptured from top to bottom in strange figures, mysterious, undecipherable, on which another race now gone once inscribed its message, its knowledge, perhaps its secrets as well. Old, old, very old, it was; none might tell how old.

Palmer pointed to the shaft as they approached. They both could see the crude but striking sculptures of that same type which so often are found in the jungles of Guatemala, Yucatan, Nicaragua—things which men risk death and even banditti to see.

Nor was this all. Just beyond the edge of the forest stood a broken stairway, the now flattened pyramid of what once, without question, had been one of the strange sacrificial temples devoted to the rites of some bygone people, whether Toltec, Aztec, Maya, or Quiche.

"Look yonder if you wish to see something," said Palmer. "I have stood here before and studied it. It's enough to make you creep. Look over at the top where the steps are broken off and the grass begins to grow. You see that stone up there? I have never been up, but I really believe that's the old sacrificial altar. See how it rounds off on top. It looks rather smooth. Well, that's where they stretched out their victim. One man each for the hands and feet and one for the head—and the old priest with an obsidian knife waiting to split his ribs and drag out his heart and hold it up to the sun! Pleasant people, those!

"They used to treat their prisoners very well—gave them everything in the world to eat and wear and allowed them the society of the most beautiful young women of the tribe. At the same time, they never concealed the fact that after a while they intended to take them up those stairs yonder. They made sacrifices to the sun—so terrible in their extent that even the Spaniards were horrified. It is more than probable that back of the sacrifices to the sun was the wish to propitiate the avenging spirit which presided over the great Valley of Madre d'Oro. That was the heart of the Aztec people. It was the core of the Aztec religion.

"Well, I suppose these steps which we see falling into decay now have seen a great many laggard footsteps in their day—the victims on their death march. And I suppose also that the heart of the Aztec empire, the core of the Aztec religion, is just as much in existence to-day as it ever was."

Palmer fell into one of his brooding silences, which Allison did not venture to break for some time. "It's strange, though, isn't it," he said at length, "that a country as rich as this should never have been explored to its last limit.

"Strange, yes, but stranger things have happened than that Madre d'Oro should not be known to-day. Have you never read Las Casas, the historian of the conquest? Did you ever hear of the lost land of Tierra Deguerra?"

"I never did," said Allison.

"Well, that strange lost land still exists! It lies between the Cordilleras and the city of Chiapas in a valley all its own. Cortes never conquered it. Some of the priests begged to be allowed to try the ways of Christianity and not of war in the subjugation of that country. It, therefore, never was fully conquered by fire and sword. To-day it is in part occupied by uncivilized and unbaptized Indians, who live precisely as they did when Cortes passed through here. Those facts were well known by the head of the Dominicans, in the city of Guatemala. It was agreed that for five years of the conquest no Spaniard should go into that country at all. None ever did. There is no Spanish civilization there to-day; and yet the government of Central America knows of that region perfectly well. It makes no attempt to extend its own government over that district.

"I have had an old padre tell me that, four days toward the great City of Mexico, starting from his old home down below here and crossing the great Sierra Madres and the Cordilleras, there is a great living city to be seen down in there, even now, and that it is just as it was when the Spaniards came in 1556—temples, houses, gardens, and all. It has in part the same old religion to-day, in spite of all the Dominicans did to set it aside in their earlier futile attempt.

"The old padre told me he had heard that story very generally, first at the village called Chajal. From that village it was not far to the top of a high ridge, and from that place the tops of the temples could be seen. He told me that once he made that climb himself, to a point about twelve thousand feet above sea level, and that at a great distance he saw that very city which had been described to him, lying white and gleaming in the sun. He said there was no doubt at all about it—that city existed then and exists to-day.

"Now, you see that is getting pretty authentic, if you want something to marvel at—this hidden city of the Quiches or Mayas or Aztecs, whatever you choose to call these people. No white man of our day has ever set foot in that city. Many have tried to do so, but the natives have killed every white man who has gotten that far into the interior. They still practice the old religion, so said my old Dominican friar. Yet those are the people who made all these images through all this country, almost down to the Isthmus of Panama. The Christian Indians who guide you in this lower country will always break off the nose of every stone idol they find hidden out in the tropic forest. The Christianized savage thinks he does that to the glory of God."

"Our course, however, does not run in that direction, does it, John?"

"No, but if that whole hidden city can exist and does so exist, protected by lack of investigation, by lack of roads and trails, why should it be any more wonderful that the still hidden heart and core of that whole civilization should also remain undiscovered to-day? There is no doubt whatever that that great body of gold did exist, and that it was known. Around it have been cast the great protective agencies of attractions elsewhere of the inland civilization. The *temblor* and volcano also have protected it. Down below here we'll cross a flood of lava buried by a flood of vegetation.

"So I say, I shall prove to you there is no marvel at all in the existence to-day of that great vein of gold. And marvel or not, I tell you, I have seen it! I don't like to talk about it, that is true—it is too terrible a thing. But you shall see it also. Perhaps you also shall be smitten dumb—I don't know.

"Of course, the valley itself is not really a valley at all. It is literally a sunken chasm due to the volcanic action of Orizaba in some forgotten day of the past. There is no great mystery about it at all. It is only chance, as I have pointed out, that no one really has taken the trouble to run down these old legends.

"Now the old padre made me a map of his lost city which he last had seen when he was a young man in Chajal. He showed me the mountain where he stood when he looked down on that city, where it lay unmapped by any hand but his. 'Señor Juan,' he said to me, 'here are men living as they did when the Spaniards first came. Cortes and Alvarado never saw them. If we could speak with those living men, they could read for us all the riddle of what the jungles yet conceal, these countless images of stone which seem Egyptian, Assyrian. They could read the words on the old pillars which we have not yet read. Ah, if we could talk with those men, what could we not learn of the history of the world!

" 'But,' he always added, 'that is another world. I don't know that they would live if we forced them to leave their own country. They could not understand us, we cannot understand them. It is like a dream city. At times I ask if I have not dreamed that I saw it. But I know I have not dreamed. The government of this republic below us knows that what I say is true. But, they have trouble enough with their own cities!

" 'But, one day,' the old friar always said, 'I'm going back there. I shall see if I can find the answer to all these riddles.'

"Well, if we want to run into riddles and marvels here's a whole settlement of the same people who once protected Madre d'Oro. There was Pedro, the old man of the lower peninsula. He was the last man, I presume, who held the actual secret of Madre d'Oro. I wonder if Pedro is still alive!

"Well," concluded John Palmer, with a deep sigh, and a wave of the hand at the old temple stairs as he turned aside, "I'm like the old padre. I shall keep on going until the end comes, I presume. If he comes out with his story—if we come out with ours—there will be enough to set this world by the ears, I'm thinking!"

"At one time, John," said his companion, "you said you might have to rely upon the Yaqui settlements if we got into actual combat with them and the government of Mexico. What hope would we have in a case like that?"

"Perhaps no very great hope," assented Palmer. "It seems to me these things will take care of themselves. The Yaquis live forty, fifty miles below my home. They have no suspicion of any hidden valley. Perhaps, after we have seen that valley ourselves, the thing may simplify—we may not want to try to move all the Madre d'Oro bodily to the United States. We may not want to go to war!"

"But, then, why do we go on—what benefit do we get of it?" demanded Allison troubled.

"You're now asking me questions which I am not yet disposed to answer," replied the older man. "I simply say we must go on to the end. Our plan then may shape itself. In things like this, one man or two or three can never shape the plan. Madre d'Oro will make its own plan for you or me!"

At this latitude, and at an elevation somewhat below that of the upper plains embraced in the great Tierra Templada of Mexico, the nights now were not so cool, the days less readily supportable in their midday ardor. These things, however, were but details for our adventurers, who were carried on by an ambition so imperative as to blot out everything that lay between the wish and the fruition. When the two women first had joined the party, practically all felt that a handicap had been assumed which might make success impossible. But Luisa, more tenderly reared than her woman, Serafina, had that courage which can rise above bodily comfort. She made her scanty couch upon the ground beyond the brush screen which Serafina erected, and youth and vitality governed her sleep.

As for the men of the party, lean, hard, and hardy, they cast themselves upon the ground this night with scarce more than the edge of a blanket over and under them. When morning came, they arose forthwith and began where affairs had ended the previous day.

Breakfast was usually the time of moodiness between them, as with all who live thus close to the edge of existence. Their supplies now were scanty; enough, as they supposed, to last them through to the valley of La Luz, where Palmer promised them something better. Serafina, in her occasional visits to the little villages, always had brought with her abundant coffee, and this morning beverage seemed to give them new heart once more.

But now the memory of the bloody and sad events of the previous day sat on the heart of each man. They had started out four friends together, knowing the risk. Now they were but three. The loss of Silsby sat on them heavily. Allison voiced the feeling of each man when he spoke.

"I can't get over it," said he. "Silsby always did his share, and he never grouched over anything. A finer chap never lived."

"Well," said John, gravely, "any of us might meet the same fate. Our chance now is to keep hidden. We have no status here in Mexico—we're worse off than filibusters if we're discovered, because they would be sure to identify us with the killing of the Rurales on the big road. If we're caught the same thing will happen to us that did to a great many army officers of our own country in the early days."

Hallock drew the little flag once more from his bootleg where he carried it. "Anyhow," said he, shutting his teeth grimly. "They saluted this, if they never saluted a bigger flag at Vera Cruz."

Allison nodded. "Still," said he, "even if we find what we're after, it is not certain that our flag would follow our rifle barrels, or that the constitution would follow the flag. We are only individuals here."

"That's true," said John Palmer. "Those men were only individuals who started the independence of Texas and took that big slice from the old government of Spain and Mexico."

"What does he say?" demanded Luisa, pointing to Hallock, but addressing John Palmer.

"He says, my dear, that this is going to be a fine day for travel through the hills. He hopes you will not find it uncomfortable. Two days more, my dear, and then we shall see the valley of La Luz!"

"Home! And then, Señor Juan?"

"And then we shall see!"

Soon they were on their way once more, boring deeper and deeper through the lower and warmer country which lay on the shoulder of Orizaba. Such broken conversation as the three men held nearly always came around again and again to the question of Madre d'Oro and the strangeness of the fact that it had not yet been discovered. But now John Palmer explained no more, reasoned no more. All he would say was, the time had not yet come. So all of that day they traveled, and that next night made encampment in the heart of a wilderness so vast that it seemed to them they never could be found, even by the most intelligent and resolute pursuers.

Afternoon of the second day and Palmer called a halt. He rode back and forth over a restricted section, looking to every point of the compass. At length he threw up his hand.

"It's all right," said he. "This is the last time we need take our bearings. You gentlemen needn't use your map, which you have on the piece of canvas, because now you could hardly miss the trail. Look yonder toward the south."

"I see it!" exclaimed Allison. "That's the last nitch! That's where we head."

"Yes, that's the gate to the valley of La Luz. When we have reached that pathway you will not need me any more should anything go wrong. It will all be simple after that; and it is simple from here to the valley of La Luz."

"How far was your place above the last settlement?" asked Hallock presently.

"I should say fifty miles—and a couple of hundred years," replied Palmer.

"Hard to understand."

"I don't pretend to understand anything. I don't understand this little gold god I have got in my pack. I can't explain it. All I say is that to-morrow night we'll sleep within a day's march of the Madre d'Oro."

An hour later he broke out uninvited once more, after his strange fashion. "After all, what right has the world to think that the last great discovery of gold has been made? They have all come without premeditation, without warning. Take the great Comstock lode—it is really the only mother vein ever found in the United States. It runs for twenty miles and it is a true mother vein, without any doubt or question. Yet it lay there absolutely without any indication. The prospectors who struck it never found any float—they just blundered into it forthright. In the same way, there has never been any trace of gold found on La Luz. There was nothing to bring any one up that valley. And yet there is the mother lode.

"I don't suppose any of you can recall the names of the prospectors who first struck the Comstock. It may be our names will be forgotten some time in the same way. Plain, simple, ordinary men, all of us, like those others. And when you actually see what I have seen, it will seem so natural and simple and easy that you will wonder why you and I ever made any fuss about it.

"Of course, I never would have found this if I hadn't had the inside knowledge from old Pedro. All ordinary prospecting methods would absolutely have failed."

"But what on earth, John, made you go all that distance to get us fellows to come with you?" Allison turned toward him curiously.

"I knew I was an old man," replied John Palmer. "I needed help. I wanted good Americans to help me—plain, simple men like myself, but younger. Always the old stories kept coming back to my mind—that the conquerors of this country always have come from the north, not from the west or from the east. That seems to be a fact, and why should you or I question that? At least, here we are, three of us out of the four. It is sad to say, but I suppose we are lucky to be three out of four to-day And even now, within sight of the very gate itself, we don't know whether there will be three of us left to see it."

"You're a cheerful sort of fellow," smiled Hallock, congenital optimist.

"Come, we lose time here," said Palmer.

Before them, at length, there lay a sharp declivity, a narrow trough piercing the enshrouding forest growth. There was no road or trail, but down the incline the treasure hunters plunged, crossing slide rock, bits of vitrified overlay. The character of the vegetation now was such that the newcomers felt themselves in a world absolutely new, like some fantastic dream.

At a point where they could make some sort of pause without too much inconvenience Palmer turned and held up his hand for a halt.

"Old Orizaba had her own way," said he. "Far back of us lies the valley which used to be the true course of La Luz. That's in a great labyrinth to the west and north. But, as I suppose, when the great valley we are seeking was countersunk in the earth crust the water that it caught bored its way out at the foot, and so built the little Rio La Luz as we knew it to-day. In matters of this sort, you see, a thousand years is but a day."

They sat now, looking out over the maze of mingled ridges, broken peaks, long and easy slopes, covered with the black half-tropic forest vegetation. Now, indeed, they were coming toward the close of their undertaking. They no longer had the apathy born of continuous fatigue. Something feverish, exciting, exalting, came into the blood of every one.

When Palmer next pulled up they were quite through the notched passage of the last ridge. Before them widened out a magnificent mountainous view. Across, beyond the valley below, appeared a succession of bold eminences, covered with heavy, dark vegetation.

"Comrade, yonder lies your Italy!" said John Palmer. "That is what Napoleon said when his army looked down from the summit of the Alps. Well, we are over the last of our Alps now. Long road, eh?

"I suppose there is no corner of the world better concealed. I don't believe any man ever would find that valley which lies below us."

"Why, nonsense, John! A good prospector can find anything, any place," said Allison, scoffing.

"Is it so? Well, there were no better prospectors than the Spaniards. But this country below us is as verdant to-day as it was in the time of Alvarado. There isn't a human habitation excepting my own within fifty miles, nor any likelihood of any. Superstition is one of the strongest influences in the world. These native people not only had superstitions, but were governed by them. There is no doubt in my mind that there was some sort of superstition which kept the natives out of exploration into this broken volcanic country. Perhaps their priests told them not to go in—I don't know. All I know is that I have lived here for many years, and I have been the only Robinson Crusoe."

He sighed, his head dropping while he sat, his hands folded on his saddle pommel. "Now that's all over," said he.

They did not press him any more. Turning, they all plunged down the last slope, their eyes exulting as they emerged at last into a flat valley that wound on away through scenes of placid beauty. This way, that, the slow turns of the rugged shoulders of the mountains cut off the view. No trail marked the banks of the murmuring rivulet which was seeking its way out into the world.

And presently they came to their journey's end, or to that last part of it which meant their ultimate encampment.

"Now we are home!" said John Palmer, after two or three hours of steady marching.

They had halted before a low clump of buildings surrounded with trees planted in order by the hand of man. Here was a little clearing, back of it a little garden, a tiny field or two. There had been flowers here, roses; palms nodded, high and aloof.

"This is the only house within fifty miles in that direction," said John Palmer, slowly. No one knows how far it would be to the west before there would show another trace. Come on in, men. There never were any locks on these doors. It is my home—that is to say, it was my home."

Luisa was the first now to enter the house. She ran on ahead, threw open the doors, uttered exclamations of eagerness, inviting all these, her friends.

Utterly wearied, the three men followed her into the interior. John Palmer sank down into a deep seat in front of the empty fireplace and sat staring. His friends, unwelcomed by the owner, stood about uneasy. Luisa beckoned them, leading to the rear door, which made out upon the walled garden, or what once had been a garden.

"She lies here," said she, sadly. "My sister. There

was a little baby also." They understood her broken English. "Me—I have been the mother of Señor Juan," she added, proudly, "these several years! Except for me he could not have lived here. He is sad now. He will not talk."

"Strange place, Barry," said Hallock, after a time, as they turned away, hushed, awed. "Spooky, I call it. I swear, if we don't get some action before long I'm going loony. All this is getting on my nerves."

"We are at the end of the world here," said Barry Allison. "I presume pursuers could come up the valley if they knew we were here, but how could they know? I'm willing to say John Palmer has led us well. As for the rest of it——"

"To-morrow, do you suppose?" asked Hallock.

"Very likely," Allison nodded. "I don't think Palmer will feel like waiting very long."

They turned back slowly toward the front door from which they just now had emerged. "Well, here we are," said Hallock, taking a deep breath. "God, what a strange place it is! We don't belong here, unless indeed we are forerunners of manifest destiny. Well, let's call it destiny. I don't know anything else which just exactly describes it."

The gentle voice of Luisa came to them. "Serafina is making coffee," said she, greeting them as they reentered. "She will show you where you may find rooms. I have not disturbed Señor Juan."

They turned back to the central room. John Palmer still sat before the fireplace, staring into it.

"Come on, John!" called Hallock gayly. "We'll have our first meal in your house."

But John Palmer apparently did not hear him. He still sat motionless in his chair.

CHAPTER XIII

THE SUMMONS

SOMETHING about the rigid immobility of the figure of Palmer before the fireplace arrested the attention of his companion. Allison stepped quickly forward and laid a hand upon his shoulder. The face of the old prospector was turned slightly toward him, his chin upon his shoulder, and eyes not closed. The hands were resting upon the arms of the chair as though he had been about to rise.

Had been? Now what had been John Palmer was no more.

In his own home, at his own fireside—bare and empty now, its cheer lacking—John Palmer apparently had heard some voice calling him; had turned as if about to rise, to make answer. But even as he did so he had passed from all earthly affairs. He had died as he sat, alone, as so long he had lived.

Their sudden cry brought Doña Luisa hurrying. She knew before she had come close. She knelt at the side of her guardian, wailing in her own sudden grief.

The immediate time of consternation, of stupefaction, passed. At length these three stood looking at one another, stunned. Serafina had come to the door and gazed wild-eyed. This was worse than death in combat. The second of them to pass within so short a time! Allison and Hallock looked into each other's eyes with sudden horror. Allison spoke first.

"He had just come back to his own home. He made it through to here. I have been noticing how thin he was. Always brooding over something. But a brave man and one of vision."

"Well, he sees further than we do now, that's sure. Only two of us now," said Hallock, a bit thickly. "Just you and me."

"No one else," replied his friend. "But now we must first take care of him."

They laid John Palmer on the long, high settle which stood at one side of the room, throwing over his face the folds of a serape. Then they turned in silence to the little table which Serafina had spread for them. Never could sadder meal come to any of these three who sat thus.

And then, after a time, they laid John Palmer by the side of the woman in the little walled garden where she once had worked among her flowers. They turned back once more to thoughts of a world which suddenly seemed to lack all plan, all coördination.

Palmer had been their chief in the natural course of things, their guide over every trail, their leader in a strange country. He had knowledge of the country and its language as well. They had not realized until now how essential had been his counsel, his leadership. Both Allison and Hallock were assailed by a strange feeling of helpfulness.

They were in a strange country with not a friend, not even a possibility of getting out word to any friend. Upon their shoulders rested the remaining responsibility of the most perilous and impossible enterprise which any man could have conceived.

"She's guarded her secret well," said Barry Allison that evening, nodding up the valley toward the mysterious world which seemed now to have shown its sudden and malicious hostility. "She has her own ways, the Madre d'Oro!"

"Yes," rejoined Hallock. "Well, for one I don't feel just like tackling it, do you?"

"No, I don't. Out of respect for a good man we ought to stop here a day or two at least. And there's the girl."

"Oh, I suppose we'll carry on—we'll get through somehow."

Allison nodded. "We've got to do that as a matter of duty to John Palmer. What a life he led! What a man he must have been! He never did go back to the States at all. I don't know what first sent him west, for he never would talk. I suppose it was a woman. Well, he found another woman. He said women make most of the trouble in the world."

Hallock nodded. But his eyes all the time were following about the place the appealing figure of yet another woman. Doña Luisa, figure of growing fascination to him whether or not he had admitted that. Allison went on musingly.

"Well, it's always a woman. I confess it was a woman sent me here. I am on a limit of one year. She's back home—Ohio, you know."

"Yes, I suppose so," Hallock nodded. "Well, you ought to have news for her in less time than that. I hope you get back home. Well, John Palmer has come home, hasn't he? He kept that little garden of hers—right up to the time he started north, it must have been. And why he ever started north I can't tell. At least he led us here—to his last gasp he did that. I swear, Barry, the whole thing makes me feel spooky—I'll not deny it.

"I suppose you and I ought to sort of compare notes," he added; "sort of fix up a plan in case of anything—in case of anything—" He jerked his head toward the little garden where John Palmer now lay at rest.

"Yes, that's true," said Allison. "Well, I'll write down my address and that of the woman in my case. Her name is Mary Westlake. She lives at Deneville, in Ohio—that's on Lake Erie. She's been waiting a good while for me. No good, maybe—not sure I am now—not sure the luck has changed."

"Well, my address—I don't just know it yet. To tell the truth," said Hallock, his fair and boyish countenance suddenly flushed, "I think it's going to depend a good deal on that girl yonder."

"So that's the way?" Allison looked at him gravely. "I'm not surprised. It happened to John. It has happened to you. There is no accounting for these things—they happen. So you have decided?"

"Yes, I'm going to marry Luisa. She doesn't know it yet, but I do. I have got to learn to talk her language a little better, but I think she would know the truth even if I couldn't."

They walked about uneasily, not talking consecutively, no actual plan for the further campaign formulated in the mind of either.

"Come to think about it, Barry," broke out Hallock after a time, "what would we do if we found the whole valley of gold? We can't carry it away. Besides, what happiness comes out of it? Old John here knew where the valley was. It didn't make him happy. Will it us?"

"You're asking me something I can't answer, friend," said Barry Allison. "I don't suppose we can cut out very much solid gold, to tell the truth. I have not thought much of that. The main thing is to put the whole proposition to the final test, isn't it?"

Hallock nodded. "And we have got to keep it a secret?"

"Surely we have. We are now the only Two Guardians of the secret, I suppose. We don't know that old Pedro, who once was the last man of the Three, is still alive. John Palmer's gone now. You and I are——" He found his eye still following Doña Luisa.

"No," said Hallock, perhaps sensing his thought, "I don't think we'll tell her anything about it just yet. First let's see about it ourselves. Not that Luisa would ever give us away. She doesn't seem Spanish to me, nor Mexican. She seems Andalusian, Goth—just like myself. Her people came from the north into Spain. We came from the north into Mexico."

"Well," Allison smiled at him, not cynically, "I shall be glad, old man. And the girl has behaved splendidly all the way down, like a thoroughbred—I'll say that."

Again some time passed before they broke the silence. "When shall it be, old man?" asked Hallock. And Allison, tactitly assigned the place of leadership, replied:

"I think it ought not to be later than to-morrow. You suppose Luisa will be afraid to stay here for a time?"

"I don't think so. She has Serafina and she'll be busy trying to find her lost chickens out in the woods. It has to come to a show-down some time, and they will have to take their chance. You and I will have to take ours."

"But what's Serafina doing with her chickens now?" queried Hallock. "Look at them, they're all flying up in the trees. Good God, what's that?"

A sort of sensation, not distinctly recognized, had come to them both. Hallock tried to laugh.

"I have heard of chickens taking to their roost when there is going to be an eclipse of the sun. Is there one due?"

"Not to my memory," replied Allison. But just then a shriek came.

"El temblor! El temblor!" screamed the old Mexican woman. She came to the door, wringing her hands, looking this way and that.

"What's that?" demanded Hallock. Once more to their senses, strained, uneasy, a foreboding lay in the air, as though something fearsome were about to happen soon.

It did happen, and soon. There came a gentle vibration, a waving movement of the hard earth beneath them, the floor of the room where they sat seemed to lie between two of the nodes. The chairs leaned forward, swung back again; a sort of rustle came from the pictures along the wall. But all the world was very, very silent. Nowhere was any sound to be heard.

And then came a strange, mysterious sound, like the low suppressed wail of the earth, a whisper, a sigh. It passed down from the head of the Valley of La Luz.

. . . . .

When Randall Trent had been a college student—for two terms; he never tarried for his degree—he came to have the name of Lord's Anointed Trent. The nick-name never gave him any concern. He had always a flair of his own. His attitude toward life was one of perfect contentment; his egotism was of that sort and extent which sometimes leaves men with no real sense of humor, no perspective. Since he was Randall Trent, what did the rest matter?

It could not be said that Trent lacked courage or, rather, that confidence in his personal star which sometimes goes for courage. What another man could do, he reasoned, that also he could do, perhaps better. It was his naïve conviction that the world was his oyster because he was Randall Trent. Not a bad mental stature for a small-town millionaire.

Trent was never actually a sportsman. He cared little for rod or gun or horse, and played golf only because some of the men whom he wished to meet did so. Risk and adventure had no special appeal to him, since they did not spell any actual return in money. With perfect health, and its attendant balance of life, with a nice instinct for good clothes and good living, he made no ill figure of a man. There do not lack abundant human beings of either sex who are disposed to accept such a man at his own valuation.

Withal, he had at his command the greatest of all arguments—money. Not that he was the sort of money-maker who increases his store by personal penury. On the contrary, he was always what is called a spender, working on large lines, thinking in terms of millions. Out of such material have arisen most of our metropolitan millionaires. What he called his luck really was his heredity, his attunement with an environment where all the leading men had sought no more than material good and material gain in life, believing that success in life could mean money and nothing else. His attitude had in it few dreams, but yet a considerable imagination of what is known as the constructive sort.

What motive actually determined this sort of a man upon the rather mad enterprise of searching for the lost mine of the Aztecs by means of the modern airplane? The make-up, the mentality, of the man perhaps might answer that. Added to that was the pressing and powerful motive of jealousy. Between him and the woman he loved stood the life of one man, a poor man, who had little to commend him to a woman of the sort most men covet. And yet that man was the hero of the woman, the only woman Randall Trent ever had loved. He had shown courage, adventurousness, willingness to take a risk—things which a woman loves in her lover evermore. Very well, if he could do these things so could Randall Trent, and perhaps better. He resolved to play the other man's game and beat him in that game. Thus he figured he might win the *spolia opima* which came ever to the winner in adventurous deeds.

If Barry Allison could seek the miracle of the lost mine, so could Randall Trent. And, whereas Barry Allison was a man of no resources, no identification with men of means, he, Randall Trent, would show said Barry Allison what a man of means and resources and ideas actually could do.

As Trent thought over all these things he smiled to himself, not cruelly, not unkindly, but simply with a feeling of superiority, a feeling that he was of the elect of life, of the winners, of the survivors of the world's best men.

His plans went forward rapidly. After the departure of the Westlake party for the States he himself hurried westward and southward, until finally he arrived once more at Magdalena Bay, upon the west coast of the Lower Peninsula. It chanced that a pair of army planes at that time were waiting at Magdalena for orders. Two army aviators had been lost somewhere in Mexico and these planes were detailed to aid in the search. These facts made appeal to Randall Trent. It occurred to him that an army airplane might find a missing mine as well as a missing man.

Trent had some acquaintance in Magdalena, and some acquaintance also in Washington, as well as in San Diego. He also prided himself as being what is known as a fast worker. It took him but a short time to explain to the two aviators that he needed one of them for a trip over Old Mexico and that presently he would have consent for such a trip. And, so far as that was concerned, within twenty-four hours he had it—by wireless from Washington. He was granted the privilege of attending an army pilot on a scouting trip over the adjoining republic of Mexico, in search for the two aviators of whom no word had come for many days.

As for young Billy Townsend of Z-78, it made little difference to him where he went or why. Young, full-blooded, fair-haired, and blue-eyed, innocent of visage, twenty-two years of age, and one of the best flyers back from France, he was rather more at home in the air than on the earth. Apostle of new days, he was proud as such men will be, and the money offered him by Trent made him flush hotly. The latter apologized. But the handful of rich pearls which Trent tossed to him, as a product of the country they now would see, seemed to Billy Townsend an excellent thing for a girl who was up north. Trent did not mention their rejection by a certain girl whom he had known. Billy took them and tucked them into a pocket of his leather jacket. Perhaps the thought of custom duties never came to his mind. As to international law and complications between the two governments—those things probably never would have stopped either him or his associate had they come to mind. Billy's one concern was that over petrol—as he had learned to call it in Europe.

"Why should we worry about that?" demanded Trent, when finally they had come to terms about the whole proposition. "A thousand miles isn't so impossible, of course, in these times. If we really get lost, or if the worst comes to the worst, there are plenty of towns where we can land. There's San Blas on the west coast of the mainland, and beyond that Guadalajara, and Guanajuato, and the City of Mexico, and Vera Cruz."

"But, good God, sir!" exclaimed Billy, "that's entirely off our line. The men we're after can't have got down there. We're supposed to work north from here, not farther south and east."

"How do you know, my boy, where air currents may have taken them? We're just as apt to find them one place as another. And what harm for a good pilot to see a little bit of this lower country while he's at it? There's another thing. There's no use cutting loose and flying wild, not knowing where you're going. Now, my real purpose——" And Trent unfolded his real purpose—as much as he thought best to tell them.

Billy Townsend's eyes began to shine. The search for the missing mine, the ancient repository of the Aztec gold, made full appeal to his youthful imagination. They talked it over for an hour or two. Before Trent was done he had taken on a partner for his own enterprise, which now seemed not so mad after all.

"You see, about our journey," he went on, talking to his pilot, "I am guided largely by an old map I saw at the Ranch of Good Hope, up toward the interior. That's an old Spanish map, and on it is marked, very distinctly, the spot where it was supposed—it was not known, it was supposed—that the Madre d'Oro actually existed. That's down here, southeast of the City of Mexico. It must be somewhere near the big volcano Orizaba—maybe just southwest of there, as near as I could tell from the map.

"Now, perhaps you don't know it, but the old Spaniards had a road between Vera Cruz and this other country where we're standing now. That is to say, it ran from Vera Cruz northwest through old Mexico, Guanajuato and Guadalajara. At Guadalajara it forked. One prong went to San Blas and the other ran southwest to Acapulco, farther down.

"Now, I think we ought to cross below the point of the peninsula and then swing in east to San Blas. I'll tell you why. The Santiago River comes in there, and we can follow that valley all the way to Guadalajara and beyond, as easily as we could a railroad track. Then, when we get to Guadalajara. we can take the railroad track and follow that through the mountains to Mexico City. When we get down there we can take our guess and our gamble as to the rest of it.

"You ask me where that mine is, and I tell you I don't know. All I say is, if we take a *pasear* around over that rough country below Orizaba, we've got as good a right to find it as anybody else. You won't have to do more than a thousand miles or so. That's a day's travel, the way you boys go. Even a hundred miles an hour will eat it up in a day—between drinks, you might say. Petrol? Well, if we do have to have it we could get it at plenty of places. I'm saying the quicker we get off the more fun and the quicker we'll be having it. And if we should by any chance fly in on that old mine or find another bunch of people who are on the point of landing on the old mine—why, you and I would be made. I'll give you all the pearls you want.

"How does it listen to you, my boy? You've got full authority from the United States government to go. You've got all the money you need to take you there and get you back. What's more, you've got orders to go out and find those two missing men if you can. Naturally, it costs us nothing more to look for those men while we're looking for our mine."

"You've been up before?" asked the young pilot.

"Oh, yes, often."

"All right. Let's start early in the morning. I always like to be up at daybreak, to see the sun come up and paint the clouds."

Trent nodded. "That suits me," said he. "We'll make an early start to-morrow morning."

And so indeed they did. The great plane, running like a clock, took off beautifully and handled gently. Townsend tooled along the western and lower edge of the great peninsula, slipping over his hundred miles or so an hour, the earth drawn like a ribbon back below him.

They rounded the point of the peninsula, swung up and beyond the horn, saw below them the tiny boats of the pearl fisheries of La Paz; then headed off directly, still in the early morning, across the Gulf of California, for the western edge of Mexico. It all seemed simple, easy, matter-of-fact.

To Randall Trent, for a time literally above the clouds and seeing the pink dawn illumining the aerial world beneath him, a strange feeling of superlative power came insensibly.

"Well," he muttered to himself, his voice drowned in the roar of the great engines, "it's no more wonderful to find the Madre d'Oro than it is to be doing just this very thing. It's a cinch, that's what it is—a cinch!"

And so, in time, as the sun rose steadily over the half-tropic land beneath them, they finished their course across the gulf, left the narrow beach of San Blas below them and swung off into the great valley of the crooked Santiago River. They were now above a settled country. Little dotted villages lay below them at times, and often Billy Townsend, full of youthful zest, would swoop low, skimming the tops of some clump of low adobes and laughing aloud at seeing the scantily-clad inhabitants scatter like quail into the cover of the thickets. What these ignorant natives thought no man might tell. Surely they must have taken the apparition for some being of another world.

As to the course of their journey, it after all proved astonishingly simple, as Trent had said. They made no difficulty in following the valley of the river far back into the Sierra Madres; and at last, even a little earlier than they had expected, they saw below them the tall spires and gleaming buildings of that marvelous city of the mountains, Guadalajara, queen of the Mexican republic.

"Not so bad, not so bad!" Trent read the message of the pilot's lips and nodded. The latter settled down and began to drive. He spiraled twice above the town, the roar of the engines without question reaching the inhabitants. They now could see all traffic stop, see hurrying to and fro, see men gazing up at the sky at this strange visitant.

Trent at the time did not understand the pilot's purpose. Townsend turned to him. "Going to land here." And this, indeed, he proceeded to do, much to the consternation of his passenger. It developed afterward that Billy fancied one of his spark plugs needed overlooking; and, moreover, he knew that at Guadalajara there must be a chance to renew the contents of his tanks. As to the danger of it, as to any international complications, these were the least of Billy Townsend's troubles.

But there was trouble in that sharp mountain country to find the proper landing field. A plane never before had flown there, so far as they could tell; never before had been dreamed there, in all likelihood. The gay young pilot got small comfort of his voyage above the ancient city. At length, however, a gleaming white expanse before him caught his eye. He headed for it, settling rapidly. What he saw was a well-cleared plaza in the center of the city of Guadalajara!

It is to be said that he had the plaza much to himself when at length the great plane, settled like a vast bird, rebounded gently, rolled, slid a bit, and came to a full stop in a beautiful environment of palms and fountains—a place once well covered with tropical growth, though now sufficiently cleared to offer a good landing field.

The population of the town by this time was anywhere but in the plaza. The galleries and windows held countless curious faces. Some of these had perhaps heard of airplanes, others had no means even of suspecting what this big creature could be which, without warning, had come down upon them.

Billy Townsend stretched his arms and casually lit a cigarette. He then explained to Trent. "Ought to look at my spark plugs," said he. "She's done fine, but you can't be too careful. Think I'll load up with petrol while I'm at it."

Even Trent, of sufficient aplomb himself, looked at the young man in silence. "You have a nerve about you, anyhow," said he. "Do you know what it means, our dropping in here? We'll never get out of here at all."

"Oh, yes, it will be all right," replied his insouciant friend. "You'll see."

From the shade of a near-by public building there appeared the leisurely figure of a man heading out to the airplane as it lay at rest. Billy beckoned to him and addressed him in perfectly good United States.

"Good morning, friend," said he. "So this is Guadalajara? How's everything?"

"Well, who the devil are you?" replied the stranger in like tongue. "Where do you come from and what are you doing here?"

Billy Townsend offered his cigarette case. "We're just strolling across," said he. "We came from up in the peninsula this morning. You see, a couple of our men—fellows of my own corps—have been flying in from Arizona way, and they've got lost. They sent me down here—this is my friend, Mr. Trent—to see if we could pick them up. I saw this place, made perfect for a landing, and dropped in. How about some petrol—gasoline? Is there any garage here?"

"You've come to the right place," smiled the other. "I'm American myself—been in business down here for about eight years. I've got the biggest garage there is and I suppose I can fix you up. How much do you want?"

"I want her filled up," replied the young pilot carelessly. "I can't drive over to your place and take on a hose. How are we going to do it?"

"Oh, that's easy," replied the stranger. "My name's Finnegan—James D. Finnegan." He handed out a card—"I've learned the ways of these people down here. Without an empty oil can Mexico cannot exist. Hold on a minute and I'll start filling up. First I've got to see the police—I see they're beginning to drift in."

He was seen at a distance engaged in rapid, violent discussion with a body of gendarmes, who now ventured upon the edge of the plaza ready for trouble. Apparently the transplanted American possessed a certain influence. He returned after a time.

"I have told them that you have brought a message of peace and friendship," said he, grinning. "Also, I have given them ten dollars apiece. Also, I have told them to send me a bunch of water-carriers with their little tin pails. We'll have you all right in a jiffy."

"You're our kind of people," said Billy Townsend comfortably. "Have another cigarette. It's a lovely day, isn't it?"

They chatted a while. Gradually groups of curious inhabitants began to edge closer and closer to the vicinity of the great white-winged bird whose ominous voice they had for the first time heard above them that day. Presently Mr. James D. Finnegan broke away through the impacting crowd, heading a little procession of carriers, each with a yoke on his shoulder, from either end of which depended an oil can filled with gasoline. And thus did the good ship Z-78 find her midday meal, as Billy Townsend explained to Trent.

"But I say," said he to his passenger, with a voice smitten half of awe, "did you ever see so many fairies in all your life? I'm here to say right now that there's more beautiful girls in Guadalajara than there is in all Europe tied together—and I investigated over there. If we ever come back alive I'm going to stop over here a couple of weeks and get acquainted.

"And look at them coming in their carriages," he added. "This is the biggest beauty show in the world. Say, I wonder if I couldn't give away some of those pearls you handed me the other day?"

In fact, Billy Townsend was all for spending the evening at Guadalajara and taking in the sights of the city, but Trent was wiser. Knowing that complications certainly would ensue if they made any longer stop, he urged the young man to take off as soon as possible. Grudgingly the latter gave his final consent, drawing on his gloves and sitting back, after motioning away the crowd in front of them. James D. Finnegan, for the first time in his life, spun the propeller of the greatest gasoline vehicle he ever yet had seen. Presently, with a vast roar and skipping run, the Z-78 once more took wing. An instant and the packed plaza of Guadalajara was passing from view.

The closely netted telegraph system of the republic of Mexico by this time was passing the news across the entire country—news which that evening reached the United States, to the effect that one of the missing airplanes had been reported at an impossible and unaccountable distance south, toward the lower portion of the republic of Mexico. And now that the danger was passed, all the alcaldes, jafes politicos, the chief of police, and all the lieutenants of police began to meet in angry concourse, demanding by what right the American airship had landed on the soil of Mexico.

CHAPTER XIV

LOVE FINDS A WAY

BELOW the two sky travelers now spread the great panorama of the Sierra Madres. A thread of steel, winding in long curves, lay discernible below them from time to time. Trent studied always his map, and Townsend his compass. They knew they were following the general course, southeastward, of the main railway, and Trent was satisfied also that that course substantially was the same as that of the highway which he most sought—the ancient Spanish road, built long before the railway was dreamed of in any corner of the world.

The great city of Guanajuato was passed far to their left. Trent dreaded lest his harum-scarum guide might wish to land here also for further prosecution of his studies in female love interest. They did not, however, vary from the general southeastern course until late in the evening, when they were well toward the great city of Mexico, capital of the republic. Here Billy Townsend, without warning, appropriated to himself a little field which lay far out at the extremities of the great interlocking canal system which feeds the old city. Once more the inhabitants left their landing place to themselves and scattered pell-mell, praying to all the Mexican saints.

"Thought I'd come down to get a little rest," said Billy Townsend. "Time to have another look at the map—we're getting pretty well south."

Trent spread the map upon a wing of the plane before them and they both bent above it.

"Just what is this proposition?" demanded the young pilot. "You say you're after a mine and an old mine. Will you tell me how to find a mine with an airship? Do we go into the mouth of it and prowl around? Maybe our wings would be a little wide."

"Well, I don't suppose it's a mine as much as a sort of valley with an open lode running across it. That's how the story came to me. It's far down in the wilderness country."

"Wilderness, eh? Well, how do you get gas in the wilderness, and how do we land if we feel like it? We've done fine so far, and maybe we have got gas enough to get back with—I don't know. We might drop in at the big city over yonder."

"That's just what we won't do," said Trent hurriedly. "You take too many chances. If they asked us what we're doing here we couldn't make any answer. They have a fashion down here of shooting you on suspicion or locking you up on the least pretense. That has been their treatment of Americans for the last hundred years. We're not going to stop anywhere now, I'm telling you. We want to go below Mexico

City, down toward Vera Cruz. We've got fuel and oil enough to put us through. As to going back, that's another matter."

"Oh, I suppose," the young man nodded, smiling. "All right. Well, lots of good times are spoiled by worrying about how you're going to get back. It's easy to follow the land so far. We leave the big city yonder, towards the canals, eh?" Trent nodded.

"All right. Then when we get in below here we'll pick up the railroad if we can, and swing off until maybe we can find your old Spanish mule road, eh? And then, I take it, we follow right on beyond here——"

His finger was following along the map, following the black line marked by the ancient maker of the map more than two centuries ago. "Ta hum! Here's where you say the mine ought to be but maybe isn't? How do we know when we leave the road?"

"We'll have to guess at that," said Trent. "We can't talk much up there. But I'll tell you what I'll do. I'll watch along the map when we leave Mexico City, and when we run down a hundred miles or two I'll have one more look at the map, and then I'll give you a tip where to pull off to the south. After that we'll be over the rough country for fair as I understand it.

"You see," he explained to his young companion, "we're after something which has been lost for hundreds of years, which indeed maybe was never found at all. But what I mean to tell you is, if we do find that old mine you and I won't have to worry about spending money all the rest of our lives."

"When I get my money," said Billy, grinning, "I'm going back to Guadalajara and stay there the rest of my born days. It looks to me as though you could get real fizz water and human food. And as for human beings—O boy!"

A certain seriousness underlay the light demeanor. "You reckon we two can get her off the ground together?" he inquired of Trent. "You'll have to get aboard mighty fast."

"Not me," said Trent, "I don't want to be left here."

"In that case," responded his pilot, "the best thing you can do is to go and hunt for two or three greasers. Try that house over there, and you'll find some one in it."

Trent wandered over and almost by main strength managed to drag to the side of the plane two or three of the villagers. Laboriously they explained to them what needed to be done in spinning the propeller. Horrified beyond measure, the natives would once more have taken to flight excepting for the threatening muzzle of a revolver. Crude work enough it was, but at last sufficiently good. The natives fell on the ground in terror when the roar of the exhaust struck them and, gently bounding over the level of the shorn field, the great ship at length took the air and rose once more into the blue. What stories of them remain along a thousand miles of Mexico no man may know.

For reasons prudential they swung wide of the City of Mexico, leaving a long track of green-lined canals below them. Now at length they caught square the wide expanse of a highway making to the southeast.

An hour passed, an hour additional; how long they did not know. Neither could they tell the distance they had traversed. Had they been advised of the nature of the country they must have known that the great Plateau of Anahuac lay to the left, to the north; that the bald cone of Orizaba now lay before them, slightly to the left; that presently they would leave the gentle plateau of the Tierra Templada and drop down, over the steep mountains through which the railroad with difficulty had threaded, to the hot levels of the Tierra Caliente. Distance was annihilated in their means of travel, and the great variations in altitude were unknown to them as they droned on and on in the evening of a brilliant day.

Now to their right lay a rugged, broken country, spread like a map done in black below them. Trent touched the pilot on the arm, turned to him a face become white, drawn. The other nodded. The nose of the great plane swung off to the south and slightly to the westward and held its course straight to the compass line. Trent tapped with his finger point upon the map. Billy Townsend knew the words, for he had seen them previously as marking the "supposed location of the Madre d'Oro."

Onward and still onward, running by the compass over an uncharted sea of broken volcanic country—a wild journey, a mad one, surely. Even Trent's abounding confidence in his star waned and failed. He knew the folly of it now, but was too proud, too angry, too much humiliated to take any action.

The twilight approached. Billy Townsend began to make wide spirals, condorlike, seeking for some variation in the vast expanse of black country that lay below them. At length, when they had but little remaining daylight, Trent touched his elbow and the pilot nodded.

Below them, in the dip of the mountains beyond a long volcanic slope, lay a little open glade or savanna wide enough to afford a precarious landing, perhaps a quarter of a mile in length, with a short level midway. Risky enough landing it was, but Billy Townsend, cool and wary, made the difficult negotiations in perfect form.

"Welcome to our home!" said he, climbing down from his seat and stretching his cramped limbs. "This is about the farthest away from home and mother I ever got in my whole life. Where do you reckon we are?"

Trent looked at him soberly. "First let me tell you who we are. We're the worst two fools in the world,

I expect. But, if we're not, we can't be forty miles, maybe not twenty or ten, from this place on the old Spanish map marked plainly, 'Madre d'Oro.' Now, which way to go, how can I tell? If we ever can take off from here again to-morrow I don't know which way we are to head, any more than you do. It's a wild-goose chase, looking for something which, as I said, maybe never existed at all. At the same time, if you have got plenty of fuel on board, we can spend a half day or so cruising around here. I'll bet we'll know more about the country then than any human being ever did before."

"Well, anyhow, this has got to be home, sweet home, to-night," said Billy Townsend, wandering about with his hands in pockets, a little disconsolately. "Chocolate is all right if you've got nothing else. Makes you thirsty, but here's a creek. Blankets we've got. Fire we can do."

"Hello, look here!" he added presently, turning off to the right and beckoning to Trent. "Somebody's been here before and not so long ago at that. I give it up—there's no place in the world you can go where there isn't some one ahead of you! If these people didn't leave tin cans—at least they left horse and mule tracks. Here's where they had their fire—there's where they slept. And look here"—he held up a strip of canvas—"is where they cut the cover off a nice chunk of American breakfast bacon. Can you beat it?"

"There's their trail," he continued. "But where it

runs the Lord only knows! We might follow them, since we've got nothing better to do, if we live through the night. I suppose they made off through that gap—horses couldn't get through, like enough.

"Well, we've got plenty of time, nothing to cook and nothing to cook it with. I'll admit we might have outfitted a little better. But, of course, this game is just to stroll down here and pick up a valley full of gold which has been lost for three or four hundred years. We didn't need bother about any breakfast bacon of our own. Lord! If I had now what has been in that canvas sack!"

In the scanty remaining light the young man strolled about the edge of the savanna with the purpose of studying the ground for the take-off in the morning. Once more he called out to Trent, who joined him at the edge of the savanna.

They stood now before a strange object which thrust up at the edge of the dense vegetation—a tall shaft of native sculptured rock. Old, old, very old, done by some Maya sculptor, no man might tell when. And yet, as they both agreed when they had made their brief study, there rose the broken steps of what once had been an ancient temple, its top now grass-grown, trees thrust out between the stones of the pyramid.

"I tell you," said Trent, with a renewed interest in life, turning to his young and carefree companion. "We may not be on such a bad bet after all! This proves to you that people have been here before—

centuries ago, these things—two or three days ago, these other things. It looks as though we were coming to some sort of focus. As for me, I'm convinced the old Spaniards were right—they did know of that great valley of gold somewhere down in this country. If they knew of it, or knew close to where it was, why shouldn't we do as well as they?"

An instant later they each turned and gazed into the other's face. "Hello, what's that?" said Billy Townsend. "Am I getting dizzy?"

"No!" exclaimed Trent. "I felt it, too! It's—it's an earthquake shock, that's what it is! I have heard they have them down in this volcanic country."

They felt it once, twice, thrice—a gentle, soft, easy wave which passed over the surface of the earth.

And then came to their ears, although they could not be sure, a sort of a great susurration, a sort of sigh of the mountains, passing down toward the lower levels on ahead.

The solidity of the earth seemed to disappear. A strange and new power seemed to lie about them in the air. Even the face of the young aviator grew serious.

"There might be almost anything in here," said he at length. He looked into the face of Randall Trent, who for once had lost much of his self-assurance.

The Spanish girl was first of all in the house on La Luz to recover. The trembling of the earth, the long, gentle wave of the *temblor* passed once, twice, and thrice down the valley, and still she stood, her lips parted, waiting. But her color came back.

"*Es nada*!" she called out to her companions. "*Muy bien.* It is nossing."

The two young men stood looking at her, less in fear than in wonder. The experience to them was altogether new. After the last trembling roll of the earth's surface had passed, Hallock for the first time found his voice.

"It's nothing? All I've got to say is, I don't want any more just like it."

Allison looked about the room, at the pictures which at length rested against the wall, the chairs which had found their equilibrium.

"I'll agree with that," said he. "I don't want any more if it's worse. But I suppose this young lady knows more about earthquakes than you and I. I hope it's stopped, so that we can get on with what we've got to do."

There was, indeed, work which must be done. The long figure, gaunt, wasted, that lay shrouded under the blankets, must be placed in its final resting place. Luisa showed them where that must be—close to the small headstone in the walled flower garden. Hither they bore all that was left of old John Palmer.

A couple of hours, and all was done. No priest was there, nor minister. It was simple, crude, matter-of-fact, savoring of the wilderness. He had lived, forgetting the world and by the world forgot; and now, by the side of the woman who had loved him, he might dream on through the long ages which rested so lightly here. Neither of the young men could say a word of any service, but, as they turned, Allison remembered a line or two of a poem:

Now dreaming through the twilight
That does not rise nor set,
Haply he may remember—
And haply may forget!

And so they left old John Palmer, and came back to the little house which he had built, huddled close down under the shoulder of the mountain in the valley of La Luz.

But now a sudden change had come to all those who met here. Doña Luisa's face had a new expression; her attitude was changed. She was young, a young woman—and here were two young men. It was far, this country. What was she to expect?

Suddenly the girl turned, put her hands against the wall and bowed her head between them. They could see her shoulders tremble with her sobs. They stood looking at her, stunned and helpless. John Palmer had been to her a protector, and now she realized it—a father more than a brother-in-law. Always he had stood between her and the actual hardships and trials of the world; this little world lost here in the hills. On all the long journey home he had been her dependence. Now he was gone. What was left for her?

She knew herself utterly at the mercy of these two

young men. Could she trust either—could she trust this one? Young as she was, she had learned certain lessons of man and woman in that far land.

Hallock genuinely moved, looked at her in dumb distress. "I say, old man," he began, turning to Allison, "what's to do? This has knocked us all aheap."

"It's sudden enough," replied Barry Allison. "I didn't realize until just now how much we all needed him. He has been our leader and our dependence right along. We need him now—and so does she."

"We can't stay here indefinitely, that's sure," said Hallock. "Neither can we go away and leave this girl. She'd perish."

Allison nodded soberly.

"Not that I'd ever think of that," broke out Hallock. "Barry, old man, let me tell you. I'm never going to leave that girl alone."

"I've had certain notions," rejoined his friend.

"All right, you've guessed correctly—as you said a while ago. She goes with me if I go; stays if I stay. I'm going to marry her as soon as we get out of here. I can't think of her staying alone here in this valley; and neither could I stay here. I'll take her out with me."

"You speak as though you know what we're going to do," replied Allison, slowly. "Go back—are we sure? Besides, we came here for a certain purpose. I'm not sure we ought to go out and leave that matter unsettled."

"You don't think I'd leave it unsettled, do you, Barry?"

"I hope not. I know that if anything held you out of it, it would be a woman—this girl. For myself, I'm going to take a whirl at it. I came down here leaving my promise to another woman that I was going to try to do something. I couldn't go back and face her, feeling that when it came to the last test, I flunked it. I'm going through."

"Of course, you know you're not going alone," said Hallock. "I'd never let you leave me."

"Have you spoken to the girl about this?" asked Allison—by now he had drawn his friend into an adjoining room.

"I hardly know a dozen words of her language yet, old man. I don't know that I need to. For two weeks, three, she must have known. For my own part, Barry, I've known my mind from the first day I saw her.

"You see, I've not many people of my own," he went on, "and there's no one to say me yea or nay. I've got a little money of my own—my lawyers take care of that for me. But I swear, even if I didn't love her the way I do, I'd be almost ready to say I ought to marry her, situated the way she is right now."

"I think you're right," said Allison, after a time. "I think you're going to be happy." Their hands met, their eyes also.

"She'll understand that before we leave her here for a day or so," went on Allison, after a time. "You'll make that clear? Then she'll let us go and finish what we still have to do. Our bargain with old John was to finish this—he wouldn't rest in his grave if he thought we didn't. We made our compact.

"To-day, as you and I stand here, we are the only two people on the surface of the earth—unless that old man, Pedro, is alive—who actually know the secret of the Madre d'Oro.

"Do you suppose that she—the señorita—knows anything actually about the valley?" he added.

Hallock shook his head. "I doubt it very much. You know John told us he never told even his wife what he himself had seen there. I hope she didn't ask him. I hope Luisa never will ask me. But here we go, talking as though we actually had found the place and got out again. And we can't tell—we can't tell, not even now."

"We'll know by to-morrow night, or the night after that," rejoined Allison, gravely. "We came here to find the truth."

They returned to the main apartment. Luisa had shrunk back into the farther corner of the room and stood now looking at them, wide-eyed, wet-eyed, a sort of pathos about her figure which must have appealed to any man. The two young men approached her. What Hallock felt was in his eyes. He trusted to Allison, a trifle more versed in Spanish than himself, to try to serve as his interpreter. His well-mean-ing friend did the best he could, explaining that it seemed well they should all rest here for the night, but that on the morrow they two must leave her for a day, or perhaps longer.

"You go try—that?" The girl did her best with her broken English. They knew what she meant and nodded.

Luisa beat her hands together, shook her head. They knew she had heard something at least of the ancient legend of the great vein of gold; knew also something of the fatalities attending its pursuit. For so the story always had come down.

Allison himself wandered out, leaving Hallock and the young girl alone. Perhaps love found its way. In a half hour they came out, hand in hand, both smiling, seeking him. Which of the two was the more tongue-tied Allison hardly could have told, but he shook hands with both. Luisa broke away from them and ran to Serafina, throwing her arms about her neck and burying a tear-stained face on the old woman's shoulder. The young men walked again apart, leaving them to their own comfortings.

"By Jove! Barry" broke out Hallock, after a long time of silence, or semisilence. "I can't tell you how I feel! Somehow, that Madre d'Oro thing doesn't seem as big as it once did. When you come right to the gate of big things, none of them seem so big, do they? I know when we had a big frontal, over across, it all seemed natural enough. Seemed natural enough when we got back. So I suppose, like enough, that—that thing we're after—is up there. All I'm troubled about is, What will we do with solid gold in case we do find it? As far as I can learn, John Palmer never brought out a stiver of it himself. If he was a miser, no one has ever suspected it, that's sure. Poor old John—to hide himself down here."

"I don't know," said Barry Allison, "but that's past and gone. None of that sort of thing for you or me, I'm sure. It's not so far from here down to Vera Cruz. We've got our passports, and we can make it out somehow."

"Agreed, then. If we live we will leave this place. Suppose we start out early to-morrow morning for the head of the valley? I want to get back as soon as I can. Luisa——"

Allison nodded. "Well, I think John would agree we've done the best we could so far. We'll finish on the same basis. It's on the knees of the gods. What would it all come to, anyhow, if it weren't for the women in the world? We always seek, I suppose, but they hold the last key."

Hallock flushed. "So you feel that way, too? I'm telling you that's precisely the same thought that came to me, and you know I'm not so much of a fellow for thinking about things. By to-morrow," he added, somber eyes showed his own determination.

"To-morrow," said Barry Allison.

CHAPTER XV

MADRE D'ORO

FOR the last two miles of their toilsome journey up the narrow and winding cañon of the little river, crossing it scores of times, picking footholds as best they might, the two riders, Allison and Hallock, had been silent, feverishly silent.

During the entire ride—begun at three o'clock that morning—they had seen no trace of man or animal. The grass lay unbroken before them. There was not the slightest indication that any trail ever had lain here. They looked from side to side now, at the closing walls, along whose face not even a mountain goat could have clung. They seemed advancing into a deep, dark tunnel of green, close and hot, so nearly now to meeting came the overhanging vegetation. There was no sound except the ripple of the little stream or the splashing of hoofs occasionally at one of the many crossings. Once in a while a little opening came and the sun fell more cheerfully; but continually they had the impression that they were going through some sort of narrow gateway, some channel, out of one world into another. An awesome experience, though neither could have been called lacking in personal courage.

At times it seemed as though they could go but little farther, for the tangled growth almost made a hedge along across the little rivulet. But always Allison, who rode in advance, found some path through. They had pushed on, now, several hours, momentarily expecting to find the end of their journey.

The end? At what, where? What was there that lay on ahead of them? The grim silence of the two men was proof enough of their own keyed-up condition. It seemed as though they could no longer endure the delay, postponement, suspense of it all. But always there was one more turn of the baffling labyrinth, some last opening through the heavy vegetation; always there came just ahead the faint murmur of La Luz, rippling over its gravel bed.

They no longer had much regard for time. Indeed, they had forgotten when they left the little rancho, supposing only vaguely that they must have come up the valley some twenty miles or more. That surely was almost far enough. Had either been alone, he would have been almost ready to throw up his hands and call the whole affair a hoax, a delusion of the brain. They bethought them, silently, how strangely aloof, how moody, how tragically stern John Palmer always had been. Had his strange life unsettled his mind? Was this story of the Madre d'Oro no more than a madman's dream?

But still they could not turn back. Always something beckoned them ahead, and there appeared a way to get ahead, farther and farther into the heart of the great mountain range.

At length—some time in the afternoon—Allison threw up his hand. Hallock spurred up. They both looked on ahead. There lay before them a slight widening of the valley, a recession of the forest growth, a place where the crowding mountains got a little breathing space. The sight of a little sunlight lying on the grass seemed heartening to these two men, adventurers perhaps where no man should be.

The same thought oppressed them both, the same chill came to the heart of each.

"Well," said Hallock at length, but his voice croaked, stuck in his throat. Allison could only make some sort of suspended sound of assent to the feeling they both had that this must be the place.

At least, surely, it was the end of all further advance. Ahead of them rose a sheer, absolute wall of rock, vertical. There was no path about it, no possibility of scaling the equally vertical wall on either side. This was the end of the trail. And, as they knew, that trail for many miles could not have been reached by means of a descent from either side, so steep had been the defile of the upper waters of La Luz.

Surely, there was little to attract any man here. Surely, no man save these two, or others alike actuated, would come here for any reason in the world. And their reason, after all, was not much better than vague peradventuring.

They dismounted, made fast their weary horses. Again certain brief explorations.

"By the Lord!" broke out Hallock, at last. "It's just as he said!"

Allison nodded. "It must be the place. Look yonder."

The entire course of the little defile was cut off as though by the face of a broken mountain which rose up abruptly for a thousand, fifteen hundred feet, or more, offering a front which no man or creature could scale. This spot was simply a cul de sac, hidden in the eternal hills. Except for the little trickle of water nothing could have led hither, and of trail of any sort there was not the slightest trace, neither any way of making one. It might as well, indeed, have been the end of the world, a place of no hence or whither.

Absolute silence, a cold and awesome silence, lay upon all the strange scene. There was no sign of motion, except that upon the little open space, the widening of the narrow trail, there passed the shadow of a great war eagle, soaring far above. Perhaps he saw these two tiny figures. Certainly he screamed down, shrilling in a wild defiance.

His voice made the only sound.

There seemed, other than this, a strange lack of animal life. The grass showed no sign of any deer.

In all the sandy edges of the little stream there were no tracks of wild animals. Once or twice, within the last half hour, there had been a soft flash of gold and green, as a bird of splendid plumage fluttered from one tree to another, the Mexican bird of paradise, the *quezal* of the Aztecs, whose plumage sometimes appeared in the royal robes of Montezuma. But strangely alone had been left the road to Montezuma's treasure.

They pushed to the head of the running water. The stream still ran over a floor of fine, white gravel. But in the gravel here, as was the case far below, there was no glitter of broken quartz, neither any trace of black sand. This apparently was the wellspring of La Luz. Any man who followed so far had only the opportunity to turn about and retrace his steps.

Every river has its ultimate source. Here, in this wild country, surrounded by these lofty mountains, was the apparent head of La Luz, the little rivulet which fifty miles below watered a few casual fields of swarthy and incurious peasants.

"Yes, it all checks out," said Allison, half whispering in the solemn silence. "It's just as he said. The rock stands like a gate—see how tight it is against the wall. That's just exactly as the old mining book described it. Great God! there must be something in this! It wasn't imagination, or it couldn't all prove out so exactly. Hallock, this is the gate of the valley. We've come to it."

Hallock stood with his arm bent across his face, as though half protecting his eyes against something which he dared not front. There came to them both a feeling that they stood in some vast cathedral, some solemn place which must not be profaned.

It was long before they stooped and peered under the rock.

"She runs almost full," said Hallock, at length. "Do you suppose—but of course old John must have gone through here, if he told the truth. There is not a crack in the rock anywhere else. There's not a mark to show that any one's ever been here, from the beginning of the world. Yes, this is the gate, the door—no doubt of that. And there's only one way through! John Palmer must have gone in here, if it ever was done. He said he did."

"It must have been done by some one," said Allison after a time. "And if by any one, why not by John Palmer? He is one of our people. You know, he told us he followed the stream, up into a tunnel, he said—always in the water."

"A man's face would be under the water, getting in here," said Hallock soberly. "I don't know that I am such a coward, but that doesn't look good to me. Suppose a fellow got in there and got caught fast. Not so much the trouble about getting down, but he'd block the tunnel and she'd flood, and then he'd drown. By every inch that his body is bigger than the space held now by the water, she raises that much.

If she stays this narrow all the way through, good night! A fellow never could get out even if he ever got in."

"But John Palmer did that very thing," rejoined Barry Allison. "He said that he saw the great lode in the valley, the open face of the gold vein. He was alone, too, and there are two of us."

"He was crazier than we are, maybe. Besides, perhaps he dreamed it all."

"He didn't dream it. We both know he didn't. We both know this is the very place. Well, if it's got to be done, it must be done. I'm going in!"

He had off his coat, threw off his boots, his shirt. He took with him only the short-handled ax which he carried at his saddle. Hallock followed his lead in every respect.

Neither of them ever had heard how far the channel actually led—Palmer had never mentioned that, so far as they could recall. Certainly, it must be a considerable distance, here under the foot of the mountain—not less than half a mile at the least, as these men, mining engineers by profession, guessed from a look at the topography. That old John Palmer had made this subterranean journey alone, unsupported, seemed to them now a marvelous and almost incredible thing. But what he had done, they now must attempt to do.

Allison flung himself on his back in the middle of the little stream, reached out his arms and hands above him, pushed himself up until he had disappeared entirely in the aperture which showed below the face of the rock. For the moment, as Hallock had said, the course of the little rivulet seemed dammed; the flow slackened, almost ceased. But, to the surprise and relief of the man who remained in the outer air, the steady flow came on again.

Hallock could hear the splashing, coming from the interior of the mountain. He himself was a little pale. But pluck they both had, these young Americans. A moment later he, too, had disappeared from the outer air.

The two horses, abandoned, stood looking at the place where their riders had disappeared. Suddenly, for no known reason, they snorted, pulled back at the tethers, as though they felt some menace actually in the air. The shadow of the great war eagle flitted once more across the little open space. Had any man now been outside this vestibule of the valley he scarce could have seen, on the little sunlit trail, any trace of human visitation.

Yet now, somewhere deep under the great mountain face before him, he for a very brief time might have heard faint sounds, splashings, a low word or two coming out of the little opening. Within, two examples of the species called man, *homo sapiens,* the most adventurous of all animals, were hitching their way into one of the most extraordinary experiences the mind of man could have conceived; crawling, pushing themselves forward, edging along almost inch by inch, scarred and bruised by the pointed rocks they must cross, these two were pushing their way into the dark tunnel which ever and ever lay on ahead. They could not turn about to look ahead. Their eyes were but a few inches below the roof of rock. Their shoulders at times touched both sides of the narrow passageway.

Now, man beneath the surface of the earth is in a situation where men do not belong. To be left alone in the dark, in an unexplored cave, is one of the most terrifying experiences that any man can be asked to sustain. How much worse was this! They had as their supporting influence only the thought that one other man, at least, had passed this way—perhaps many others, at some time in the history of the world.

They never knew how long they were in that awful gorge—never could retain accurate impressions, never were able to describe their own feelings as to the lapse of time and space. Allison said that his last memory was that of the gold and green bird of paradise which had flitted across the defile below the opening in the rock face. He kept in his mind, so he said, the description which John Palmer had given him of those gold and green birds flying in the valley.

And truly, almost the first thing which he saw in the sunlight was the same flash of green and gold, a bird flitting. He felt rather than saw the sunshine come, thrust head and shoulders out into an open space, stood erect, weak and trembling, truly, but still upon his own feet once more. He was drenched with water, dripping, half naked.

He dared not look about him yet. There passed above him, with a querulous cry, dipping down from some unknown space above, a bird of gold and green, yes, so he thought. But he did not turn. His eye was fixed upon the dark little opening from which he had emerged. He heard Hallock coughing, splashing. He stooped and gave his friend assistance to emerge, to stand as he himself stood—at last fully within the magical valley of which they had dreamed!

Never, until now, had either of them actually believed it could be a possible thing. They dared not face it just at once but stood looking into each other's faces. Allison saw that Hallock's face was pale as death beneath his tan and felt that his own face also must be like that for surely he felt gripping at his heart a feeling of absolute terror—fear! fear! that was what they both felt now. And they were young men, and brave.

"He did that!" croaked Hallock, after a time, nodding at the black hole from which they had emerged. "Good old John!"

Allison nodded. "A dozen times I thought I was gone. Except I thought that he had been through, I never could have done it. Could you?"

Hallock shook his head. "Great God!" said he. Then he began to tremble. Allison himself had to lean against the rock wall, also. They dared not lift their eyes.

They stood for a time, they could not say how long a time—for in some strange way all their known values of life had left them—waiting for strength to come to them. Strength they knew now they needed.

The blessed sunshine gave them their first grace. They began to feel the gentle air of heaven, began to realize that out of the wet gloom they had come into an actual world which they could comprehend, a world not wholly unkind. Slowly they loosened their hold upon the rock face, loosened even the support each of the other's shoulder; began to turn, to look. Then each drew a long, deep sigh.

The story of John Palmer had always been broken, disconnected. Apparently, he did not desire, or did not dare, to tell in detail all that he had seen in the valley of the Madre d'Oro. So what now appeared before the eyes of these two was, after all, unexpected, impossible, incredible.

The descriptions which they had read of the ancient valley of the Aztecs—the descriptions which John Palmer had given them of the place—tallied precisely. The sheer face of the rock walls rose straight up, above a thousand feet, perhaps two thousand, shutting off all view across the surrounding country, whose nature they could only guess. The face of the broken rock apparently had been shorn off by some great convulsion of nature. The thread of water, lying silvery in the sun, as it wound on midway of the valley, was just as Palmer had described it. Unquestionably, this was drainage of some watershed above. It had worn through countless ages its own pathway here under the face of the rock, which made the lower dam of this great indentation of the earth's surface—this valley, gorge, chasm, countersunk into the fabric of the hills. The walls were as clean-cut as though a giant chisel had wrought them.

There was a short, thin grass which grew close to this little stream; a few scanty green trees of no great stature stood along the edge, as though some seed of conifer had been pushed in from above and taken root. The air was soft, gentle, warm. There seemed to be no animal life, except that, flitting across from time to time among these infrequent trees, they saw others of these mystic birds of the Aztecs, the *quezals,* vibrant, flaring of gold and green in the brilliant air.

As for the air itself, it seemed molten gold and honey mingled, so gentle was it, so comforting. Now a vast peace seemed to fall upon them. Their terrors had vanished. They felt as gods. A sudden exaltation, born of their assurance of success, came to them.

Hand in hand now, like two children, they walked slowly ahead into the strange expanse that lay before them. The entire width of the valley did not exceed, by anv great degree, a half mile. Perhaps a quarter of a mile on ahead, an inthrust or shoulder of the right wall cut off a clear view of the entire valley.

They had not yet come to the point where they could see the little waterfall coming in at the upper edge, flung over the rim, as John Palmer had described it, as the legend of the Aztecs always had described it—as the story of the Book of Mines had described it. Nor yet did they see the other thing which they had come to seek.

So far the floor of the valley lay flat before them. Only they had the feeling that they were utterly alone, and that none ever could come here, so awe-inspiring was the sheer uplift of the walls which almost closed about them. Yes, this was the place.

John Palmer had told them it was like a great dent, crushed into the body of the mountains as by some giant die. Orizaba's work, they said to themselves. Yes, earthquake or volcano, or both, had chiseled out these walls.

The general feeling that came to them, as they advanced into the lower portion of the valley, was that Palmer's report had been correct. He must have been here. He must have known. It was no dream.

The soft air on their cheeks, the gentle ardor of the sun, came to soothe them. Their keyed-up feeling, their dread, their fear, gradually began to disappear. If they were here, surely there was some protecting power that had brought them hither. Even the wild scream of the eagle, which seemed to follow across the mountain top, came to them now, not so much in warning as in triumph and assurance.

There was not a footprint in the sand. Not a blade of grass had been disarranged. If man ever had been here he had left no trace, absolutely none.

They paused below the inthrust shoulder of the hill, which made a sort of curtain to the great stage. The sun was now westering. There came not the great upflung flash, the blaze of refracted light, from the face of the Madre d'Oro itself, which some traditions had it must be seen from the rim of the valley at a certain hour in the morning. They saw no indication of anything extraordinary, beyond the feeling that they were in some new world, with a new air, surrounded by new fences, floored by new fabric. Even as their fears passed from them, there came back the old feeling that they must be adream.

They did not even dare look in each other's eyes now; but at length, after a long pause, each felt the other's hand tighten in his own. Once more now, two children newborn into a mysterious world, they stepped forward, slowly, hesitantly.

They walked into or under—they could not tell—a sort of lambent wave of what must have been light, reflected, not shrewdly punishing the eye, but a thing soft, gentle, not uninviting. They knew that now the thing they sought was close at hand.

And so, rounding the last veil of the inner temple,

they paused, fell back a step—hand in hand stood agaze at what they saw.

The ancient stories had been true! Strangely accurate to the last detail, they had all been true! John Palmer had told them the truth. Every one of the old Guardians of the great secret of the Madre d'Oro had told the truth to his successors.

It was like a dike. They could not surmount it, so they thought. The face of it, as it lay, like a gently sinuous dam from edge to edge of the great valley, disappearing into the solid rock face at either end, must have been a dozen feet—fifteen—twenty—more—they did not dare guess—from the foot to the top of the widespread gentle cascade which poured down from above.

They could at this place—when at last they had slowly ventured to the foot of the little waterfall—see nothing of the valley above. As though in a dream they had seen a picture from their first vantage point, the enduring, sharp-cut rock-faces closing the upper end as the lower end of the little valley; the veil of white water falling, deep, deep, a thousand feet, two thousand feet, from the inner mountains over the rim of this great chasm.

The strange feeling of animate life, of existence conveyed by this tremendous ledge no doubt was due to the thinly spread water, moving a little bit in the air currents, which covered the upper face and the bared edge of the great ledge. The whole thing never got to their minds at all, so they said. They could not think. The sound of the water dropping into the little pool, into a great bowl of some solid material, no larger now than it had been ages before, came to them in a strangely comforting way. They thought that, except for the sight of the little waterfall, they must have gone mad utterly. Upon this they were agreed. Indeed, neither would credit his own memory. Always, afterward, each would question the other and say, Was this true? Could it have been true? And he would not believe until his friend again assured him.

Before them lay Madre d'Oro! This, indeed, might have been the mother of all the gold in all the world. Whatever made it, by whatever alchemy in the great crucibles of nature, far below the surface of the earth, by what titanic fires melted and assembled, by what super forces flung up bared to the eyes of the gods, if not to the eyes of man, this thing may have been fabricated, at least, here it was!

And what a secret it had been to keep! Was the religion of the Aztecs, jealously preserved, after all so far wrong?

The two seem to have called aloud at first, in a sort of terror, when they reached out their hands and actually touched the great, chill wall, yellow, half-luminous, cold to the feel, wetted as it was by the little water stream. They both swore that they heard some sort of strange sound, something like a confused humming, which ran along the whole face of the Madre d'Oro. A strange thing, perhaps not to be credited, though both of these credited it, and each assured the other that he had heard it—the sound—the voice of the gold itself! That might have been due to the event which after a time they were to note. But as to that soft humming, gentle, not menacing, these two, the only men alive who could speak of it, were absolutely agreed.

CHAPTER XVI

THE LOST MINE

ALLISON and Hallock paused for a considerable space after their first actual view of the great ledge. They had remaining only enough of their own human instincts, attributes, reasoning, to feel at length that something yet remained to be done.

They both agreed that something was there about them; something which had a voice, a presence. They never could explain precisely what they meant. Perhaps they were overstrained. For instance, it was strange they should agree that they had heard that humming sound, not unmusical.

They said that the great line of yellow metal wavered a little in its course, but were sure it entirely crossed the deep valley, and sure it disappeared in the farther side, as certainly it did at the end where they first approached it. It seemed almost level along the top. How far back it ran they could not tell, because they never scaled the actual face of the ledge itself. They had the feeling, so they said, that it ran back quite a way.

They saw no lake, nor any body of water dammed up by it, so apparently there was some lever or upper face, whether of this same material or another, into which the course of the stream never had cut at all. They thought there were two stages, or floors, in the valley, their own and that which lay above, at the level of the ledge itself.

As to the direction, they were both agreed that they saw the sun approaching the upper end of the valley, so they concluded it was late in the afternoon. Yes, they thought, a man could by remote possibility look down into the valley, if by any chance he could have stumbled through the mountains and blundered upon the rim.

They both were sure, from their mutual recollections, that the place seemed as though done by some freak of volcanic action; but as to the character of the rock they became confused. In truth, they had forgotten all about geology, all about science. All their expert training went for naught. Indeed, they said, all the rules and laws of the world, as they had known them, had disappeared from their thought, utterly and absolutely.

The only thing upon which they agreed in their geology was that there could have been no quartz broken off from the ledge. This accounted for the fact which John Palmer had mentioned—there was not a color of gold in all the valley of La Luz. Water may wear away quartz, drill its way through a mountain; it does not hold gold in solution, and does not cut into gold—does not create any particle, no matter how small, does not divide it by any agency of its own. All that water can do is to carry gold in its envelope, its chrysalis. But here was the great cocoon from which the web of phantasy has been spun, ages and ages, in the longing and wondering history of the world.

They said they had come in at the right-hand side of the valley, and that it seemed natural to work off to the right along the face of the ledge. And then they saw, close to the right-hand wall, the final proof that the old stories were true. Here upon the face of the ledge were the marks of tools!

An actual excavation had been made into the solid front. And here—hidden as though but yesterday by the men who had used them, pushed back entirely from the light into the cavern, which they, perhaps in centuries of time, themselves had wrought, by the tools themselves.

These implements were three in number, three adze-like tools, short of handle, the wooden shafts polished none might know how long. They had been kept perfectly dry in this air—might have lain there for hundreds of years for aught one could say. The blades of the adzes themselves were not of steel, but of black obsidian—the same glasslike substance of which the ancient Aztecs made their sacrificial knives, their razors, their fighting weapons. These heads or blades were bound with rawhide to the short shafts of dense wood —mesquite wood.

They said they could find no trace of any kind of human work, because there was no sand, no dirt, no detritus of any sort. The floor and the walls and the roof of this cavern in which they found the adzes were of gold. There was no earth; there was no vegetation. It might have been made yesterday, or a hundred years before, or five hundred, or a thousand. They said that their first impressions was that not so much gold could have been taken out. But when they began to figure the weight and the value of the cubic foot of the precious mineral they saw how tremendous had been the excavation, how enormous the amount of actual wealth which must have been transported from this spot. Ages and ages it must have been, they said.

But by that time they were so dull that nothing much impinged upon their minds. Only they were agreed about the short-handled adzes or axes and about the low, musical humming which they heard, as though the Madre d'Oro were talking, crooning, to herself—which, of course, was the most absurd of all.

This little cavity had been hollowed out by the hands of men, that was sure. They figured that it must have covered all the wealth of the Aztecs, however ancient had been that people. That so much gold as this had ever come into the circulation of the world they doubted very much. Not all the galleons of Spain ever had freight like this, that was sure. But this was the Aztec gold.

Who knew whence these ancient peoples came, one race succeeding another, into this far corner of the world? And if they came, did not tradition spread back along their trail to yet all the other and older races of the world, from which they came? Hence these tremendously separated legends of the Madre d'Oro, located now at one corner of the world, now at another—now in Alaska, now in Siberia, now in Africa. Might that not after all have been entirely natural and logical? Might not all of them have originated at this very spot? That was what these two men felt as a conviction. They never had any doubt whatever of the foundation of the widely separated stories of a Mother of All the Gold. They had seen it—touched it with their hands.

They seem now at first to have fallen upon the adzes of these forgotten workmen, and to have splintered them at the solid gold face of the ledge. They could not do much at it, could not understand these tools, felt helpless after a time. Then reason came to them, and they knew that, although they had found all the gold in the world, or the mother of it, they could not take it away!

They threw down the broken implements, at length, desecrated as they were, flung themselves down in the soft, gently illuminated interior of this hollowed-out partial drift into the face of the ledge. It was Allison's hand, scraping around in the angle of floor and roof, which struck a little mass of smaller objects, detached.

Now, indeed, they both agreed, they almost lost their reason at what they saw. Here, hidden actually in the face of the ledge itself, was the secret hiding place of the jewels of the Montezumas—no doubt brought here as the one safe place of concealment, perhaps soon after the Spanish invasion. Now, indeed, they had treasure at their hands, portable, visible, indestructible—wealth of the sort which they could use!

There were many emeralds, far more emeralds than diamonds, which latter gem was but sparsely represented. Some of the gems were roughly cut, but most of them lay but roughly faced out—only enough to indicate what they actually were. A great quantity of beryls was there, and a certain amount of turquoise, and many stones of a deep greenish-blue, very heavy, which experts lately said were zircons. Of rubies there was some store. The emerald was the stone most abundant of all. Of these—they paid no attention to the masses of opal matrix which had been faced out—they took as much as they felt they could transport from that spot. It seemed to them they had not made so much of an imprint in the actual mass of these royal jewels. How they had been cut, how they had been faced in this way, they never quite could tell. But as to the great worth of the gems themselves—later proved by the circumstances of them both—there could be no doubt whatever.

So at length their dream, if it was a dream, their deeds, if there were deeds, lay not unrewarded after all, although the great Madre d'Oro they must leave behind them, still smiling, still talking to herself, much as it had lain these many, many years.

They had come to the valley almost naked, stripped to underwear and trousers. They had not much means of transport with them. They said that at first they were helpless, until they bethought them of an old mountain expedient. They stripped off their trousers, tied tight the rents in them, and made them fast at the bottom with strings which they found in the pockets. Thus they had sacks of a sort which they could carry over their necks or over a saddle horn, or in a pack. They filled these receptacles and tied them at the top—with how much wealth neither of them ever knew; for in the vicissitudes even of their painful travel back to the ranch of La Luz they lost a part of their store out of the fragile enveloping which was the best they could afford. The best of the pearls—many pink, a number of pure black—they happily got at the bottom of their packs, so that most of these were preserved; a fortune for each of them.

It all seemed as simple and matter-of-fact to them, so they both said, as though they were shoveling so much gravel or sand for a later proving. They did not think that they had any actual idea at the time of the value of what they took away. Nothing impinged on their dulled minds, which by this time were almost beyond the power of receiving impressions. They moved, they both said, like automata—as though they still were in a dream. It was only later proof which made them sure they had found the ancient treasure chamber of the Aztec people. Then the full value of the tremendous tale, the mystery, the magic of it all, the solemn, the tragic method of preservation of this great secret, made itself plain; when at length they were able to think, to reason once again.

They said they hardly knew when they emerged from the little room, or cavern, of the Aztec treasure. They now had burdens as heavy as they dared make them. In some sort of way they felt that it was time for them to be going.

It must have been well into the evening now—they had no ability left to measure time—were not even sure there was such a thing as time any more. But surely they had left the great vein, had made their way partly down toward the protecting shoulder which hid the sight of it from the lower entry to the valley. Then came those other experiences, regarding which neither of these two ever cared to talk; their attitude in this regard being precisely that of John Palmer, who always had seemed smitten half dumb by the terrifying experiences through which he had passed.

Certain it is that, midway of their journey back over the lower part of the valley, they heard once more what seemed to be the gentle sigh or breathing of the world, distinctly passing from the west toward the east and south. And once more they felt the tremble, the distinct wave of the earth beneath their feet. Now the same terror seized them which they had known the previous day—a terror which was intensified because suddenly they felt a sense of culpability, of guilt in being here at all.

It was the culmination of the earthquake of that year, which now for some days had given its warnings in advance—in these repeated waves, gentle, not violent, of the earth's surface, passing through this mountain range toward the southwest, well below the southern rim of the plateau of Anahuac. El Temblor had come once more, as though to protect, to avenge the Madre d'Oro!

As they stood they felt the ground rise and sink beneath their feet distinctly. Terrified, they let drop the burden which they had; but later, as the immediate menace seemed to pass, they picked up their packets and turned once more toward the lower end of the valley. They knew that was the only chance ever to emerge again into the world they once had known. Whether they ever thought of the danger of the closure of that terrible passage beneath the foot of the mountain, neither of them ever could distinctly recollect. The impressions of their minds seemed to have been made distorted, broken, confused. They perhaps had no distinct reasoning—only a sort of continuing function of what had been their reasoning faculty, the survival of the metabolism, the habit of the processes of nature, still clinging to her own. The extreme shock which they both underwent made some sort of break between the world they once had known and this which, so they said, always remained to them only as a sort of lurid dream.

Neither could agree with the other at just what moment they lost sight of the Madre d'Oro, but that must have been as they turned the inthrust corner of the rock wall, upon their left-hand side as they descended the valley. But they both knew that the first trembling of the earth was no more than a warning, and both knew that an earthquake was coming.

They saw the falling inward, the crumpling, the massing up of the walls at the upper and narrower end of the valley. They said it seemed to them as though a card house were falling in toward them, crumpling up, mingling. They both swore that the great ledge itself never was broken through, that it never was folded up or down. They said it must have sunk, intact—that is to say, it must have been covered deeply by the incoming walls on either side. They thought that perhaps, if these walls actually did fall in, one edge toward the other, they must have covered, or almost have covered, the entire valley. The latter, itself, was little more than a strange, sharp gash, thrust down through the average contour of the mountain range. But while they both retained the feeling that they had seen the Madre d'Oro sink away, draw about her the cover of the mountains forever and forever—they both remained of the mind that they saw something else;

and but for that sight they must indeed have gone mad and have perished where they stood.

They both denied hotly that the sound which they now heard could have been confused in their minds with what they called the "voice of the Madre d'Oro." But they heard it now—a throbbing groan, distinct, rising almost to a roar. They turned back, looked toward the upper end of the valley, whence this sound came distinctly.

They both saw, coming toward them, dropping swiftly, some vast winged creature. It had broad white wings and had a voice. It was flying. Of these things there could be no mistake. And it was coming directly in at what had been, though it was no longer such, the upper end of the Madre d'Oro.

"My God!" cried Allison. "My God!"

Hallock said his voice sounded wholly unlike his usual voice.

"It's a plane—Look!—Look! It's going to crash!"

Dear Barry [so wrote Hallock to his friend, Barry Allison], since we parted at Vera Cruz, a good many things have happened to me. All I can say is, I hope this finds you the same, for I am very, very happy—happier even than I was at Agua Prieta, where we found the priest on the lower La Luz, and where you were my best man. Speaking of dreams—this is the real dream of my life.

I can't speak so very much Spanish yet, but I am learning some. Luisa can say, "Si, señor." I don't care whether she ever learns much more than that.

THE LOST MINE

You see, when you took the boat for New Orleans, I headed back by rail the other way. You can get all the way through to Guadalajara pretty comfortably, so we enjoyed our wedding journey well enough. Then I was lucky enough to get a boat from Acapulco over to La Paz, on the peninsula; and from there it was not so hard to find our way north and toward the interior.

We passed a strange rancho, called the Ranch of Good Hope, run by an odd old buck they call Father Ernesto. Luisa knew him and he knew her—remembered her from the time she was a child, you might say. He took us inland, to the big ranch and mining property owned by the Martinez family, and there we found papa and mamma. They didn't kill me, but they wanted to, until I had done a little explaining and told them I hadn't taken their daughter away, but brought her back to them.

As you know, I was able to prove to them that I could support a wife. After a time they concluded they didn't want to lose their daughter a second time. They sort of adopted me. I make a bluff at running the ranch, although the most I do is to make love to Luisa. From the first time I saw her I knew I was going to marry her. I tell you, it's almost like a dream.

I think I can now tell you what plane it was that crashed in the valley just after the big shock came. It was Z-78, an army plane that went over from Magdalena. The pilot was Billy Thompson, one of the best. He had along—some sort of mysterious thing it was, all around—a chap by the name of Randall Trent, a rich young man from somewhere in Ohio—did you ever hear of him? Z-78 has been missing, anyhow; and old Father Ernesto says he is sure Trent got Billy Thompson to try some fool sort of thing off to the southeast. The pretense was that they were hunting for a couple of lost aviators who disappeared in Mexico, south of the Arizona border. Of course, they couldn't have got 'way down where we were, and there was no reason for going there, unless what Ernesto told me was the truth—and he said that Trent was looking for the lost mine of the Aztecs! He wouldn't talk much more than that. I don't feel much like it myself. There are some things which are just as well let alone.

There was at this rancho a girl and her mother—Mary Westlake was the name of the girl. Did you ever hear of her? It seems to me you named her once. She came from somewhere in Ohio, too. They seemed to have plenty of money and were fine people. Well, Trent was crazy over that girl. To thicken things up a little, there was old Pedro, an old beggar that lived here on the Martinez ranch for goodness knows how long. He was said to be the oldest man in the world, and goodness knows, too, how many generations of children survive him around here. Well, old Pedro messed up the game by dying while all the people were in here. Ernesto says that Trent told Pedro something, or Pedro told him something—I don't know what, but it was about a lost mine. Can you guess the rest?

Well, just to clear up a few things in my mind, I went straight to Ernesto and had it out with him about Pedro. I found that Ernesto did know something about the old story. He says that Pedro told him he was the last one of the last Three Guardians. Don't you see where Palmer got his hint? And don't you see what Palmer did when he took the sister of my wife away and went down to that country? Well, those two never came back. I brought back Luisa. I think, in time, they really will be reconciled to me because of that. As to how the mother feels about Dolores—I'll not try to write.

The story of the course of the Z-78 is rather plain.

They took off at Magdalena and made a landing at Guadalajara—some fool sort of thing, no one knows why. They were reported from the edge of the City of Mexico—in fact, they were traced by telegraph all the way across the country. How much they really knew of the lost mine they were after no one will ever be able to tell. No one knows just where they left the old Spanish Road—which they seem to have followed to the southeast. No one ever will know how they came to be just where you and I saw them for those few minutes in the evening, the last evening either of them ever was to see.

Of course, as you know, they must have smashed not so far back of the edge of the big—you know what. There must have been, when the walls of the valley began to fall in, some sort of air pocket or down suction which pulled them in. You know that old place didn't conform to any sort of natural laws. I wouldn't try to explain it—and no one else can.

But doesn't that bear out the old stories about that awful place that you and I have always heard? The Aztec legend was that more than one man had located that place and seen down into it but not one of them ever got away with it. Men had been found wandering around blind; others had been found starved to death back in those mountains, so those tales go—saw the reflection from the valley and that gave them the trace of it. What saved you and me, do you reckon, Barry? I have often wondered about that. If there was in all the world another woman like the one I married—if you knew also, and loved, as I do this one, any other woman—why, then I could understand it. I'd say that on their account, just because they were women, just because there is such a thing as a good, clean love in the world, that is why you and I ever got out of there alive!

As for what we brought with us, that's just as crazy as anything else. I don't try to realize how much our little treasure pile may come to—don't care much about it, anyhow. If I had had only enough to bring me here, safe back to Luisa, I wouldn't have asked any more. As for what we didn't get and what's gone now forever—I say good riddance of it! Its time has not yet come, after all.

I have the strangest feeling about that whole experience, sort of vague, sort of daze, all confused up. I have to reason back to prove it out. We came off pretty well, didn't we? I have a notion that before the entire earthquake shocks were done that whole valley was pretty much filled in, or, anyhow, all made over again. For one thing, thank God!—we didn't have to try to crawl through that infernal crooked tunnel with the water all around us. We would never have got our loads through there without tearing them all to pieces, and, once in there, I don't think you or I would have turned back for a peck of Kohinoors.

For myself, I can just barely remember sliding along the bottom of that crack which opened at the foot of the valley. Whether it closed our water tunnel or ripped it open I don't know and don't care. And what became of our two horses, I have often wondered—I suppose they broke away when the first shocks came. I never saw any tracks of them—I don't remember anything—I can't tell how you and I got back to the rancho and found the old woman and Luisa crying and wringing her hands—well, waiting, I suppose.

Of course, Luisa asks me sometimes to tell her what you and I were doing up there. I've tried to, but I can't get coherent enough so she will believe me—and I'm glad she doesn't. It makes me feel creepy, even yet. But, at least, Luisa knows we were somewhere—the entire Martinez family knows that. They have a few family jewels and a little family plate of their own, back here in this marvelous country, which some of them found a couple of hundred years ago; but if they hadn't we could start on those things right now. I rub my eyes—I can't believe it. It's not true. But sometimes Luisa comes—well, I don't care whether it's true or not. If we ever were there, and if we ever got out, and if you are you and I am I—well, it's Luisa did it for me and some other girl for you. Of course, I knew all the time that there was such a girl—you told me—don't you remember?—that that was why you had come—to find your fortune. Well, I hope you found it, old man. My own is entirely secure. And happy? That's not just exactly the word.

I came out a little gray around the edges. Did you? When I look in a glass I seem older, and different—do you?

Well, anyhow, I am settled down. I don't seem to want to wander around the world any more at all—I don't think I ever shall. I am not so much of a hermit and a recluse and a misanthrope as old John. But, I tell you, I have learned that there isn't so much in this living business, after all. After he'd seen that valley he never went back again, and, as you know, he told us he was content with what he had—three meals a day and a tight roof and the woman he loved. Has what you brought out got much more than that for you? For me, I don't want much more than that for my own self.

The sun is brilliant here for the most part, but the nights are fine—the evenings, especially, marvelous. We have a little stream of water here close to the house—it heads up just opposite the rio which runs past the Ranch of Good Hope, where Father Ernesto lives, forty miles to the west. We have every fruit in the world, and palm trees grow here, and we raise all we want in our valleys, and there are cattle and sheep and everything—wild sheep in the hills, and deer, so that we can have all the sport we need when you come down to see me. It's world enough for me. I told you I don't want to hunt any further; and I want to tell you this—any man who wants the rush and hurry of the big cities in our beloved country can have them if he likes. Not for me. Not any more do I want to get back into the past that you and I knew once when we were boys—a year or so ago when we were boys, and not old men, as we are now.

Why, think of it, Barry! Everybody crazy after more money, and still more money, and a little more than that—and what do they buy with it? Ask me and I'll tell them—not much!

Surely not any more than I have right here. And surely, old man, not more than you have, or, I hope, will soon have.

Tell me about things, won't you? Luisa is calling. "Yes, dear." (That's me to her.) And what I've said to you is for you only. Write me for the sake of the old days. I don't know just when I'll be coming north. Yours, as always. PUG.

Address: P. B. Hallock,
Rancho Del Camino Real,
Baja California, Mexico.

CHAPTER XVII

THE GREAT MIRACLE

THE cablegram of Barry Allison from Vera Cruz found Mary Westlake at home at Deneville—where he thought she had remained during his absence. The message itself was noncommittal, brief:

Safe. Successful. Coming direct.

Mary Weslake met that message at the door. She turned, the paper crumpled in her hands. "Mother!" she cried. "Mother! Look! Look!"

Mrs. Westlake, who, in spite of her only partially restored health, had returned to her household duties, gave up her exercise with the carpet sweeper.

"Well, daughter, what is it now!" she inquired.

"Why, it's Barry! Barry! He's alive! He's coming back!"

Her mother smiled slowly, a smile conveying her doubts.

"He says he's successful. I suppose——"

"Yes, I suppose, too! He hasn't been gone quite a year. If he has made a fortune in that time he has made it mighty quick. I would rather know where he is than what that is, if I were you."

"I don't even know where he is, mother."

"Vera Cruz. That's in old Mexico, on the gulf. He's coming over. Yes, I suppose so. He'll explain everything to you once more and all over again, won't he? Well, I'm glad we got out of Mexico alive. That's no place for such as me. I'm not going to foreign parts ever again—home is good enough for me."

Her somewhat enfeebled hand began once more to push the carpet sweeper. She turned, however.

"You haven't heard anything from Randall Trent, have you? I see in our papers right along something about how he seems to have disappeared with a young fellow in an airship. They left from some place—Magdalena, I think it was—not far from where we were. Then the bottom seems to have dropped right out, and no one seems to have known what became of him or the young fellow that went with him. That was Thompson, they say in the papers—William D. Thompson, a young chap, he was—and their airship was Z-78—right out of the army fleet, it was. And it's disappeared. The army's right anxious to know what's become of it.

"Now, what do you suppose made Randall Trent get in an airship and fly off that way across Old Mexico? No man ever made his fortune that way, that's sure. But Ranny didn't need any fortune. His father left him plenty, and he's been successful in business ever since. He's got a fine house ready built and waiting. You know whom it's waiting for, too. And you know what your Pa and I want you to do. And here"—she turned once more, desisting from her labors on the parlor carpet—"you come to me with a message from that other man! You say he's alive; and you act right glad about it!"

"I am glad, mother! Why shouldn't I be? It's everything in the world to me. I can't tell you how I felt—waiting all these months, and not a word."

"Mary, tell me one thing." Her mother faced her fairly. "Are you going to marry Barry Allison? I hope not. He's somehow trifling, according to my way of thinking. Gone a few months and made a fortune! Oh, no! Things don't happen that way, my dear. And this sort of thing that you've got, saying he's alive and successful, that don't buy no potatoes, daughter."

"But wait!" said the girl. "Wait!"

But she herself would not longer tarry for the old arguments with her mother. A sudden mad impulse came to her once more. She flew off to her own room, opened a certain little-used drawer, and drew out from it the crystal sphere, by gazing into which, always with a feeling of guiltiness, she sometimes had sought the comforts of amateur divination.

She put the clear crystal on the black cloth on the empty table top and sat before it, as once, twice, she had done before. Long, long, she gazed, and was almost at the point of despair, when there began to appear the faint, white threads, the films within the center of the sphere. But what she saw was no picture of anything definite. Only turmoil was there! The mysteries of milky white moved as by some hidden force. But there was nothing coherent. There was no form. It was a jumble and confusion. It was chaos!

The girl wondered how this could be, since always before she had been successful in these efforts at her scrying. But at length she gave it up and hid the sphere forever.

But what did this mean in regard to Barry Allison? Surely not much of peril could have come to him, since he had sent his message from the gulf coast. And surely he would send other messages—and she must wait. Tears came to her eyes. Silent and moody, she went on with her own household routine, not speaking much with either of her somber and dour parents, who had their own opinions of their daughter and her wisdom in the serious affairs of life.

She heard her mother at breakfast the next day discussing the daily dispatches with her husband.

"Sure enough," said Mrs. Westlake, "it's time they got word about those folks, if they are ever going to. They have been lost for days and days. Now, that's a big country, and we know it's right wild. I wouldn't put it past to have happened that they'd come to some kind of trouble down there—no one can tell what. Now, no word has come out. And yet——"

Her husband's eyes, turned moodily upon the daughter just entering the room, ended what she was about to say.

But Mr. Westlake also knew that Barry Allison, not wholly *persona grata* here, might be expected one of these days to arrive, to enter that very door, perhaps to expect a place at this very table. That, however, did not come out in the event precisely as Mr. Westlake had forecast, although the essential truth remained.

Mary Westlake did get further messages—one from New Orleans, one from Memphis, one from Chicago. And so, one evening in the early autumn, when the leaves of the maples were just beginning to show a different color on their edges in the little city park, when Mary Westlake heard the whistle of the incoming train from the west, she rose without any word to any one of the household, quietly donned street wrap and hat and gloves, went out the front door, and walked down the brick walk to the front gate. Walking slowly, with her own easy dignity, she turned along the sidewalk that led toward the business portion of the town.

Came now sudden wheels of a taxicab. Perhaps she suspected something of the sort. And then, as she turned, her eyes shining, there happened what she must have expected.

A young man flung open the door, sprang out, hurried across the pavement to her side. He was a tall young man, thin, eager-eyed, brown with sunburn. His hair was edged with gray. His cheeks seemed much sunken. Could it be he—the man who had left her less than a year ago? Why, this man seemed older by years! Yet it was he—her lover—Barry Allison!

He saw the startled look, wistful, yearning, almost pathetic, in the girl's eyes. But he answered all her questions by the sound of his voice, the clasp of his hand. Indeed, forgetful of all conventions, he caught her to him in one swift embrace, his lips against her cheek.

The taxi driver smiled, but waited gladly enough. After a time the young man led the young woman back, entered the car. "Drive around," said Allison. "Pull up over by the city park after a while—it can't be so cold!"

But now reason and propriety had come to them both. They sat, silent, not even venturing a glance, one at the other, until after a time they found themselves altogether alone in the little formal space above the lake bluff, dignified by the name of park. The band concerts now had been discontinued. Blown easily along the ground, the red leaves made the only sound; the little iron seats were empty. Beyond lay the wide blue of the lake itself, marked with its usual long trails of steamer smoke.

Allison dropped his handbag at the end of the seat—all the luggage he had with him.

"You've come to stop over the week-end, haven't you, Barry?"

"I've come to stop over until the end of the world, my dear," he rejoined, evenly.

Neither of them dared ask the great questions which were in their hearts. He seemed content just to let his hand rest on hers, and to look out over the lake at the blue smoke trails. She was the first to speak.

"You're back, Barry, aren't you? That's fine! I'm so very glad. And successful! Are you sure?"

"Are you not here, my dear? Yes, I'm sure. I am successful, if you let me sit here by you."

His eyes regarded her face. He did not see one flicker of regret or surprise. Yes, she seemed as content as he.

So at length, himself contented now, he went on: "You shall judge about it all, my dear," he said. "We found the great treasure—I don't know that I can ever tell you all about it. But, so far as merely being rich is concerned, why, yes, I am rich. I've got in that little handbag enough to keep you and me as long as we live. You can have everything you want, my dear, now. We can travel, we can see the wealth of the world, and the art of the world, and the good things of the world. Yes, I reckon maybe we can help the misery and the suffering of the world, as well. It would be like you to want to do that if you were rich, wouldn't it, Mary?"

She nodded. He could not see, in the corner of her lips, in the corner of her eye, any interest in this. Only her hand was not withdrawn from his.

"You don't believe me, do you?" Reaching down, he lifted up the little handbag, set it on his knees, opened it, asked her to look in.

Her eyes opened in wonder, then almost in terror. "Barry!" she said. "What have you done—what have you done!"

"This is only a part, my dear," said he, quietly, for by this time he had become somewhat used to the feel of these precious condensations of wealth which he had carried with him all this time. "I have got some in safety vaults in New Orleans, and some in Chicago.

"It's the treasure, my dear—we found a treasure house the Aztecs had—we found that other thing—but I am not going to tell you about it—we can't understand it—I can't understand it—I can't believe it, or even remember it—I don't trust myself at all beyond this, right here, that we can see and feel and know is true."

He went on, stumbling, blundering, his hand still upon hers, clasping the long fingers closely, trying to tell her something of the experiences through which he had gone.

"It was true, Mary," he said; "what you saw in the crystal ball was true. There is such a valley—or was at one time such a place. Two of my friends who started with us never saw it. One was killed; the other died. I'll tell you all about it. But the other—that was Hallock—and I stood in that very place and we saw the treasure of the Aztecs. Here is a part of it. Of course, it's all a lie—it can't be true. It's all a dream—it can't possibly be true. I don't ask you to believe it. All I ask you to believe, Mary, is—I love you. Is that enough?"

She nodded slowly, gravely, as her wont. Free of coquetry, of all pretense, as ever had been her way, "Yes," said she, distinctly, "that is enough."

It was enough for Barry Allison also. For a long time they sat, the treasure casket open before them, neither looking at it, neither thinking of it. There seemed in the world something far more worth while, far more marvelous. At length, after a long time, he turned up the collar of her coat.

"You mustn't get cold," said he. It seemed to her the first time that any one ever had really cared for her, really had tried to do something for her, to try to add to her personal comfort. Her father and mother lived in a word where each creature fended for itself. They were practical. They saw things as they are, so her mother always had said. But now Mary Westlake was beginning to see things, not as they always are—but as they always ought to be.

After a long time, she brought herself to ask him certain questions—spoke of Trent and his strange disappearance. At first, she could not understand her lover's sudden silence; but at length he turned to her.

"My dear," said he, "we've been working in miracles. There have been forces carrying you and me and all of us along—things we never will understand. Listen,

Randall Trent will never come back to you! The world will never know what has become of him. I would far rather that some other man had to tell you this than myself."

"You don't mean——" she turned her face, horrified, upon him.

"No, no. I had no hand in it. But what I escaped he did not escape."

And now, haltingly, brokenly, confusedly, he tried to tell her of what he had seen on the evening of that terrible day, which came to him in memory now only as an awful and broken nightmare, a distorted dream which gladly he would have put out of his memory forever.

"Let it stand as it is!" said Barry Allison, at length, solemnly. "I shall give no story to any one but you. Let it be said that he disappeared somewhere in Mexico with that young man of the army. I can tell you now —could tell them all—that no word will ever come back from Randall Trent, or the man who carried him on his last journey."

For a time they sat, looking out, a trifle moodily, at the steamers' smoke. One or more of Randall Trent's own boats might be plying out there—plying its way in the accepted commerce of the world about them. The girl herself, always self-controlled, reticent, made no comment at all; nor could her lover find much ability or much need of speech. They did not know how long it was before his voice again broke the silence.

"Why, gold!" said he, and he spread out his hands.

Still shy, silent, not knowing what to do with love, now that it had come to her, Mary Westlake did not speak. Only the firmer grasp of her fingers within his told her actual emotions.

"Well, I took my chances," said Barry Allison at length. "I risked everything I had in all the world. I might have lost. It was worth the risk. I have been saved by a miracle, my dear—it was the marvel and the miracle of——"

"What is it, Barry?"

"It is love, my dear," said he. "That's the only thing in the world that sent me out; it's the only thing in the world that's brought me back. It's the only thing in the world worth while."

"Don't kiss me yet, Barry, please," said she. "I want to think for a while."

Her fingers, infinitely gentle, infinitely tender, were brushing at the gray edges of his hair.

At length she drew a deep sigh. "You've been through something, Barry," said she. "I'm not sure that I can understand all of what it was. But I know you're back again. Yes, it's been a miracle!"

"A very great miracle, my dear—the one great one—the greatest that ever happens in all the world."

THE END